A LETTER

Years before Ha... ...r first cookie at Th... ...ls called "psychologic... ...nately, or perhaps fortunately for the books, my characters became very real to me, and writing about their demises scared me half to death! *Winter Chill* is not an exception, and it definitely lives up to its title. It's truly chilling, and not just from the freezing temperatures.

It's true that Minnesota winters are beautiful, with the sun sparkling on gleaming white snow, glittering icicles hanging from stark tree branches, and skies so blue, no color chart has ever been able to capture the color. Children bundled up like colorful mummies in parkas and snow pants make snow angels and build snowmen, while their older brothers and sisters put on skates and glide across the surface of a frozen pond. It's a lovely picture, but not everything about winter in Minnesota is lovely.

Winter can mean gray skies, snow blowing so hard in the cold North winds that you can't see to walk from your door to the mailbox, and temperatures so cold that ice forms on the inside of windows. "Cabin fever" strikes when your car won't start, the cable goes out, and there's nothing to do except shiver through the long, dark nights alone. It's not a rosy picture, and being trapped in a small house while winter weather rages outside can cause the imagination to take such a bizarre twist that even the sanest mind starts to unravel.

When I wrote *Winter Chill,* I had just moved to Southern California, and it's true that you can take the girl out of the Minnesota winters, but you can't take the Minnesota winters out of the girl. I'm still in Southern California, and even though it almost never gets below freezing, I still have my parka, snow boots, and mittens . . . just in case, don'cha know?

Books by Joanne Fluke

CHOCOLATE CHIP COOKIE MURDER

STRAWBERRY SHORTCAKE MURDER

BLUEBERRY MUFFIN MURDER

LEMON MERINGUE PIE MURDER

FUDGE CUPCAKE MURDER

SUGAR COOKIE MURDER

PEACH COBBLER MURDER

CHERRY CHEESECAKE MURDER

KEY LIME PIE MURDER

CANDY CANE MURDER

CARROT CAKE MURDER

CREAM PUFF MURDER

PLUM PUDDING MURDER

APPLE TURNOVER MURDER

DEVIL'S FOOD CAKE MURDER

GINGERBREAD COOKIE MURDER

CINNAMON ROLL MURDER

RED VELVET CUPCAKE MURDER

JOANNE FLUKE'S LAKE EDEN COOKBOOK

VIDEO KILL

WINTER CHILL

Published by Kensington Publishing Corporation

WINTER CHILL

JOANNE FLUKE

KENSINGTON BOOKS

http://www.kensingtonbooks.com

ISBN-13: 978-0-7582-8977-3
ISBN-10: 0-7582-8977-4
First Kensington Mass Market Edition: August 2013

eISBN-13: 978-0-7582-8978-0
eISBN-10: 0-7582-8978-2
First Kensington Electronic Edition: August 2013

10 9 8 7 6 5 4 3 2 1

Printed in the United States of America

WINTER
CHILL

PROLOGUE

Her cheeks were red from the cold, and she grinned up at him as he turned on the seat. "Come on, Daddy . . . just once more. Please?"

"Better make it quick." Ronnie Powell snapped his visor down and glanced at his watch. "It's coming down pretty heavy, and you two are novices. Five minutes more and we start for home."

"You heard the boss." Dan put his machine in gear as Laura clasped her hands around his waist. "Hang on tight, honey. Here we go!"

They left Jenny and her dad in a cloud of white snow. The wind rushed past her stinging cheeks, and she laughed out loud. Jenny was right. Riding on a snowmobile was almost like flying. The cold took her breath away, and she narrowed her eyes to slits, squinting into the frozen brightness. They were rounding the far corner of the trail now, between the tall pines, and she didn't want ever to go home. If only she had wings and could fly through the snow forever!

She gave a delighted squeal as the machine made a sharp turn to the right, cutting across uncharted snow between the trails. They were taking a shortcut directly through the center of a deserted field. She could barely see now, the snow was swirling so fiercely. The wind tugged at her blue and white stocking cap and threatened to blow it off her head.

"Oh!" Laura let go for an instant, pulling at her knitted hat with both hands. It was an early Christmas present from her mom, and she didn't want to lose it.

"Hang on, Laura!" Dan turned for only an instant, but that was enough. The heavy Snow-Cat crashed headlong into an innocent mound of snow covering an abandoned harrowing machine.

"Daddy!" He sensed rather than heard her cry. Somehow he managed to hang on to the snowmobile with one hand, but she was gone, tipped out in a tumbling arc, propelled forward by the force of the crash. There was a sickening lurch as the machine toppled, and he heard a snap like a firecracker as pain exploded in his head. His last sight was of his small daughter's body caught fast, impaled on the old farm implement's sharp, rusty prongs. It seemed to take forever for the darkness to come, rolling over him in deep, compassionate waves.

* * *

The wind picked up around two thirty and blew the snow in rattling gusts past the kitchen window. Soon ice crystals were pinging against the glass, and Marian peered out into the blinding swirls, listening for the car in the driveway. They should be on their way home by now. It was rotten weather for snowmobiling. She put on the coffee and poured milk into a saucepan for hot chocolate. Dan and Laura would be cold when they came in.

An hour passed as she paced between the stove and the window. Perhaps they had stopped on the way. It was just like Ronnie Powell to convince Dan that they needed a hot brandy. Laura and Jenny were probably munching hamburgers at the truck stop right now, while their fathers sat in the bar. There was really nothing to worry about.

Why didn't he call? At four o'clock Marian began to worry in earnest. She tried dialing Sally to see if she'd heard from Ronnie, but the lines were down. The phone was dead, except for a faint mechanical crackling. It was turning bitter cold now, and the wind chill factor was rising. Marian wished that she'd given in and let Laura wear her new blue coat. It was warmer than the old parka. What if they were stuck out there in the middle of the frozen snow?

Marian forced herself to calm down. Of course they were fine. She was just borrowing trouble. But the heavy curtain of snow outside the glass was an impenetrable barrier, and she couldn't help feeling that somewhere in that wall of icy white, her husband and daughter were in trouble.

Her worst fears were realized when the patrol car

drove up outside. They were hesitant about getting out of the car, Sheriff Bates first and then Sally. There was something they didn't want to tell her, something awful about Dan and Laura. Marian threw open the door and stood waiting, alone and fearful in the numbing cold.

CHAPTER 1

"Lord, we commit unto Thee this body . . . ashes to ashes, dust to dust . . ." Marian shuddered, turning her face away from the small white coffin. Freshly falling snow left her face wet with the tears she could not shed. She leaned against Sally Powell's supporting arm and shut her eyes tightly. This wasn't real. It was only a dream, and she would wake soon to put on the coffee and call Laura and Dan for school.

Last night she had driven home from the hospital after hours of watching Dan in his merciful coma. As she turned past the small cemetery, she saw with horror that one section was in flames. The men at the fire department were kind. They explained haltingly, embarrassed at her ignorance. The ground was frozen; it had to be thawed before a new grave could be excavated.

In the darkness of her living room she had peered through the windowpane, watching the banked fire cast a flickering red glow on the fresh snow. She had hugged herself there in the empty house, pretending that Laura was upstairs sleeping in her yellow-curtained room, that it was all a terrible mistake. But when she looked again, the fire was still there, thawing the ground for her baby's grave.

"Hang on, Marian. . . . It's almost over." Sally's arm tightened around her shoulders. Tears were running down her friend's face, and Marian felt a stab of resentment. She should be the one to cry, not Sally. She had lost her baby, and Jenny was still alive. But it wasn't right to resent Sally. Her grief was real. Sally had loved Laura, too.

It popped into her mind with sudden clarity, her high school's production of *Our Town*. She had played the part of Rebecca, Emily's sister-in-law. The night of the performance was a revelation. These were the same friends she had shared sandwiches and class notes with. Then, in costumes and stage makeup, they were total strangers.

It was the same feeling she had now, the same sense of unreality as she faced her neighbors and coworkers. She was playing the part of a grief-stricken mother, delivering the correct lines, making the proper gestures to an audience of nameless strangers. She was incapable of honest emotion. This was merely a performance. It was not real. She was not real.

He had been aware of the voice for some time now, but he was too tired to care.

"Vital signs are normal, Doctor. Are there any further instructions?"

"Continue with the IV, and turn him once an hour. The funeral's this afternoon. Marian's coming in later. Run the blood work again, and call me immediately if there's any change."

He tried to open his eyes, but there was something heavy on his eyelids. All he could do was listen, barely breathing, as footsteps receded. There was a stabbing pain in his arm and the realization that the voices had been talking about him!

This time it worked. He opened his eyes and stared at the white-clad figure leaning over him.

"It's Joyce Meiers." The nurse leaned closer. "Just relax, Mr. Larsen. You're doing fine. I'll get the doctor."

He was in a hospital. It was clear now, the small room with white furnishings. He was in a room at the Nisswa Clinic, on the far edge of town. But what was he doing here?

"Well, well . . . you finally decided to join us!" Dr. Hinkley's face swam into focus. "One more little pinprick and we'll talk . . . all right?"

There was another stab in his arm, and Dan flinched. "What am I doing here? What happened?"

As he asked the questions, he knew. The snowmobile. The sudden storm. The accident. And Laura. What had happened to Laura!

"She's dead, isn't she?" His voice was slow and thick as the shot took effect. Tranquilizer. "You said something about a . . . a funeral. Laura's dead."

"I'm afraid so, Dan." Dr. Hinkley reached for his hand, practiced fingers taking his pulse. "Would you like something to put you back to sleep?"

"No." Even though his voice was weak, the word was definite. "I've slept enough. How long?"

"You've been in a coma for three days." The doctor's voice was kind. "You had a nasty blow to the head, Dan. Now that you're awake, we'll do some tests."

Laura was dead. His baby was dead. Dan tried to think, but his mind was fuzzy. "Marian?" he asked. "Where's Marian?"

"She'll be here in a few hours." Dr. Hinkley released his wrist and wrote something on the chart at the foot of his bed. "Don't try to think about anything now, Dan. Just concentrate on getting well."

Was he dying? His body was numb. His legs felt like lead. He tried tentatively to move, but nothing happened.

"My legs!" Dan's eyes widened. "They're gone!"

"No . . . It's all right, Dan," Dr. Hinkley said soothingly. "Your legs are fine . . . nothing wrong at all. You're just experiencing some difficulty in moving, that's all. It's probably a simple blockage caused by the accident. Nothing to worry about. Now, relax and let us take care of you."

Just as panic started to set in, there was another prick in his arm and a wave of soft grayness settled down over his mind. *Another shot. Don't think.* It was all a bad dream.

The sun reflecting against the highly polished desktop hurt her eyes, and Marian shut them for a moment. She wished the sun weren't shining. Something should be changed, in honor of her grief. The scene outside the plate-glass hospital window was straight out of a Currier & Ives Christmas card, but her baby was dead. How could this afternoon be so beautiful when Laura was lying in the frozen ground?

"Marian?" Dr. Hinkley pushed a box of Kleenex across the desktop, and Marian realized that tears were running down her cheeks. Why now? And not at the funeral?

"Do you want a tranquilizer for tonight? It helps sometimes, just to get a good night's sleep."

"No, thank you." She had the insane urge to giggle. He sounded as if he were offering her a pastel mint at a party. *Would you like a mint, Marian? No? Then perhaps you'd care for an after-funeral pill.*

Marian realized with a start that she wasn't paying attention. Dr. Hinkley was trying to tell her something.

"We think it might be conversion hysteria, Marian." She tried her best to concentrate. "That's a term for acute anxiety converted to dysfunction of parts of the body. In Dan's case the problem is his legs. He regained consciousness briefly this morning, and we immediately ran tests. There's no sensation in the lower extremities. Even though the paralysis is only in his mind, it has the same effect as a break in the spinal column."

"Wait a minute." Marian tried hard to understand. "Are you saying Dan can't walk?"

Dr. Hinkley nodded slowly. "I'm afraid so, Marian."

It was just too much to take. Laura was dead now, and Dan was paralyzed. The bright room was closing in on her. There was a sound growing around her, a thin, high-pitched wail. She was shocked to find it was coming from her own throat. And then the afternoon sun began to darken alarmingly, and she was pitching forward, falling into Dr. Hinkley's arms.

There was a metallic taste in her mouth as Marian struggled to open her eyes. She must have made some sort of sound, because suddenly a nurse was there beside her.

"Good morning, Mrs. Larsen. We had a wonderful night's sleep."

The nurse was holding a glass of water to her lips. Marian gulped thirstily. Her lips were stiff. The words formed slowly in her mind.

"Dr. Hinkley? I need to see him."

"He'll be here in a few minutes." The nurse smiled. "You can doze off again, if you want. Dr. Hinkley said to give you the royal treatment."

She must have responded somehow, for the nurse left and she was alone again. Marian made herself sit up straighter. She knew she had to play a part again, the part of an alert, competent woman. Then the doctor would let her go home. It was important that she didn't let anyone guess how helpless and frightened she was inside.

Things were better when she applied the light makeup she carried in her purse. The hospital coffee was weak, but it helped. She was ready when Dr. Hinkley came. This time she would not faint.

"The X-rays show no spinal damage, Marian." Dr. Hinkley was sitting in the chair by the bed, and Marian nodded alertly. "In Dan's case, the paralysis is definitely a form of hysterical neurosis. Only his lower extremities are affected. That means he can use a wheelchair, Marian. And he can go home tomorrow, if you think you're up to it."

"Yes . . . of course I am." Marian drew a deep breath. "But when will he recover? You said it wasn't physical. When will Dan be able to walk again?"

"No one knows, Marian." Dr. Hinkley reached out to pat her hand. "Dan's body is punishing him for the accident. He blames himself for Laura's death. In some cases of Dan's type, spontaneous remission has occurred almost overnight. But, Marian . . . Dan may remain paralyzed for the rest of his life."

"I have to help him." Marian straightened her shoulders. "What can I do, Dr. Hinkley?"

"Good girl!" Dr. Hinkley nodded. "You're a fighter, Marian, and that's precisely what Dan needs. Take him home with you tomorrow. There's no reason why he can't go back to work in a week or so. He has a commitment to that hockey team of his, and that might just pull him out of this. I talked to Jim Sorensen at the Conoco station, and he says he can rig your van for a wheelchair. You drive it down there this afternoon, if you feel up to it, and Jim'll work on it tonight. And don't stay alone in that house of yours. I've had calls from half the women in town, offering to stay with you until Dan gets home. You take somebody up on that, Marian. Or I can move an extra bed into Dan's room, if you'd rather stay here."

"I'll stay here with Dan." Marian's voice was strong. "He'll need me if he wakes up. And thank you, Dr. Hinkley. Thank you for being so kind."

* * *

She sat in the chair by the window, looking out at the gathering darkness and hearing the deep, even sound of Dan's breathing. He had opened his eyes once and had seen her sitting there. It seemed to satisfy him, for he had gone straight back to sleep without a word. Marian turned to study her husband's sleeping face. He was a handsome man, rugged and muscular. They'd called him "the Viking" when he'd played hockey in college. But Dan had never wanted to be a professional hockey player. He'd wanted to teach history and coach hockey on the side. He took the job in Nisswa because of Harvey Woodruff's persuasion.

Harvey was a principal in danger of losing his school. There was talk of dissolving the Nisswa district and busing the students to Brainerd or Pequot Lakes. Dan's job was to add prestige to the school and make the community proud to have a winning hockey team. There was no way Harvey wanted the local kids bused away. The Nisswa School was his life. He'd built it into a fine academic institution, and Dan could help him save it.

Dan had been coaching for two years when Marian joined the Nisswa staff. The hockey team was winning, and Dan was the town hero. There was no more talk of busing. Nisswa was proud of its school and even prouder of Dan. It had been exciting to date the most eligible bachelor on the faculty.

Marian hadn't dated much in college. Her particular combination of femininity and brains had served to scare off most of the college men. And she had to admit that she wasn't all that interested in beer parties in student apartments. Marian was convinced she was destined for something more worthwhile than becoming a simple wife and mother. She had dreams of an academic career, perhaps a place on a college faculty, the respect of her colleagues, the publication of her innovative teaching methods.

Then he'd asked her for a date, Marian Walters, newly graduated, her head filled with theories of education, her heart dedicated to bringing enlightenment to the children of America. And Marian realized what she had been missing by pouring every waking hour into her lesson plans and her research. Dan Larsen was fun!

She remembered telling Dan her dreams, how disappointed she was in not landing a job in a warmer climate, how she longed for a break from the endless snows of Minnesota winters. But jobs in better climates were at a premium, and elementary school teachers were a dime a dozen. She was lucky to get the position in Nisswa. After two years she thought she would try to move on, perhaps to California, where the days were sunny and warm, even in the winter, but there was Dan, and then there was love and marriage . . . and Laura. Painful tears squeezed out behind Marian's swollen eyelids. Her baby was dead, and Dan was paralyzed. It was too much.

"Would you like some coffee, Mrs. Larsen?" A white-uniformed nurse came into the room on silent feet. "I'll sit with Mr. Larsen if you want a little break."

"Thank you, yes." Marian rose to her feet stiffly. She had been sitting in the chair for hours now, just thinking.

"There's coffee at the nurses' station at the end of the hall, and there's a sandwich machine there, too. I'm Joyce Meiers, Mrs. Larsen. I had Mr. Larsen for history when I was a senior."

"Thank you, Joyce." Marian forced a pleasant smile. She remembered Joyce now. Dan would be pleased to see her if he woke up, she thought as she began to walk down the hall.

In a way, he was glad she was gone. He loved her so much, and he didn't know what to say. He had opened his eyes in the early evening to see her sitting there, head bowed slightly, eyes vacant and weary. Somehow it was wrong to interrupt her solitude. They had always been so close, but now what could he say?

I'm sorry I killed your daughter, Marian.

Oh, that's all right. It was an accident.

It was better to say nothing at all. They would talk later, heal the breach, start over. But not now. Now he was too heartsick to try. And his grief was too new. It was best to pretend to go back to sleep until the pretense became a reality.

She felt better after the coffee and sandwich. There was a candy machine at the end of the hall, and Marian reached into her purse for change. She should take Laura a Nut Goodie. It was her favorite candy bar.

Marian stopped suddenly, a quarter balanced against the coin slot. A hard, racking sob shook her slender body. She leaned her forehead against the cool, impersonal glass case and held it there until her legs stopped trembling. She couldn't break down now. She had to be strong for Dan. He needed her. It wasn't fair. Life would go on and time would pass, whether she wanted it to or not.

CHAPTER 2

The jangling summons of the little bell made her headache worse. Even upstairs, in their bedroom, the noise was jarring.

"Marian? Is there any more coffee?"

Marian sat up. She must have fallen asleep, and Dan needed her. She had to go to him, even though she was so tired, she wanted to sleep for a week.

That was how long it had been. One week of Dan settling in, getting used to the den downstairs, which they had converted into his domain. One week of waiting on him hand and foot. A week of plumping pillows, smiling lovingly, running back and forth to fulfill his every need. But soon all that would change. She couldn't put it off much longer. Soon she would have to go back to work, take her coffee break in the morning with the other teachers, pretend interest in their lives and their work, and appear normal. She would have to start a new group in reading, put up a colorful bulletin board, sing songs with her class, and convince everyone that everything was just fine. Marian was terrified that she couldn't do it. Everyone would see that she wasn't really competent Marian Larsen. She had turned into someone else, some colorless impostor who was no good for her students, no good for Dan, no good for anyone ever again.

Marian hated making excuses to be alone, but she couldn't let Dan see how unhappy and frightened she was. It wouldn't be fair to burden him with her problems. Up here, alone, it was all right to cry.

She reached for the bottle of pills on the table and took another one. Dr. Hinkley claimed they would elevate her spirits. She hadn't told him the pills didn't work. He had prescribed several types already, and she couldn't ask for more. Dr. Hinkley might give up on her and tell Dan. She couldn't let Dan know how desperate she felt. Life wasn't worth living without her baby. If only she could think of a decent way to end her torture.

"Just a minute, honey!" Marian slipped her feet into moccasins and ran her fingers through her short, brown, curly hair. "I'll make a fresh pot of coffee. Then we'll watch a little television together."

Dan could hear the click as she pushed on the alarm button. She was setting the clock now. There was a rustling as she settled down on the bed and covered herself with the blankets. It made him sad that she was so careful not to touch him.

There was something wrong with Marian. Dan had been watching her all week. She was too controlled. . . . *Brittle* was the word that came to mind.

He wished she would break down, just once. He'd never seen her cry, and that wasn't good. He knew she cried alone, but she wouldn't share her grief. She was always kind and cheerful, a model wife. She was playing a part; the real Marian was hidden. That scared him.

Dan stared up into the darkness. He despised being helpless. He lifted his head and peered down to see if his feet were covered. That was a little thing most people took for granted. If your feet were cold at night, your blanket had slid off. Now he couldn't tell if his feet were cold or not. It bugged the hell out of him.

He reached under the covers to squeeze his leg. Nothing. He concentrated until beads of sweat were lining his forehead, but nothing moved.

He concentrated again, trying by sheer force of will to make his leg move. He tried again and again until tears of frustration ran down his face. If he was going to be like this for the rest of his life, he'd rather be dead.

Marian was not sleeping. She heard a rustle from the living room and a thump as Muffy jumped off the couch to pad softly across the rug. The little dog ran upstairs to take her place at the closed door to Laura's room. Suddenly the thought of Muffy, waiting with sweet animal patience outside Laura's door, made the tears come.

"Marian? Honey. What's wrong?"

Marian tried her best to stop crying, but it was

no use. The sobs shook her whole body as Dan reached out to draw her closer.

"It's Laura, isn't it?" Dan's voice was soft. "Tell me, honey. Talk to me."

This time she couldn't hide. The anguish was too keen, the racking sobs too violent to pretend that everything was all right.

"Yes." The word was muffled as he pulled her against his shoulder. "I can't live without her, Dan! It's too hard. I . . . I just can't stand it anymore!"

There was a long silence as he held her in his arms. There should be something he could say, some way he could give her comfort. He had known this moment was coming, but he was still unprepared for it. Somehow he had to give Marian the courage to go on living.

"You have to go on, Marian." Dan's voice was firm. There was no hint of the desperation he felt. Marian didn't want to live without Laura. He knew how she felt. But he had to say something to change her mind.

"Think about Laura for a minute, Marian. Do you think Laura would be proud of you right now? Would Laura want to see her mother acting this way?"

Marian was silent. At least she was listening to him now.

"She'd be disappointed in you, Marian. I know she would. And I believe that Laura's there somewhere, listening to every word we say. She isn't gone forever, Marian. I can't believe that. She's just in another place, waiting for us to join her someday. You don't want Laura to be sad, do you, Marian?"

It was a full minute before Marian spoke. Then her voice was shaking and full of doubt.

"Do you really believe that, Dan? That Laura can hear us now?"

"I believe it, honey." Dan's arm tightened around her, and he sighed deeply. "And you can believe it, too, if you let yourself. Try it, Marian. Try to believe. Will you try it for me?"

"If only I could, Dan." Her voice was a whisper. "Yes. Darling . . . I'll try."

The words still echoed in his mind long after she'd dropped off into an exhausted sleep. Had he deliberately misled her? Dan wasn't sure if he believed in an afterlife or not. But believing in life after death certainly couldn't hurt Marian. She had to have something to hold on to, something to pull her out of her terrible depression and make her want to live again. He hoped he had given her that much, at least.

The phone rang again as Marian was making a fresh pot of coffee. She wiped her hands on a towel and hurried to answer it.

"Is there anything Ronnie and I can do to help?" Sally's voice was anxious, and Marian winced. What could she say? There was nothing anyone could do.

"I don't think so, Sally. I guess Dan and I will just have to struggle through somehow."

"So when are you coming back to work?" Now there was a deliberate cheerfulness in Sally's tone. "Your class is going crazy without you. The first thing Ricky asks every morning is when you're coming back."

A smile flickered across Marian's face. Ricky Owens, the terror of the second grade. The substitute must be making him toe the line.

"Soon, I think. I haven't really discussed it with Dan yet. I still have two weeks of sick leave coming, Sally."

"Oh, don't make it that long!" Sally sounded distressed. "Your kids miss you, and I miss you, too. Edith makes lousy coffee."

"I'll let you know just as soon as I decide," Marian promised. "I have to get back to Dan now. Dr. Hinkley's with him."

She sighed as she hung up the phone. Three calls today, one from Harvey, one from Edith, and now the call from Sally. And all three of them wanted to know when she was coming back to work.

Dr. Hinkley smiled as she came into the den. "Well, Marian. You look chipper. Getting ready to go back to that class of yours?"

They were ganging up on her! Dr. Hinkley meant well, but couldn't he see that she just wasn't ready yet?

"I'm trying to talk her into going back on Monday. I don't think it's good for her to stay in the house like this, do you, Dr. Hinkley?"

And now Dan was getting into the act. For a moment Marian had the urge to scream. Her baby was dead! Couldn't they see she wasn't ready to go back? She might never be ready to go back!

"Why don't you try it for a half day on Monday, honey? The substitute can take the morning, and you go in for the afternoon. Just see how you feel, say hello to the kids again. If it doesn't work out, everyone'll understand."

She was just too tired to fight with all of them. Marian sighed and gave up. They were making her decisions for her, and she guessed she'd have to go along with them.

CHAPTER 3

It was Saturday morning, and Marian was washing dishes. She was in good spirits this morning. Perhaps Dan was right. She needed something to believe in.

She wiped the last of the plates in the drainer and bent over to get Muffy's bowl, next to the refrigerator. It was still full. Marian stopped, puzzled. Poor Muffy had eaten practically nothing last week.

There was a slice of cold roast beef in the refrigerator. Marian took it out and cut it into bite-size pieces. She'd tempt Muffy with her favorite treat. Muffy loved roast beef.

"Muffy? Come here, Muffy!"

There was no sound of running feet. Marian put the beef in the bowl and carried it to the living room, looking for Laura's pet.

"I haven't seen her all morning, honey," Dan called out. "Maybe she's upstairs."

She found Muffy lying by Laura's door, head down, eyes closed. The little cocker spaniel looked up as Marian placed the bowl of food next to her.

Her tail thumped against the floor once, and then she whimpered.

"What's the matter, Muffy? Aren't you hungry?" Marian reached down to pat her silky head. "It's roast beef, Muffy . . . your favorite."

Muffy sniffed once at the bowl, and then her head lowered again. It was clear the little dog wasn't going to eat.

"I'll leave it right here for you," Marian promised. "Now be a good girl and eat something. We can't have you getting sick on us."

Marian turned to go back downstairs, and then she stopped by the phone in the upstairs hallway. Muffy was losing weight. Her coat had lost its shine, and her eyes were dull and listless. It might be a good idea to call Roy McHenry, the local vet.

It was late afternoon before Roy got back to them. Marian was right. Muffy was definitely ill. The little puppy had lost too much weight, and she was suffering from dehydration. But Roy couldn't find the cause of Muffy's malaise. He suggested a change of scene, perhaps a visit to a family with a child. Marian knew he was trying to tell her that Muffy was grieving for Laura.

Dan had come up with the solution. They would take Muffy to the Powells'. It was practically her second home anyway. And Muffy loved Jenny.

"Time to go see Jenny!" Marian called the puppy to her and snapped on Muffy's leash. "Jenny's waiting for you. You're going out to the country for a nice little visit."

Muffy looked up at her with large, brown eyes. Marian thought she could see a glimmer of excitement in their liquid depths. Perhaps this was best for Muffy. If she adjusted well at the Powells', she could stay with them. Sally had promised.

Marian picked up Muffy and hurried to the garage. Sally would have a cup of coffee waiting. Dan would have a good time talking with Ronnie, and in the Powells' huge, cheerful farmhouse, she might be able to forget her cares for a while.

Muffy whimpered as Marian put her in the passenger seat and started the cold van. The small puppy was shivering, and Marian draped a blanket around her. As soon as Laura's pet had settled in a bit, she backed the van out of the garage and went back after Dan. He was waiting for her just inside the front door.

"Ready for your first outing, Mr. Larsen?" She smiled as she wheeled his chair out the front door and around to the back of the van. The hydraulic lift Jim Sorensen had installed worked perfectly, and in a matter of seconds Dan's chair was clamped into place.

"I could have stayed home in comfort," Dan grumbled. "It's thirteen below, Marian. Of course, that's not bad for December. The weatherman said it's going to be a mild winter."

Marian could see his smile in the rearview mirror. Dr. Hinkley was right. Both of them needed to get out of the house more often.

Marian shivered a little as she backed out onto the street. She had never liked driving at night, and winter driving terrified her. She was glad Dan was with her. Of course, he couldn't help with the driving, but it gave her comfort just knowing he was there.

The roads were slippery tonight. Marian could

see the buildup of ice in the glare of her headlights as she made the turn onto the highway. She had to concentrate on her driving now.

Muffy whimpered piteously and pressed her nose to the cold window. Marian gritted her teeth and swerved just a bit as she turned to look at the cocker spaniel. If Muffy whimpered all the way, she'd be a nervous wreck.

"Drive out to the truck stop and pull in, Marian. Then I'll take Muffy on my lap. She might ride better that way."

The snow beat against the windshield in staccato swirls. Marian peered through the glass and ducked her head a bit to see better. The windshield wipers would have to be replaced. It was really difficult to see. The wind was whipping up loose snow and driving it against the side of the van. The gusts came harder and harder and Marian slowed to a crawl. It would take forever to go five miles this way.

At last the lights of the truck stop were visible. Marian gave a sigh of relief and took the corner just a bit too fast. She fought with the wheel as they skidded, and the van responded sluggishly. Then the heavy vehicle straightened, and she pulled into a parking space in front of the café.

"Just take it easy, Marian. . . . You're doing fine. If you can hand Muffy to me, it'll make everything a lot easier."

Muffy was still shivering and Marian handed Dan the puppy and blanket. "Keep her wrapped in this, honey. I heard that's supposed to be comforting."

"It'll be comforting for me, too." Dan grinned. "It's cold back here!"

"Oh, God! The heater vents!" Marian groaned as

she opened them all the way. "I'm sorry, Dan. I'm not used to anyone riding in the back."

The heater was on high now, both vents aimed toward the expanse of space in the back. At least Dan would be warm. That made it a little cold in the front seat, but she could take it. They'd paid extra for the auxiliary heater, but it didn't do much good at thirteen below. A van this big was almost impossible to heat in the winter.

Muffy was blessedly quiet as Marian put the van in gear and drove back onto the highway. Only a mile to go before she reached Ronnie and Sally's turnoff. Then there were three miles of gravel road to navigate before they got to the farmhouse.

It seemed as if she were crawling. The speedometer read fifteen miles an hour. It would take forever, going this slow, but Marian was afraid to speed up. The wind drove the snow up against the windshield, and Marian shifted her gaze from one side of the road to the other. If she stared straight into the blowing snow, she'd become hypnotized by the patterns and go off the road.

"We're close, Marian. . . . I spotted mile marker forty-seven. County Road Five should be just ahead."

"Yes, I see it." Marian turned right, and the van bumped onto the gravel road. It was growing darker, and that made the blowing snow glare in the beam of her headlights. The familiar road changed in the winter. Landmarks were covered; shapes changed and drifted until it was almost impossible to see the plowed road. Several times Marian slowed to a near stop before she realized where the side of the road was.

"Only about a mile to go, honey."

Dan's tone was encouraging, and Marian gave a quick smile. Muffy still whimpered every time the van lurched, but that couldn't be helped.

"Is it warm enough back there?" Marian called out. "I don't want you to get cold."

"It's fine, Marian. Don't worry about me. I'll warm up when we get there."

Marian doubted that she would ever be warm again. With both vents blowing warm air to the back of the van, it was frigid in the driver's seat. Her toes burned with the cold, and her fingers, even inside gloves, were stiff and chilled. Marian gritted her teeth to keep them from chattering and gave the van a little more gas so she could plow through the drifts without stalling.

"I think I see their light." Dan sounded grateful. Another minute of driving and Marian saw it, too. The Powells' yard light was shining in the distance. Relief washed over her in a wave as she turned in at the driveway and pulled up in front of the house.

"I made it. . . . We're here." Marian shut off the ignition and sighed deeply. At least she hadn't landed in the ditch. Poor Muffy was whining again. The little dog didn't understand what was happening, but she would be fine as soon as she saw Jenny.

"I'll help!" Jenny raced from the house to take Muffy's leash. "Hi, Mrs. Larsen. Hi, Dan. Mom says to go straight in the kitchen and thaw out. She's baking fruitcakes."

The little redhead was clad in a bright green parka and moon boots, complete with a scarf tied around her neck. Jenny was already lifting Muffy out of the van, hugging the little dog tightly.

"Well, well. You decided to come out and see us at last!" Ronnie opened the back of the van and grinned at Dan. "Was he a backseat driver, Marian?"

"I didn't say a word." Dan chuckled. "I figured it was best not to distract her, so I did a lot of praying instead."

"Got something to show you, Dan." Ronnie unhooked the chair and pressed the button for the ramp. "I'm working on a new project. You're going to love it."

Marian turned to watch as Jenny walked the cocker spaniel through the snow. Muffy plodded along, her head hung low. She looked dejected, displaced. Somehow Laura's puppy reminded her of the orphans she had seen in those ads: ADOPT THIS ORPHAN. ONLY FIVE DOLLARS A WEEK WILL KEEP THIS CHILD FROM STARVING.

That kind of thinking was ridiculous. Marian hurried to the house and opened the door. Dan and Ronnie were already inside, and she heard Dan laughing. There was no need to be depressed now. Dan was having a good time with Ronnie, and Muffy would be very happy with Jenny. What the little dog needed was a normal family life again. Jenny would give her plenty of love and attention, and Muffy would be back to normal in no time at all.

"Come on in, Marian!" Sally called out from the kitchen. "I'm up to my elbows in candied fruits, so you'll have to pour your own coffee."

"It smells wonderful in here." Marian breathed in deeply and grinned at her friend. "You must have a couple of fruitcakes in the oven already."

"Actually, it's leftovers from two months of

dinners," Sally confessed with a grin. "I just haven't had time to clean the oven. Well? What are you waiting for? Pour yourself some coffee and sit down."

The kitchen was so bright and cheerful that Marian felt almost like crying. Sally was wearing a big white apron, and she looked happy and content. This old farmhouse suited her perfectly. Marian could imagine Sally as a farm wife, baking bread every day and milking the cows.

Marian leaned back in her chair and then quickly sat up again as it gave an alarming *creak*. Most of the Powells' furniture was from swap meets and garage sales. And it was always in very tenuous repair. Sally said Ronnie kept promising to get around to fixing it, but he never had the time.

"Ronnie must have Dan in the workroom." Sally shook her head. "You won't believe what that man of mine is building now!"

"Two coffees, Sal." Ronnie appeared in the doorway, grinning. "Dan's looking over the plans right now. Then I'm going to wheel him around the outside and take him to the basement. His eyes are going to pop right out when he sees my boat."

Ronnie hugged his wife so hard, he lifted her right off the floor. Sally laughed and tipped her face up to his, clearly enjoying the moment.

Marian looked down quickly and stared at the red and white checked tablecloth on the table. Dan wasn't as affectionate as he'd been before the accident and neither was she, but Marian knew how hard they were both trying and the thought of their effort warmed her.

"Just holler if you need anything." Ronnie snitched a handful of nuts and raisins and headed for the kitchen door. "And don't come down to the basement. I want to surprise you when it's all finished."

Sally put her finger to her lips until she was sure Ronnie had gone. Then she laughed good-naturedly.

"I was afraid you were going to ask about the boat. Ronnie's building what looks like a schooner in the basement. Jenny and I went down there the other day to take a look. The way Ronnie's building it, it'll never fit through the basement door. At first we were going to tell him, but you know how stubborn he is. I swore Jenny to secrecy, and we're just waiting around for the explosion when he finds out for himself. I guess he'll have to tear down a wall to get it out."

"Another Ronnie Powell project at its best?" Marian started to laugh. "Remember the bookcases on the porch?"

"Exactly the same," Sally sighed. "But that one wasn't so bad. At least he put in a sliding glass door when he cut the hole in the wall. This time we're hoping he'll enlarge the basement and turn it into a rec room."

Marian laughed, but even to her own ears it had a hollow sound. Sally turned to look at her sharply.

"How are you really, Marian? You're sitting there, wound as tight as a mainspring."

"Oh, I'll be fine." The response was almost automatic by now. Marian forced a smile that wavered a bit, and she was sorely tempted to blurt out all her problems to her warmhearted friend. Sally really wanted to help her.

"It's been a tough day." Marian forced out the words. "Tomorrow will be better."

"It'd better be!" Sally buttered a pan and poured in batter. "My kids were awful today. Robbie Benton upset the sandbox right before the bell, and Jane Herman cut her knee on the playground. I thought I'd have a little relief at nap time, but there was no sleep for my bunch today. They were like a herd of little wildcats. There's only one thing that keeps me going. You're coming back on Monday. I think that's just fantastic, Marian!"

This time Marian's smile was genuine. Talking about school was safe and easy.

"Are you going to the teachers' Christmas party?" Sally opened the oven and popped four fruitcakes inside. "Ronnie won't go. He says he was too hungover last year. I thought if you wanted, we could go together."

"I'll think about it," Marian agreed. "It all depends on Dan. I don't like to leave him alone for long. And I know he won't go with me."

"Got the perfect solution for you." Sally wiped her hands on a towel. "Ronnie doesn't like to stay home alone, either, and Jenny's spending the night at her cousin's house. Why don't we lay in a supply of beer at your house and set the guys up playing cards? Then we can go and enjoy ourselves."

"Well . . . maybe." Marian took a sip of coffee and tried to look pleased. She didn't think she was up to any party, but she didn't want to say so.

Sally crossed to the table and sat down facing

her. "I get the feeling there's something you're holding back."

There was no way Marian could resist the sympathetic look on Sally's face. She had to take a chance and ask Sally. Sally wouldn't betray her.

"Sally . . ." Marian cleared her throat. "Do you . . . I know this is personal, but . . . do you believe in life after death?"

"Yes." Sally nodded emphatically. "I didn't believe before, but I do now. Do you want to know what changed my mind, Marian?"

Marian felt a lump in her throat, and she swallowed hard. She was too anxious to speak, so she nodded.

"My mom died right after Ronnie and I were married. I still remember how I felt, Marian. It was awful. I loved her so much, I almost wanted to die myself. First I felt terrified. I was numb all over. I couldn't believe she was gone. I'd go to the phone to dial her number, and remember, and then I'd cry all over again. Ronnie tried to help, but that was when he was in the service. He was only home on leave for two weeks. Then he had to go back, and I was alone, really alone, for the first time in my life."

"Sally . . . don't!" Marian felt the tears gather in her eyes. "You don't have to talk about it, Sally, really you don't."

"No, I want to. I want to because it was all right after awhile. I remember one morning I was sitting in the kitchen, staring out the window, wondering what to give my dad for his birthday, and I heard Mom say, *Handkerchiefs, honey. Your father always wanted monogrammed handkerchiefs, and I never got around to buying them.* That was when I started believing, Marian, and I've believed ever since. Even now, when I've got a problem, I talk to Mom. And she's always there, right inside my head, giving me advice and loving me."

"Thanks, Sally." Marian spoke past the lump in her throat. "Thank you for telling me."

"Well . . ." Sally cleared her throat and got up. "More coffee, Marian? I have a feeling the guys'll be tied up for quite a while. Ronnie's got a captive audience, and he's going to take full advantage of it."

Ronnie had gone to start the van, and then he would come back to wheel him out. Dan sat stiff and straight in his chair. Ronnie was being nice, but Dan couldn't help but resent this whole evening. Ronnie had wheeled him around like an invalid, and that had made him feel even more helpless. Now Ronnie was starting the van. What kind of man was he if he couldn't even start his own damn car?

There was a sound from the living room, and Dan turned his head to see. Jenny was stretched out in front of the TV, Muffy beside her. She was laughing at some program, stroking Muffy's head absently with her hand. It made him sick to see Muffy and Jenny together. Muffy was Laura's dog! Laura should have been there petting Muffy, and instead it was Jenny. Jenny was the lucky one. Jenny was still alive. If he had the power, he would have changed things. Jenny would be gone, and Laura would be here, happy, alive, laughing at the program on television.

Shame made him wince. It wasn't right to think

this way. Jenny was a nice little girl. He liked Jenny. But Laura was his.

"All right, let's go!" Ronnie came in the front door with a bang and took his place behind Dan's chair. "Marian'll be out in a second. Sally's wrapping up a couple of fruitcakes for her."

The cold was chilling as Ronnie pushed him down the shoveled walk and out to the driveway. Dan felt cold all over, now that he knew the truth. He wasn't fit to socialize with anyone. He resented Sally and Ronnie, their closeness as a family. Watching them hurt too much. If this kept up, he'd hate all the happy people, and that was sick. He was much better off staying by himself with only his painful thoughts for company.

Muffy was stretched out on the rug when Marian walked through the living room. The little dog turned to stare at her with sorrowful eyes.

"It'll be all right, Muffy." Marian reached down to pat her soft golden hair. "You be a good girl now and play with Jenny."

Muffy's pink tongue came out to lick Marian's hand. There were tears in Marian's eyes as she let herself out the front door and hurried to the van. She felt as if she'd left a part of Laura here at the Powells'. But soon things would be better. Sally had helped. Now she had new hope. It was all just a matter of time.

Sally watched the van pull down the driveway until it turned at the road. She was worried about Marian. There was something wrong, and she couldn't quite put her finger on it. Marian had changed, and it frightened her. Of course, she had expected that Marian would be subdued and sad. That was normal. But now there was something about Marian that made Sally desperately uneasy.

Sally stood at the kitchen window and looked out over the snowbanks. Jenny's snowman was near the edge of the driveway, looking comically disreputable. How would she feel if Jenny were dead? The very thought was so painful that Sally winced.

How about Ronnie? What if he were paralyzed? Sally shivered in the warm kitchen. What would she do? How would she cope, knowing that her husband was confined to a wheelchair?

There was no answer for that. Even though she tried, it was impossible to put herself in Marian's place. She was sure she'd go crazy without Jenny. And if Ronnie were an invalid, she'd break down for sure. She wouldn't even have the strength to pretend. She'd curl up in a ball and hide from reality.

Maybe that's what's happening to Marian. Sally gasped as it hit her. Marian could be having a nervous breakdown, and no one would know. There were people who went quietly crazy, and no one knew about it for years, until they did something horrible.

"Did Marian have a good time?"

Sally whirled to see Ronnie standing in the doorway. Without a word she ran across the kitchen and flung herself into his arms.

"Hey!" Ronnie hugged her and stepped back to look at her face. "What got into you?"

"I . . . I'm just glad I'm me." Sally's lower lip

trembled. "And I'm glad I have you and Jenny to love."

"Well, good." Ronnie placed a kiss on her lips. "Hey, Sal . . . are you going to let me go back to work?"

"No." Sally hung on fiercely "I think you're all through for the night. Let's go to bed."

"I think I like this." Ronnie grinned at her and flicked off the kitchen light. "Maybe you ought to bake fruitcakes more often."

CHAPTER 4

Both of them were glad to get home. Marian took care of Dan first. When he was comfortable and settled in bed, she took her shower and got into her robe and slippers. They could have French toast for breakfast. That was easy. Marian opened the refrigerator door to make sure they had eggs and milk.

The sight of a ham bone, carefully wrapped in plastic, made tears roll down Marian's cheeks. Muffy was gone.

She didn't want Dan to know she'd been crying. Marian turned off the light before she got into bed. She tried to sound cheerful as she said good night.

There was a quaver in Marian's voice, and Dan pulled her close. He knew what was wrong. He missed Muffy, too.

"Don't feel bad, honey. Muffy's better off at the farm."

"I know." Marian drew a deep breath. "But,

Dan . . . it's almost like losing Laura all over again."

"Don't look at it that way, honey. Muffy's happy now. And that's the way we have to feel about Laura. We miss her, but we've got to believe she's happier and better off in another place."

"Yes . . . I suppose so." Marian's voice was sad. "I think I'll go out to the living room and read for a while. I'm too wound up to sleep."

Dan knew she shouldn't be alone. He pulled himself up in bed and switched on the light.

"Stay here, Marian. I'll read too. Find me a good book, and we'll keep each other company."

"How about that mystery I read last month?" Marian got out of bed and pulled a book off the bookshelf. "I'm through with it."

"That's fine. Do we have any snacks, honey? I'm a little hungry."

"Just the fruitcake Sally sent, but that has to age until Christmas." Marian frowned. "I'm sorry, Dan. I meant to go to the store this morning, and I forgot."

"It doesn't matter, honey. I'm really not that hungry." Dan could have kicked himself for saying anything. He could tell that Marian was feeling guilty for not doing the shopping.

He took the book Marian handed him and flipped through it. A piece of ruled notepaper fluttered to the bed.

"Hey . . . what's this?" Dan picked up the paper and glanced at it. "How about this, Marian? It's a note from Laura."

Without thinking, he handed it to Marian.

Another mistake. Laura's note might make Marian feel even worse.

"It says, 'Mommy, I love you.'" Marian smiled down at Dan. "She must have put it in my book to surprise me. Isn't that sweet?"

There was nothing but pleasure on Marian's face, and Dan sighed in relief.

"It's funny, but I feel so much better now." She leaned down and gave him a quick kiss. "It's almost as if Laura's alive again. I'm so glad you found it!"

Marian looked positively radiant. Now Dan was glad he'd given her the note.

"I think I'll bake some cookies." Marian slipped into her robe and pulled on her slippers. "Now that I think about it, I'm hungry too."

As she hurried from the room, Dan gave a contented sigh. Marian was back to normal. All traces of her earlier depression were gone.

In a moment she was back, leaning against the doorway, her expression thoughtful. "I just wish Laura could write me a note now. Wouldn't it be wonderful to know that she was happy and at peace?"

Dan nodded. What could he say? Then she was gone again, and he heard the dishes rattle as she got out the mixing bowl.

A frown crossed Dan's face. It was really far-fetched to think of Laura writing notes from the grave. He must have misunderstood Marian. Perhaps she was speaking figuratively.

Marian found a package of chocolate chips in the cupboard and mixed the dough from memory.

Chocolate chip cookies were Laura's favorites. She'd made them so often, she didn't need a recipe. Marian took down the brown sugar and broke up the lumps with a spoon. Then she reached for the kitchen matches she kept in a box by the sink and knelt down to light the oven.

The stove was old, but Marian loved it. It had come with the house. Dan had been after her to order a new one, but Marian couldn't bear to give it up. The white enamel finish was wearing off in spots, but it was still serviceable and it was a genuine antique. Hand-painted flowers in yellow and red decorated the door of the large oven. There was a smaller oven next to it, with a broiler beneath. Marian had never seen a stove with six burners before. Of course, it didn't have a pilot light, but that was a minor inconvenience. She was very cautious about making sure the gas was off when the stove was not in use.

She turned on the gas and struck the match. The stove lit with a whoosh. By the time she finished mixing the dough, the oven would be ready.

In a few minutes the smell of baking cookies filled the air. Marian smiled. She felt so much better now. She really should make an effort to spend more time in the kitchen. It was a cheerful room with bright yellow walls and white curtains at the windows. Their house was the last one on the block, nestled up against the side of the big hill. Folks still called it Heidelberg Hill after the people who had built this house in the twenties.

Marian pulled aside the curtains and looked out toward the wooded hill. The wind had died down, and the moon was almost full. Tall pines dotted the white snow, and the crest of the hill was slick with frozen ice. As soon as Christmas vacation started, children would be sledding on Heidelberg Hill. The far slope was gentle, and there was a small pond at its base. Dan had always gone out to sweep the pond and reglaze the surface for the skaters. Perhaps she would do it this year.

The cookies were ready to come out of the oven. Marian smiled as she put them on the wooden board to cool. She wrapped up the extra cookie dough and put it in the freezer. She wouldn't be caught unprepared again. By the time she had washed the mixing bowl and spoons, the cookies were cool.

"Honey, here's some . . . oh!" Marian stopped as she caught sight of Dan. His book had dropped to the floor, and he was sound asleep. He looked peaceful and boyish, snuggled up in the blankets, and Marian didn't have the heart to wake him.

The Reverend Harris was pontificating on *Sermonette for Tonight,* and Marian turned off the television with the remote control. She supposed she should let Dan sleep. He must be tired to have fallen asleep with the television blaring and the light on.

She set the plate of cookies on his nightstand and placed the remote control next to it. If Dan woke up to watch a movie in the middle of the night, he could have his snack.

Dan didn't wake as she turned off the light. Marian climbed into bed beside him and smiled up into the darkness. She was tired, too. They would both get a good night's sleep tonight, and tomorrow was a new day. For the first time since the accident, Marian found herself looking forward to tomorrow.

"Marian! Wake up!"

It was seven in the morning, and the winter sun was shining weakly through the window. Marian sat up quickly, fearing the worst.

"Call Dr. Hinkley!" Dan's voice was urgent. "I walked, Marian. . . . I know I did! I got up in the middle of the night and I walked, but now I can't move again. Tell Dr. Hinkley to come right away!"

Marian rushed to the phone in a panic. With shaking fingers, she dialed the doctor's number. Dan was hollering in the background for him to hurry, and Dr. Hinkley promised he'd be right over.

The doctor arrived in less than fifteen minutes. He pulled off his overshoes and handed Marian his coat.

"I'll go right in." Dr. Hinkley patted her hand. "Why don't you make us a pot of coffee? Give me a couple of minutes, and then join us."

Marian hurried to the kitchen and put on the coffee. Then she ran upstairs and dressed. She was just running a comb through her hair when the doctor called her.

Dan was sitting up in bed, alert and hopeful. His face was flushed, and his eyes were bright. It had to be true! Marian's heart pounded in her chest. Dr. Hinkley had to tell them that Dan was recovering!

"It's possible you walked, Dan." Dr. Hinkley

closed his bag and snapped it shut. "There's no evidence of any change in your condition, but that really doesn't prove anything. I'm sorry I can't be more positive, but there's no way I can tell whether you actually walked or whether it was a very real dream. I won't even hazard a guess. We'll just have to wait and see if it happens again."

"It was so real!" Dan's voice was eager. "I just don't see how it could have been a dream."

"Dreams can be very real. But even if it *was* a dream, it's a good sign." Dr. Hinkley patted Dan's shoulder. "Subconsciously, your body wants to walk. And the subconscious is very powerful. You may have several of these dreams before your body actually responds. Keep your hopes up, Dan. And try to relax. You'll walk again when your body's ready."

Marian could see the disappointment on Dan's face. He had been so sure. Dr. Hinkley was being kind, but it was clear he didn't believe Dan had walked.

"Is that coffee ready, Marian? I could use a cup before I make my rounds at the hospital."

The doctor followed Marian into the kitchen. She turned to him just inside the kitchen door.

"What do you think, Dr. Hinkley?" she said softly so Dan wouldn't hear. "Did Dan walk?"

"I can't say, Marian. Hysterical paralysis is a tricky thing. Let's assume that Dan *did* walk. It's symptomatic that it happened in his sleep. Remember, everything hinges on his guilt about the accident. Dan's an active man. His body is too restless not to walk, but his guilt won't let him walk when he's awake. It's entirely possible the incident happened, but it's much more likely it was only a dream."

Marian sighed. "Dan was so happy this morning, and now he's crushed. What can I do to help him?"

"The best thing you can do is to keep him calm and hopeful. And don't let him get too anxious if he has these episodes again. I think we're better off assuming they're dreams. It'll be easier for Dan to cope with them. If he thinks he's sleepwalking, it might frighten him."

Dr. Hinkley stayed for an hour, visiting with both of them. They talked about the hockey team and Nisswa's chances for the championship. Marian could tell that Dan wasn't really listening. Finally, the doctor left to go to the hospital.

"You're disappointed, aren't you, honey?" Marian sat on the side of the bed and held Dan's hand.

"Yeah." Dan didn't look at her. He looked down at his legs and sighed. "I guess it was only a dream, Marian. The doctor's right. I'm sorry I got you all excited for nothing."

"But you didn't! It's a good sign, Dan. You heard the doctor. I think this dream of yours was a rehearsal. You have to go over hockey plays in your head before you get out on the ice, don't you? Your mind's rehearsing how to walk, and pretty soon your body will do it. All you need is patience, darling. And you shouldn't push yourself. You'll walk again, Dan. I'm sure of it!"

Dan was relieved when Marian went to the kitchen to make breakfast. He wasn't hungry, but he wanted to be alone. Had he walked? He still wasn't sure. If it happened again, he wouldn't say anything. It wasn't fair to drag Dr. Hinkley over here for nothing. And he wouldn't mention it to

Marian. There was no sense in disappointing her if it was only a dream.

He reached down and touched his legs. There was no feeling. He made a fist and smacked his thigh, hard. Nothing. It was like hitting a punching bag. He hit his leg again and again until his arm was tired. His leg should hurt like hell, but he didn't feel a thing. The doctor was right. It must have been a dream.

CHAPTER 5

It was noon on Monday, and Marian had spent most of the morning getting her books and papers together.

"Well, I'd better get going." She put on a cheerful smile for Dan's benefit. "Are you sure you don't want me to get the wheelchair, honey? You could move around down here if you weren't stuck in bed."

"No!" Dan's voice was sharp. "I'm fine here in bed, honey. Leave that damn thing in the closet. It just takes up space in here."

Dan's face seemed so suddenly vulnerable. Marian tried to understand. The wheelchair represented sickness, disability. It was the symbol of all the things he didn't want to face. If only Dan could think of it as temporary, he might accept it. He had to believe he wasn't going to be in a wheelchair forever. Dan needed to keep up his spirits if he wanted to recover.

"I'll put the phone right here." Marian plugged in the extension and placed it on the bedside table.

"Call the school if you need anything. Mary said she'd send a message to my room right away."

"Have a good day, honey."

She turned back, but Dan's eyes were closed. He'd been silent and thoughtful ever since his walking dream. She wished she could shake him out of his quiet mood, but she had to start for school. It wouldn't do to be late on her first day back.

Marian felt empty and sad as she picked up her books and papers, and retrieved the car keys. They used to leave together. Dan would warm up the van, and they'd ride together to the school. They would kiss good-bye in the parking lot and meet again for lunch in the faculty dining room. Sometimes they'd stopped at the grocery store on the way home or taken Laura out for a hamburger. Now all that was over. Now she was alone. Marian warmed up the van herself and carried her own books and papers. Life was so very different now.

The brilliant sun glancing off the fresh white snow did nothing to erase Marian's loneliness. She backed the van out of the garage and turned onto the plowed street, trying not to breathe too heavily until the defroster kicked in. Already the windshield was beginning to cloud on the inside, and she wiped her glove over the surface, melting a space large enough to see through. It was slightly warmer today, but she felt chilled to the bone. It was a cold born of loneliness, and she hoped going back to work would help. At least the kids in her class would be glad to see her.

* * *

"Yes, Jenny?" Marian had purposely dressed in a bright yellow pantsuit this afternoon. She wanted to appear as cheerful and normal as possible. Her second-grade students were bound to be uncomfortable, and it was up to her to reassure them. She gave Jenny Powell an encouraging smile as the tiny redhead raised her hand. Jenny got quickly to her feet and cleared her throat.

"Uh . . . Mrs. Larsen . . . well, the whole class wants you to know how sorry we are about the accident, and if there's anything we can do to help you, all you have to do is ask."

Jenny got to the end of her obviously prepared speech and sighed dramatically. "My mom wrote that for us, and I practiced last night. I feel so awful, Mrs. Larsen, and so do the rest of the kids. We really loved Laura, and it just isn't fair!"

"Thank you, Jenny." Marian swallowed hard. "That was very sweet, and thank your mother for her help. Actually, I think the best thing you can do to help me right now is to take recess five minutes early. You wouldn't mind that, would you?"

"No, ma'am, Mrs. Larsen!" Ricky Owens spoke up from the back of the room. "Can we stay out until the regular bell? Then us guys could play King of the Mountain!"

Marian winced at his grammar, but she nodded. "Until the regular bell. Now button up those coats. It's cold out there."

Two minutes later it looked as though a tornado had swept through the second-grade classroom. Marian picked up a forgotten textbook and placed it neatly on top of a desk. Then she took a deep breath and headed for the teachers' lounge. No doubt they'd all be wondering how she was doing her first day back at work.

"Do you think we should say anything?" Midge Carlson's voice carried clearly out to the hall.

"It might be easier if we just acted the same as always," Edith Peters, the music teacher, chimed in.

"Let's play it by ear." Sally was speaking now. "We'll take our cue from Marian."

A ghost of a smile touched Marian's lips. They were worried about her. She'd have to set them at ease immediately, or there would be more than a few uncomfortable moments.

"No, you shouldn't say anything." Marian opened the door to the teachers' lounge and walked in. "And I wish you would act the way you always do . . . especially if someone made coffee."

"Oh, Marian!" Edith looked embarrassed. "We didn't expect you so soon. We just didn't know the best way to—"

"I know." Marian smiled at the assembled group. "I'll be sure to call out for help if I need it, so don't worry about that. Right now I'm more interested in having a cup of this terrible coffee than anything else. Is it left over from last Friday?"

"I made it fresh this morning." Edith hurried to pour. "Have a couple of cups, Marian. Consider it your civic duty. If someone doesn't drink it, we'll have it again tomorrow."

For just a moment, with her hand on her coffee cup, Marian considered telling her friends how she really felt. She could say she was alienated, stuck in a nightmare that wouldn't go away. It had started with Laura's desk, the front desk in the second row.

It was so empty now. She kept glancing at it, knowing that she should move another child to Laura's place, but somehow she couldn't. No one could take Laura's place. Then there were the papers, the best artwork displayed on the bulletin board, with Laura's picture among them. And the roll book, with Laura's name in black ink. An efficient teacher would reassign Laura's seat, file away her artwork, erase her name from the roll book. But how could she wipe out all traces of her baby when Laura was still so alive in her heart? If there was nothing left of Laura in her classroom, would the wonderful memories die, as well?

Marian wanted to confide in her friends, tell them how frightened and alone she felt, but of course, she couldn't do that. Oh, they would be sympathetic to poor, poor Marian, but not one of them, not even Sally, would really understand.

She was quiet for a moment, and the conversation went on without her. They were talking about the Christmas program now. That was safe. Marian joined in gladly. Her class was scheduled to sing three carols. She would hold a practice right after recess.

"There goes the bell." Marian rinsed out her cup and set it to drain on the small sink. "I promised to get the children started on their Christmas presents today. I guess we'll make candles this year."

She paused for a moment just outside the door. They were talking about her again, saying how brave she was, how well she managed. Marian smiled to herself as she walked up the hall, high heels clicking against the old, wooden floor. They hadn't guessed she was playing a part. No one knew the truth. Now all she had to do was never let anyone know how desperate she really felt.

For once, the faculty meeting started on time. Marian pulled out her notepad and pen, prepared to write down any schedule changes for the holiday season. There was a murmuring as the principal walked in and took his place at the lectern in the front of the library. Harvey Woodruff was a small man, dressed in a traditional brown suit, an ever-present white carnation in his lapel. He was a picture of frustrated authority as he cleared his throat and banged the small, wooden gavel on the stand for attention.

"Worse than the senior study hall." He paused for a moment and smiled at the predictable burst of laughter. "Now that I have your attention, the December all-school faculty meeting will come to order. The secretary will read the minutes of the November meeting."

As Miss Pepin, the home economics teacher, droned on in her colorless voice, Marian found herself staring out the window at the playground, absently noting the "angels" the younger children had made. She remembered making an angel with Laura last winter, helping her fall backward in the fresh snow, laughing as she swept her arms and legs out in arcs, and lifting her carefully to her feet to see the wings and gown she had made.

"Marian?"

She came out of her reverie with a start. Harvey was calling her name. "We'd like a report on how

Dan is doing, Marian. Mrs. Baltar says she got at least a dozen calls last week from concerned parents."

Marian stood up and nodded at the twenty-five faces turned her way. "Dr. Hinkley says there's been no change in his condition as yet, but he's very hopeful. Dan is in good spirits and sends his regards. He misses all of you."

"Well, he doesn't have to miss us for long!" Drew Burns stood up. "Tell Dan his hockey team is suffering from a lack of expert attention and they've written up a petition for him to come back. They say they don't care if he can get out on the ice with them or not. They'll rig up some way to get him out to the rink and back, if he'll just be there for practice. Those kids miss him, Marian. Try to convince Dan that it's his duty to come back right away."

"That's my feeling exactly." Harvey nodded. "Dan could certainly handle his history classes, and we'd work out something for hockey practice. The important thing is to keep up morale. The state championship is only eight weeks away, and we've got a good crack at it if Dan comes back. Do you think he's well enough, Marian? We'd make every concession possible."

"I'll ask Dr. Hinkley." Marian nodded. "Yes . . . I'm sure Dan could handle it if everyone cooperated. It might be a good idea to send over some of the boys from the team to talk to him. If he knows they need him, it might help."

"It's as good as done." Drew was grinning, and Marian smiled back. Drew would be relieved to have the hockey team off his back. The basketball championships were coming up too, and Drew had his hands full with his own department.

"That's it, group." Harvey Woodruff dismissed them. "Only two weeks until Christmas vacation. And let's watch the tree lights this year. Last year's power bill was definitely out of line."

"Do you think Dan'll come back right away?" Edith picked up her stack of papers and walked with Marian to the door. "I think getting right back to work is the best medicine. Look what it did for you. You're amazing, Marian. I always knew you were a tower of strength."

"Thank you, Edith." Marian put on a smile, but her heart wasn't in it. She just hoped Dan wouldn't feel everyone was pressuring him. He had a kind of stubborn pride. She knew he'd never go back to work if he thought he couldn't do the job. And then he'd turn bitter and disillusioned if he stayed cooped up in the house day after day with nothing to do but watch television. Somehow she had to convince him to go back to work. It was the only solution.

As she stepped out into the icy twilight, Marian drew in her breath sharply. Fear, deeply hidden in the depths of her mind, came crashing to the surface. What if Dan wouldn't go back to work? What if he never got better? Could she even pretend to be strong enough for both of them?

"They're coming tonight?" Dan frowned as Marian gave him the news. "Oh, honey . . . isn't there some way you could put it off for a while?"

"They're anxious, Dan. Drew says they even signed a petition for you to come back."

Dan sighed. He supposed there was no way to get

out of it now. He'd have to talk to them whether he was up to it or not.

"I'll make supper right now, honey." Marian smiled brightly, and Dan tried to concentrate on what she was saying. "Would you like pork chops or steak?"

"Either one's fine. It really doesn't matter, Marian. How about some scalloped potatoes? We haven't had those in a long time."

The scalloped potatoes were a stroke of pure genius. Dan was proud of himself for thinking of it. Now Marian would be tied up in the kitchen, and he'd have time to think. He had to come up with something to say to stall the team. There was no way he was going back to work in a wheelchair. The boys might not understand, but certainly Drew would have a little consideration for his feelings!

Dan raised himself up in bed and leaned against the backrest pillow Marian had bought him. His shoulders ached, and he was tired. He'd tried to be cheerful for Marian, even though he hadn't felt like it. Poor Marian. It had been a rough afternoon for her. She'd cried when she told him about Laura's empty desk, and he had felt like crying right along with her. It must have been painful, facing all Laura's friends and classmates. Dan knew he couldn't have done it.

Dan knew Marian would worry about him if he confessed he hated the children who were Laura's age. He had tried, but he couldn't control his feelings. They walked past the house in the mornings, laughing and throwing snowballs on their way to school. They were so damn happy! It just wasn't fair.

Why should they be happy when Laura was dead? It should have been one of them and not Laura!

The boys filed out the door, full of enthusiasm and spirit. Drew pulled Marian to the side, out of the cold draft from the open front door, and draped a friendly arm around her shoulders.

"Talk him into it, Marian." He stood close to her, and she could see the fine lines of concern on his face. "He told the boys he'd give them an answer by the end of the week, but it doesn't look good. The kids think he's coming back, but I'm not so sure. Dan's changed. Oh, he smiled and kidded with them, but he's not the same Dan."

As Marian nodded, Drew pulled his stocking cap over his sandy hair and sighed deeply. "Frankly, I'm worried. If we don't get Dan out of the house soon, he's going to hole up in here like a hermit."

"I'll do my best, Drew," Marian promised. Drew did look worried. His usual carefree expression was gone, and the tips of his small mustache seemed to droop. Everyone was worried about Dan. She wondered if Drew was worried about her, as well.

He seemed to sense her unspoken question. Drew slipped his arm around her shoulders again and hugged her close. "It'll work out somehow, Marian. Don't despair."

Tears came to Marian's eyes, and she blinked them away. "I . . . I don't know what to do." She faltered. "There's got to be some way of convincing Dan to go back to work."

"Is there anyone else Dan would listen to?" Drew

frowned slightly. "How about someone he's close to? A real friend?"

"Ronnie Powell's a friend," Marian began hesitantly. "Do you think I should ask Ronnie for help?"

"Sure." Drew flashed his easy grin. Marian could tell he felt better with a plan of action. "Call Sally, and get the Powells in on it. Ronnie can talk some sense into him. Dr. Hinkley might be able to help, too. I'd talk to him if I were you."

Drew turned on the top step and looked back at her. "If you need anything, Marian, just give me a call. I'll be here over the Christmas break."

Marian almost asked, but he was already halfway down the snowbanked sidewalk. Just today the teachers' lounge had been full of gossip about Drew's Christmas vacation. Everyone thought he was going to Aspen with his stewardess girlfriend. One of Drew's legendary romances must have suffered a setback.

She stood staring after him until he turned the corner. She didn't want to go back in the house and face Dan just yet. She felt unprepared and defenseless. She needed a little time to herself before she talked to him.

Marian shut the heavy front door and leaned against it wearily. A burden far too heavy to bear had settled on her shoulders. She had to be strong for Dan now. She had to make him see that hiding here in the house would do nothing but hurt him more in the end. Dan had always been the decision maker, and now she was faced with an unfamiliar role. She had to decide what was best for him and do it.

Quietly, almost stealthily, Marian climbed the

stairs to the phone in the upstairs hallway. She called Sally, and Ronnie promised to come in to talk to Dan on Friday. That was his day off. Then she dialed Dr. Hinkley's number.

"You're absolutely right, Marian." Approval was clear in the doctor's voice when she finished her explanation. "I'll get in on it too. When I see Dan on Wednesday, I'll tell him to go right back to work. He's brooding, Marian, and the best cure for brooding is work."

"And how are you getting along, dear?" Dr. Hinkley's voice was kind. "You went back to work today, didn't you?"

"Yes." Marian smiled wryly. "It's good to be back, and I'm fine. Or I would be if I weren't so worried about Dan."

"Just leave Dan to us," the doctor reassured her. "We'll shake him out of that house. Do you have enough pills, Marian? You have to be careful to get your rest. I'm concerned about you, too."

Dr. Hinkley sounded so kind that for one shaky moment, Marian almost blurted out the truth. She wanted to tell the doctor that things were not as well as they seemed, that she was suffering, too. This morning she had awakened to find herself clutching the pillow as if it were a life raft, and the only way she could make it through the lonely hours was to rely on her secret hope, her crazy fantasy that Laura was not really gone, that any day now Laura would write her a note from the other side.

"Yes, I'm just fine, Dr. Hinkley." The moment for confidences passed. "Now, I'd better get back to Dan. And I'll tell him to expect you on Wednesday."

Marian sat down on the top step and cupped her chin in her hands. She had seen Laura sitting this way many times, staring off into space, lost in her own secret world. Marian wondered what her daughter had thought about in those quiet, reflective moments. Did Laura have dreams? Did her mind take secret flights to faraway places? Was Laura in such a place now? Watching her and listening to her concern about Dan?

A worried expression settled over Marian's face. She had to believe that Laura was out there somewhere, not really dead but waiting. It was the only way she could go on. Dan believed. And she had to believe, too. But it would be so much easier if she had another note.

Her legs were stiff when she got up at last. Marian gripped the banister and steadied herself. Her eyes were drawn to the end of the hall, to Laura's door.

She knew she shouldn't, but the room drew her like a magnet. Marian hesitated for a moment in the upstairs hallway, then pushed open the door to Laura's room. Faint light spilled in from the hallway, and she didn't have the heart to switch on the lamp in the room. She knew what she would find. There would be a fine cover of dust on all Laura's toys and books. The room would be empty, neglected. In her weaker moments, Marian thought that perhaps her friends were right; she should pack away Laura's things and put the room to other use. Sally had suggested a sewing room or a guest bedroom, but Marian couldn't bear that. It was so cold . . . so final.

Marian swallowed hard as she gazed around her

daughter's room. The brightly patterned clown wallpaper mocked her with its cheerful motif, and Laura's sweater was draped over the edge of the bed, where she'd tossed it before the snowmobiling trip. Her flannel nightgown was folded untidily on the top of the dresser, and her shoes peeked out from beneath the chest of drawers. Everything was exactly as it had been, untouched and empty without Laura's bright presence. Tears began to form in Marian's eyes, and she squeezed them shut tightly. She had never felt so bereft and alone.

She sat down in the rocker, the same rocker in which she had cuddled Laura when she was a baby. She remembered the little, downy head pressed against her breast, the sweet, tiny fingers that clasped hers, the first time Laura smiled up at her. The birthdays, Laura's first Christmas, the memories came in a flood. And now Christmas was coming again. Marian couldn't bear to think about Christmas without Laura.

Her tears were an endless well. Marian pressed her hand to her mouth to muffle her sobs. The rocker moved as she cried, squeaking against the old floor. The familiar motion of comfort had turned into unbearable pain.

There was a noise upstairs. Dan turned down the volume on the television and listened. Marian was in Laura's room. He could hear the old rocker creaking and the sound of her muffled sobs. Dan wanted to run up the stairs and take her in his arms, smooth back her hair and dry her bitter tears.

He had to do something to comfort her. He couldn't bear to hear her crying like this.

What could he do? He was stuck down here, a prisoner in his bed. There had to be something!

Another note from Laura would comfort her. Dan picked up the book by the bed, but there were no more pieces of folded paper stuck inside. He wished he could write one and say it was from Laura. Would it be wrong? It was a deliberate deception, but it was a small price to pay to ease Marian's grief.

The pen was in his hand before he had made up his mind to do it. Then he was writing, forming large block letters on the notepad he found in the drawer.

Be happy Mommy. I love you, Laura.

There was a cookbook by Marian's side of the bed. Dan opened it and stuck the note inside. Then he called out for Marian as loud as he could.

Her eyes were red and puffy as she came into the room. Dan felt an almost physical pain as he came face-to-face with her grief. It didn't matter whether he'd done the right thing or not. He'd do anything to see her smile again.

"It's another note, Marian! I found it in your cookbook."

Her hands were trembling as she reached for the note. There was a long silence, and then she sighed. It was a sigh of peace, a sigh of contentment. Then a radiant smile transformed her weary face.

"It's true, Dan." Her voice was shaking with happiness. "Laura's here, watching us. I never really believed until now. Oh, Dan! She's not dead! This note proves it!"

What was she talking about? This note was like the last one. It was supposed to be an old note he'd found in her cookbook.

"Don't you see, darling?" Her eyes were shining as she smiled at him. "That cookbook is new! I got it in the mail last Friday. And look at the printing. This isn't an old note. The letters are perfect. Laura's written me a note from the other side!"

For a moment he was stunned. What had he done! Now Marian thought Laura was writing her notes from the grave!

He had to say something, do something, to clear up her misunderstanding. Dan was mute as he gazed into his wife's ecstatic face. There was no way he could admit he had written the note. That would force her back into a terrible depression. She'd never trust him again if he told her the truth.

"Dan? What's wrong, honey? Don't you believe that Laura wrote me this note?"

"Of course I believe it." Dan made his lips smile. "It's just a shock. That's all."

Now her arms were around him, her lips on his. "I love you so much!" she whispered. "Everything's going to be all right, Dan. I'm sure of it now."

A moment later she was up, smiling and happy. "I haven't done a thing for the holidays. We really ought to set up a Christmas tree in here. Laura would be upset if we didn't. How about that corner, Dan? Do you think a tree would look nice there?"

"Sure." Dan nodded. "Whatever makes you happy, Marian."

She was already in the doorway, face radiant, eyes sparkling. "I'll run out and buy a tree right now. The Red Owl's still open. A small Scotch pine would be just perfect. It's Laura's favorite!"

After Marian left, the worry began to grow in Dan's mind. Had he unwittingly fostered an unhealthy fantasy? Then he remembered her happy smile as she ran out to buy the tree. With the hope he'd planted in her mind, Marian was full of cheer and energy. Maybe now she'd be all right. He didn't know what he'd do if Marian expected more notes from Laura!

CHAPTER 6

Marian awoke with a smile on her lips. It was a quarter after six, and she was wide awake. In this hour, just before dawn, the room was filled with a half-light. Solid objects were dark shadows against the dimness.

She slid out of bed and stretched, her body tingling with energy. Then she picked up her robe and slippers and tiptoed out of the room. She'd let Dan sleep until the coffee was ready. This was a perfect time to have the house to herself, to think about Laura, to rejoice in her happiness.

Laura wanted her to be happy. She'd said so in her note. Marian patted the pocket of her robe, and the paper crinkled reassuringly. She would carry the note with her today so she could look at it whenever she felt lonely.

By the time she had finished dressing, the coffee was ready. Marian poured a cup and sat at the table, savoring its steamy flavor. The kitchen was light now. It was almost seven. The sun was hiding behind storm clouds, and more snow was predicted. It could turn into a blizzard, but the weather had no effect on her happiness. The day was beautiful. Laura was here.

"I hate these gray days!" Sally set her tray down next to Marian's at the long Formica table. "Are your kids restless today?"

"No." Marian smiled happily. "We finished our Christmas candles this morning. They turned out even better than I expected. And after lunch we're going to start a new unit in reading."

"What's your secret? I haven't been able to accomplish a thing. Are you taking a new kind of pep pill?"

Sally was joking, and Marian laughed. In a way, Sally was right. She *did* have a secret, but she couldn't tell Sally. Marian knew why things were going so smoothly today. Her good spirits and enthusiasm were all due to Laura's note. Everything was easy now that Laura was here.

"How's Jimmy Dahl doing this year?" Sally tried the stew and made a disgusted face. "Roger just got back this morning. He was out for two weeks with the measles. Do you think Jimmy could help him with his makeup work?"

"I think he could handle it." Marian waved at Harvey across the room. "I have to talk to Harvey for a minute, Sally. My grade book's right there on the table. Why don't you check for yourself?"

Sally paged through Marian's grade book. Jimmy

was above average in every subject. He'd make a fine tutor for his little brother.

Marian was deep in conversation with Harvey. Sally flipped to the attendance page and found Jimmy's name. He hadn't missed a single day this year. The measles must have passed him by.

Her eyes skipped down the page. Laura Larsen. There was a check mark for "present" in today's column. *Present?* Sally frowned. That was certainly strange. She could understand Marian's reluctance to take Laura's name off the roll, but to mark her present? Marian must have made a mistake.

The Red Owl was crowded, and Marian didn't bother to get a cart. All she needed was milk and some cereal. She avoided the crowd of shoppers at the produce section and cut around the back of the magazine rack to the cereal aisle. She grabbed a box off the shelf and hurried to the dairy case to pick up the milk. A moment later she was in the ten items or less line.

There were five people ahead of her, and the milk was cold against her arm. Marian shifted it to her other hand and juggled the box of cereal. Suddenly the picture on the box registered in her mind. Froot Loops. Laura's favorite cereal, the only kind she would eat. Marian and Dan hated it.

The box of cereal slipped from her nerveless fingers. What was she doing? Laura was gone. There was no reason to buy Froot Loops now.

Tears came to her eyes, and Marian blinked them back. It was no use. She was going to cry right here in the store. She set the milk down in a stray shopping cart and ran out the door. She didn't stop running until she was safely in the van.

It was a long time before she raised her head from the steering wheel. Then she glanced around her fearfully, hoping no one had noticed her dash from the store. The parking lot was full. People were doing their last-minute shopping after work. No one was staring at her. Everyone was in a hurry to get home.

Tears were still running down her cheeks. Marian reached into her purse and took out the note from her baby. It was too dark to read it, but she knew the message. Laura loved her. Laura was watching her. Laura would think she was silly to cry over a box of Froot Loops.

"I'm sorry, baby," Marian whispered. "Mommies are silly sometimes. I just forgot for a minute, that's all."

The street was full of traffic as she pulled out of the parking lot. Marian waited for a break in the traffic and drove toward home. It had been a long day, and she was tired.

It was late. It seemed he'd been sleeping for hours when the noise awakened him. Marian was standing by the bookcase in her robe and slippers. She took an armload of books off the shelf and carried them into the living room. Something about the quiet way she moved disturbed him. He heard pages rustle. There was a series of thumps as she stacked the books on the table. Was this some sort of strange dream, or was Marian really dusting the bookshelves at this hour?

Now she was back again, moving stealthily. She replaced the books she had taken and left with another armful. What was going on?

He was about to call out to her when he realized what she was doing. Marian was looking for another note from Laura!

What could he say? Dan tried to think of something, but he was just too sleepy. He heard her replace the rest of the books, and the light in the living room clicked off. When she slid into bed beside him, he reached out to cuddle her close. He was still trying to think of the right thing to say when he dropped off to sleep.

In the morning she was cheerful, smiling as she brought in his breakfast. It was Wednesday. Dr. Hinkley was coming today. Marian was full of last-minute instructions, and there wasn't time to say anything then. She had to hurry off to work. And now he was waiting for her to come home, hoping to see a smile on her face.

Dan pushed the backrest to a more comfortable position and poured himself a cup of coffee from the thermos Marian had left this morning. Dr. Hinkley was concerned. He said Marian was worried about him in the house alone. He'd spent the entire time of the examination urging Dan to go back to work. Everyone seemed to be nagging him about work. Harvey and Drew wanted him back for the team's sake. Dr. Hinkley wanted him back for Marian's sake. And Dan admitted he should go back for his own sake. He was growing bitter and despondent cooped up in the house. All those arguments made perfect sense, but he couldn't seem to force himself to go back.

Dan tried to be objective. He honestly didn't think a man in a wheelchair could coach hockey. They all wanted him back out of pity, and that was a damn poor reason. "Isn't he brave?" they'd all say. "Poor man, he looks so pathetic. Did you know he used to play hockey in college? Now he can't do a thing, but he's still got his job. One thing about Nisswa. We take care of our own."

It was enough to make him sick! Dan knew his attitude wasn't healthy, but he couldn't seem to rise above it. If it weren't for Marian, he'd give up for good.

It was late. Mrs. Owens had stayed well over the half hour allotted for parent-teacher conferences, and then Harvey had wanted to talk. Marian hung her coat in the closet and pulled off her boots. She had to check on Dan. Perhaps he was in better spirits today.

She'd been so full of hope yesterday, after Dr. Hinkley's visit. But Dan refused even to talk about going back to work. He said he was thinking about it. And this morning he had been quiet and uncommunicative. She had been worried about him all day.

He was asleep. Marian stood in the doorway and blinked back tears as the wave of despair she had been battling all day hit her with the force of a physical blow. Dan was unmoving, uncaring in his slumber. The small Christmas tree she'd set up at the foot of his bed was dark. She should have thought to put it on a timer. It was almost more than she could bear, seeing her husband here in the dark, with no cheerful lights to lift his spirits. She tiptoed to the foot of his bed and switched on the tree, hoping that he would wake with a smile and they could talk. But Dan's eyelids didn't even flicker as the tiny, colored bulbs cast a rosy glow over the room. Suddenly she had to get out, get away from the wasted man who was once her strength.

The day's mail was still in the box. Marian ran out the front door and dashed down the icy side-walk to the mailbox. The hinge seemed to be stuck, and she pulled with all her strength to open it. There was a tiny plastic bottle of shampoo inside, a new-product sample. It had burst as it froze. Now there was shampoo ice all over the inside of the mailbox. When would out-of-state companies learn about Minnesota winters?

She wiped off the mail as well as she could and carried it back to the house. There was a power bill, a campaign letter from their congressman, and a preprinted postcard.

It was the final straw. Marian stared at the writing on the postcard, and tears came to her eyes. It was from Laura's dentist in Brainerd, a reminder of her six-month appointment. She tried to stop crying, but it was no use. Laura was gone. She was foolish to pretend any longer.

Marian climbed the stairs and opened the door to Laura's room. She felt as if her head would split. She was on a roller coaster of emotion, and she had to get off.

There were brief periods when she was happy,

secure in her knowledge that Laura was with her. She would smile and laugh then. Her energy was high. Then her mood would change abruptly, and doubts would return. Was it foolish to believe that Laura was still here? There were no more notes. Had something happened to take her baby away forever?

She stood in the doorway and closed her eyes, trying to bring back the comforting feeling that Laura was with her. The room seemed empty now, deserted. Marian picked up a dust cloth and wiped the top of the bookshelf. Then she rearranged Laura's toys, as if the act of cleaning her baby's room would bring her back.

This time nothing helped. She couldn't shake her terrible loneliness.

"Where are you, Laura?" Her forlorn whisper hung in the silent room long after the words were spoken. There was no answer. Marian switched off the light and shut the door behind her, plunging the room into darkness again. Laura's room. Laura's toys. Laura's clothes. Life was all so empty without Laura.

Somehow she made it through supper, putting on a cheerful act for Dan. Then she sat at the kitchen table, correcting papers until the childish printing swam before her eyes.

"I'm going for a walk, honey." Marian raised her voice so Dan could hear it over the sound of the television. "I'll be back in a few minutes."

"Wear my parka, Marian. It's warmer than your coat. I just heard the news. It's five below tonight."

* * *

It was clear and cold, a perfect December evening. Marian's boots squeaked as she walked past the lighted houses. The Murphys were still up. They were probably waiting for Barbara to get home. She worked at the Tom Thumb until ten on weeknights.

Marian's breath sent up icy clouds of moisture that condensed in the air like smoke. Dan's parka kept her toasty warm inside. It was made for sub-zero temperatures. She'd walk around the block once. Then she had to get back home.

Irma Mielke hadn't shoveled today, and her house was dark. Marian wondered whether she was visiting her son in Florida. Irma usually spent the month of December there. She always came back with a suntan that was the envy of everyone in Nisswa.

The snow was trampled with the boot prints of neighborhood children. Marian could pick out Ricky Owens's path. His boots were unique. Ricky's father had carved initials in the bottom of the rubber.

Marian followed the trail of *RO*s to the end of the block. Ricky had stopped at the park on his way home from school. There was a cluster of footprints near the Viking monument. Two other children wearing moon boots had joined him there.

The park was deserted at this hour. Fir trees stretched up to tower over the surrounding houses, and the green-painted benches were covered with snow. Marian brushed off a bench with her glove and sat down for a moment. It was so quiet, she could hear her heart beat. There was only the sound of her breathing to mar the silence.

She sat for long moments, staring up at the streetlight. A few lazy flakes of snow were falling, whirling and dancing in the circle of light. The snow stuck to her eyelids, and she brushed it away. The night was still and waiting. Was Laura up there somewhere, watching her?

The park in the winter was a lonely place. Marian shivered slightly. Her toes were numb. She could feel the cold creep through the leather of her boots. She stood up and stomped her feet. Then she pushed her hands into the deep pockets of the parka and walked back the way she had come.

"You know how I feel about it, Marian." Dan's voice was firm. "I won't go back to work if I feel I can't fulfill the terms of my contract."

"But how about the team, honey?" Marian made an effort to be cheerful as she brought in his morning coffee and sat next to him. "The boys simply won't accept a substitute. They're convinced that no one else can coach them. You could coach from the sidelines, couldn't you? They really need you."

"Sure, I could coach from the sidelines." Dan gave a bitter grin. "That'd be fine if I coached basketball or baseball. Hockey's different, Marian. You've seen me out there with the team. You know how critical it is to demonstrate everything. How am I going to skate from a wheelchair? Tell me that!"

"Now, honey, don't get upset." Marian tried to be calm and reasonable. "Why don't you get Cliff Heller to do the demonstrations? I'm sure the boys will cooperate. They're so anxious to get you back."

"It wouldn't be the same, but it might just work." Dan frowned thoughtfully. "That's not a bad idea, Marian. I think Cliff could handle the demonstrations if I gave him some extra time. It might even be good for him. He wants to be a coach someday. I don't know, Marian. . . . The thought of getting pushed to practice in a wheelchair is pretty hard for me to handle. Maybe I should give up coaching for good."

"Now, don't be silly!" Marian reached out to take his hand. "You're a wonderful coach, and it's just plain ridiculous to talk that way. Before you know it, you'll be right back out on the ice with the team. Dr. Hinkley's sure your condition isn't permanent. Wouldn't it be dumb to give up your coaching job and then find yourself all recovered a week later?"

"Maybe." Dan met her eyes and then looked quickly away. In that brief contact, Marian saw his despair. Dan was convinced he wasn't going to get better. He had lost hope.

"I've got to run, or I'll be late." Marian got up and headed for the door. "Don't forget that Ronnie's dropping by this afternoon. I baked the rest of those cookies, and they're in the jar in the kitchen."

"Have a good day, Marian."

She turned at the doorway, but Dan was already switching on the television. He sounded so sad and lonely that she hated to leave him. At least he'd have company today. Ronnie was coming in this afternoon. She hoped Ronnie would be persuasive. Going back to work was the only thing that would perk up Dan's spirits.

* * *

Dan switched off the television the moment she left. He needed to think. Marian was trying to hide it, but he saw how depressed she had been. He'd heard her moving around in Laura's room when she thought he was asleep, and he knew exactly what she was doing. Marian was looking for another note from Laura. It had become an obsession with her. If he wrote another note, she'd be happy again.

No. He couldn't deceive her again. The notes might be bad for her in the long run. There had to be some other solution, some other way to bring her out of her depression.

He knew what she wanted. Dan winced as he came to a painful decision. He had to conquer his fear and go back to work. It was the only thing that would help. If he went back to work, she could stop worrying about him. He'd be there, in the same building with her.

There was a knock on the door, and Dan called out. Ronnie was early. In a way, he was glad Ronnie was here. He needed something to take his mind off his problems.

"Hi, Marian!" Dan's cheerful voice greeted her as she opened the front door. "Ronnie just left."

"Sounds like you had a good visit." Marian rushed to the den and stopped at the doorway in sudden confusion. The formerly neat little room was a total disaster. Newspapers were spread out all over the bed, an open package of Doritos was leaning against the lamp, and the wastebasket was full of crumpled balls of notepaper. In the midst of it all, Dan was sitting propped up in bed, writing something on a clipboard.

"Good heavens!" Marian leaned against the wall, staring at Dan. A smelly cigar was clamped, unlit, between his teeth. "What happened?"

"Oh, I guess we made a mess." Dan grinned up at her. "Ronnie was here all afternoon."

"And the cigar must be Ronnie's contribution." Marian wrinkled her nose as she picked up several beer cans and forced them into the overflowing wastebasket. "What are you doing, Dan?"

"Ronnie saved all the sports pages for me." Dan grinned and handed her the cigar. "Throw that away for me, will you, Marian? I don't know how Ronnie can smoke these things."

"You're working out hockey plays!" Marian bent over to look at the clipboard. "Does that mean you're going back to work?"

"I have to," Dan said cheerfully. "Ronnie talked me into it. He laid down a fifty-dollar bet on the championship, and he can't afford to lose it. If I don't get back to work on Monday, he says he'll switch his bet to Brainerd."

Marian stood still, staring at Dan's clipboard. She could hardly believe her ears.

A smile of genuine amazement flooded over her face. Dan looked so much better. Thank God for Ronnie Powell and his disgusting cigars!

"Ronnie told me a new joke." Dan gave her a rakish wink. "Did you hear about the Brainerd hockey team? It seems they all drowned."

"And why did they drown, Dan?" Marian played the straight man with a grin.

"Their coach sent them out for spring training!"

Marian groaned. "That's about what I expected from Ronnie."

"Now, run off and let me go back to work." Dan waved her away with a grin. "Oh, those cookies were good. Ronnie raided the cookie jar for us, so I won't be hungry for a couple of hours. And, Marian? I really love you, honey."

She was still laughing as she went to the kitchen. The joke wasn't really that funny, but she felt wonderful. Dan was going back to work. She'd make something special for supper to celebrate.

Marian ran some water and washed the coffeepot. She took a roast from the refrigerator, seasoned it, and popped it in the oven. Next she'd roll out a piecrust and make Dan's favorite apple pie for dessert.

There was a Popsicle in the freezer, left over from summer. Yesterday the sight of Laura's treat would have desolated her. Tonight it had no effect at all. She was happy. Dan was going back to work.

Marian stopped and listened. She stood perfectly still and let the feeling of closeness wash over her.

"Hello, baby!" she whispered. "Your daddy's going back to work!"

CHAPTER 7

Dan arranged his books and papers again and looked up at the clock. His students would be here in five minutes. Marian had driven him to school early so he could get everything organized before his first class. Maybe it wouldn't be as bad as he had anticipated. His wheelchair fit neatly behind the desk. If he tried hard enough, he could almost make himself believe that he was sitting in a regular desk chair. Of course, he couldn't get up and pace the way he usually did. And he supposed he'd have to appoint a scribe for each class, some student with good handwriting to make notes on the board.

All in all, he felt much more confident than he had anticipated. Teaching history should be fairly easy, even from a wheelchair. The big problem would come in hockey practice.

The bell rang, and students began to stream into the room. "Welcome back!" Ginny Davis gushed. "We really missed you, Mr. Larsen."

Jerry Lindstrom spoke up. "We had Mrs. Hendricks last week. She must be at least ninety. All we did was read."

"I'll have to remember that if I'm ever gone again." Dan grinned. "Somebody in this school should teach you boneheads to read."

There was a groan, and the class faced him expectantly. For a second Dan felt real panic. What did they want?

Oh, yes. The absence slip. He got out his class roster and read off the names. It was strange how quickly he'd forgotten the routine.

"Do you want me to write on the board, Mr. Larsen?" Ginny raised her hand. "I volunteer."

"Fine." Dan beamed at her. He'd never been wild about Ginny before, but today she was a real sweetheart. "Write down 'the Industrial Revolution. England. Eighteenth century.'"

It was a total surprise when the bell rang. Time seemed to fly this morning. Dan dismissed his class and took a second to relax. So far, everything was going just fine. It had been a good lecture, and his class was attentive. Maybe this wouldn't be so bad, after all.

The door opened in the middle of second period. Harvey Woodruff stuck his head in, waved, and backed out again. Dan shrugged, and the class laughed.

It happened again ten minutes before the bell. This time it was Tom Woolery from across the hall. A smile, a wave, and he was gone.

"Tomorrow we'd better discuss the open door policy," Dan quipped. The class seemed to find his humor uproarious, but he still managed to quiet them down in time to give an assignment before the bell.

Third period was even worse. Lois Scott, Dave Bartleman, and Mary Baltar peeked in. Dan knew everyone wanted to say hello, but couldn't they wait until lunchtime? It was difficult to teach with these constant interruptions.

He had just dismissed his third-period class when he figured it out. They were checking up on him!

"Leave the door open, Hank," Dan called out loudly. "It seems my fellow faculty members are all checking up on me today. Maybe they think I'm showing dirty movies in here."

The class enjoyed his joke, but he had to fight to keep his mind on his lecture. Dan did a slow burn all through fourth period. Four teachers passed his room, waving cheerily. What did they expect? Did they think he was going to fall out of his wheelchair and break his nose?

At last it was lunchtime, and Dan stayed in his classroom as the students filed out. He'd really prefer to take his lunch in here, away from the stares of the other teachers, but Harvey had vetoed that idea. He said it was important to get right into the swing of things.

Dan propped his elbows on the desk and closed his eyes. He was tired, and he didn't feel like socializing. Marian would be waiting for him, and she'd want to hear all about his morning. He wished there were a broom closet he could hide in.

Marian poured herself a cup of coffee from the giant urn on the counter and carried it to the table.

She was much too nervous to eat. Voices buzzed all around her, but she took no part in the conversation. Any moment now, Dan would be here. Harvey Woodruff had promised to bring him to the lunchroom personally.

There was an excited buzz, and the door to the teachers' lunchroom opened.

"He's back!" Harvey pushed Dan's wheelchair through the door. "Somebody get a tray for Dan, and it'll be like old times."

He wheeled Dan to an empty table and held up his hand. "And let the man eat before you bombard him with questions. I don't want any complaints about short lunch hours."

Marian took her place beside Dan. He looked tired. His face was white and drawn, but he seemed to be in good spirits.

"How was it, honey?" she asked softly.

"Pretty good." Dan gave a little grin. "Actually, my bonehead history class was better than they've ever been before. They must have felt sorry for me. Maybe being a cripple has some advantages."

"Oh, Dan . . . don't talk like that. You're not a cripple. This is just temporary. Remember what Dr. Hinkley said."

"Sure." Dan looked up to smile at Dorothy Pepin as she brought a tray. "Mmmm . . . steam-table macaroni and canned peas. My favorites! And yellow pudding for dessert. Just look at what I've been missing."

"They really could make a more appetizing meal." Dorothy peered down at the tray over her silver-rimmed glasses. "Even my seventh-grade girls can do better than this. I'll send you up some cookies later, Dan. My seniors are doing a unit on nutritional snacks."

"Granola and sorghum," Dan muttered as Dorothy went back to her table. "Or safflower and wheat germ. I know Dorothy's nutritional snacks. They're practically inedible."

"It was sweet of her to offer." Marian grinned a little. "She probably thinks they're wonderful, Dan. See how thin she is? That's because she cooks nutritious foods."

"Oh, for a TV dinner!" Dan groaned. "Compared to Dorothy's recipes, even this stuff looks good. I guess I'd better see how much macaroni I can get down before the bell."

"I'll stay until you're through with hockey practice," Marian offered. "Just have one of the boys come to my room when you're ready to go home."

"Fine." Dan scooped up a spoonful of peas. "It'll be a short practice today. The wind's starting to blow."

"Don't get cold out there. And make sure you wear your gloves." Marian stopped suddenly, her face coloring with embarrassment. "I'm sorry, honey. I know you're perfectly able to take care of yourself."

"Yes." Dan pushed his tray back and checked his watch. "I'd better get going so I can beat the rush in the halls."

"Let me push you." Marian got up and moved to the back of his chair. "It'll be faster that way."

"No." Dan's tone was flat. "I don't want you doing everything for me, Marian. I'm going to have to get used to this, and it might as well be now."

Without another word, he clumsily turned the

wheelchair and headed for the door. One of the other teachers opened it, and he propelled the chair through.

The bell rang loudly, and Marian picked up her cup and carried it to the trays against the wall. She could hear the shouts of students racing to class as she left the lunchroom and entered the corridor. Dan was just turning the corner in his wheelchair. Several students were clustered around him, and Cliff Heller was pushing. For a second, Marian felt a stab of unreasonable jealousy. He hadn't wanted her to push his chair, but it was fine if Cliff did. She felt like an outsider with her own husband.

"Your kids are in." Sally rushed past her with a quick smile. "They came back from the playground a little early. It's cold out there!" Marian quickened her pace and arrived at her room slightly out of breath. Her class was back indeed. And they were shouting like a bunch of wild animals.

"That's enough!" Marian flicked the light switch for order. "Let's all calm down now, and I'll read us a story. How about another chapter in *Charlotte's Web*?"

"Marian?" Drew called to her across the crowded room. The teachers' lounge was always hectic this time of day. "Come over here a second, will you?"

Drew pulled out a chair for her and patted it. "Take a load off your feet. And smile, for God's sake. You look terrible."

"Just tired, I guess." Marian tried to force a smile, but it failed miserably. She'd been on pins and needles all afternoon. Even her class knew that something was wrong. She'd lost her place in the reading text and assigned the wrong problems for math.

"You don't have to worry about Dan." Drew patted her shoulder. "I checked on him fifth period, and he was in top form. They were discussing Waterloo when I poked my head in the door. Dan was Napoleon, and the class was Wellington. I think the history books are wrong. It really sounded like France was winning."

"Dan could teach history in his sleep." Marian smiled. "It's hockey practice that worries me. Dan's out at the rink right now."

"We could always check it out." Drew flashed a conspiratorial grin. "Why don't we go for a walk and just happen to drop by the hockey rink?"

Marian frowned. "I'm not sure that's a good idea. Dan's a little upset about coaching in a wheelchair. An audience might embarrass him."

"Don't be silly, Marian. Dan's a good friend of mine. He won't be a bit upset if I drop in to take a look. And he certainly couldn't object if you came along. He'll probably be glad to see you."

Drew was persuasive. Marian wrapped her coat tightly around her and waited for him to join her. She tied her scarf securely and slid her hands into warm gloves. It was growing cold. The big thermometer attached to the side of the building stood at fifteen above zero.

As she walked across the playground with Drew, Marian had thoughts of turning back. Would Dan be angry if they dropped by without an invitation? She needed reassurance too badly to back out now. They could take a quick peek and then go right back to the school. She had to make sure that Dan was all right.

They stood at the very back of the wooden bleachers, partially hidden by the crossbeams. Dan was on the sidelines, shouting out to the team. He was wearing his huge winter parka, but he looked small and defenseless in the distance. Marian wanted to rush to him and give him her long, woolen scarf, or at least turn up his collar. He was all alone, the wheelchair a dark blotch against the gray winter sky.

Marian shivered slightly. The wind was cruel today, and watching Dan made her icy inside. He had always been the strong one, streaking across the ice with exuberance. He was the one who told the boys they weren't tired, that they were weaklings if they couldn't keep up with a thirty-three-year-old man. Now, suddenly, he looked frail.

"Cold?" Drew turned to look at her. "Come on, Marian. . . . Dan's doing fine. Let's go back inside, where it's warm."

"Just a second more." Marian saw Cliff Heller skate over to Dan. There was a little conference, and Dan turned his head their way. He had seen them. Dan beckoned to her, and she left Drew standing there as she hurried to the edge of the rink.

"Coming out to check up on your crippled husband?" Dan smiled coldly.

"Dan!" Marian blinked back sudden tears. He was really angry. Now she was sorry she hadn't stayed inside. "I'm not checking up on you." Marian's voice shook. "I just thought I could save you some time. I'm through in my classroom,

Dan. Now you don't have to send one of the boys to get me."

"Go back inside, Marian. And take Drew with you. We'll talk about this later."

Dan turned away and blew a sharp blast on his whistle. He totally ignored Marian as the team came in from the ice.

"Let's do that last play again." He reached out to slap Gene Watson on the arm. "This is hockey, Watson, not figure skating. It doesn't matter if you look pretty. All you have to worry about is speed."

"Okay, Coach." Gene grinned. "I think I got it now. Give me another crack at it, huh?"

It was clear that Dan had dismissed her. Marian walked quickly back to Drew, her back rigid.

"He's really mad," she explained. "He told me to go back inside."

The crust of the snow was hard, and their boots crunched with every step as they walked back toward the school. Drew patted her shoulder awkwardly.

"We shouldn't have gone. He was furious, Drew. I guess we embarrassed him, after all."

"Aw, you're imagining things." Drew gave her a grin. "Dan's all right. He's just tired, that's all. He shouldn't have taken on all his classes and the hockey, too. They offered to give him half days, but he refused."

They reached the teachers' parking lot, and Drew headed toward his car. "See you tomorrow, Marian. And don't worry. Dan'll be fine as soon as practice is over."

* * *

Marian was busy in the kitchen, and Dan turned up the volume on the television. They'd have to talk soon. He couldn't stand the silence any longer. But how could he explain the awful surge of anger he felt when he saw her standing there with Drew?

Of course, he was being unreasonable. Dan knew that. He was sure Marian hadn't deliberately set out to hurt him when she came out to the rink with Drew. The problem was in his own mind. Something had snapped when he saw them standing there, his pretty little wife and Drew.

Dan gave a bitter laugh. Marian was so innocent. She'd never guess that Drew had designs on her. Hadn't she heard the stories about Drew and his female conquests? It was the favorite topic of discussion in the faculty lounge.

The tension built with every moment that passed. Marian was a nervous wreck by the time she stacked the dishes in the sink. Dan hadn't said a word all through their meal. Now it was bedtime, and Marian could stand the silence no longer. It would only be worse if she didn't get things straightened out.

"I'm sorry I came out to the hockey rink, Dan." Marian's voice was shaking. "I never meant to embarrass you."

Before she realized what was happening, tears fell down her cheeks. Then Dan held out his arms, and she rushed to him, sobbing openly.

"It's my fault, Marian. Don't cry. I acted like a real bastard today. I can blame it on the fact that I was afraid, but that doesn't excuse anything. I never should have taken it out on you."

"You were afraid?" Marian raised her head to look at him. There was a pained expression on Dan's face.

"When I saw you at hockey practice, I was afraid of losing you. I saw you standing there with Drew, and it was like someone stabbed a knife through my heart. You and Drew look good together, Marian. I saw the two of you walking through the snow. Then I thought of us, you and me, and how we'd look. You'd have to push me in the wheelchair, Marian. We'd look like some kind of freak couple. Everyone would pity you because you were stuck with a cripple!"

"No! That's not right, Dan! No one would . . ."

Dan put a finger to her lips. "There's more, Marian. I probably won't have the nerve to say this again. Let me finish . . . please?

"You're beautiful, Marian. No one knows that better than I do. And you deserve a man to love you. I can't do any more than hug you at night. That's why I'm afraid of Drew. He can give you what I can't. Don't you know the kind of reputation he has?"

"Oh, Dan!" Anguish was in Marian's voice. "All I want is you, darling! I don't want Drew. You should know that. I think you're being unfair to him. Drew's always been your good friend, and nothing's changed. Just because he's been nice doesn't mean he wants to sleep with me."

"He'd be a fool not to want you." Dan gave a sad little smile. "I trust you, honey. And I believe you'd turn him down. But how will you feel a year from now? There's no guarantee I'll ever walk again."

"Dan, I love you." Marian took his hand and squeezed it. "I'm not looking for anyone else. I'll never look for anyone else. Drew means absolutely nothing to me, and I won't even talk to him again if it bothers you. I want you, Dan. You're my husband. The vows we made mean something to me, and I intend to obey them."

He reached out to hold her then, and Marian cuddled up against his chest. She stroked his cheek with her fingers and kissed him softly. His body was tense, and she rubbed his neck, fingers working lovingly to ease the tension.

Dan's breathing deepened with sleep. She could feel his tense muscles relax. Poor Dan. All this was her fault. She had been so busy thinking about her own problems, she'd failed to see the terrible burden he was carrying.

Marian turned off the light and stared up at the darkness. Was Dan right, after all? She *did* miss the physical closeness they had shared. No, Dan was wrong. She was his wife. She didn't want another man. She would never want another man.

She could see the moonlight sparkle on the surface of the water. She was . . . yes . . . in a bedroom, walls lined with pine, giving off a faint scent of freshness in the still night air. There was a light burning in another room, the hiss of a lantern, the soft thudding of summer bugs against the screens. It was hot, but there was a breeze gently cooling her body. She was naked, lying comfortably on crisp, white sheets.

A sound came from the other room, the pop of a cork, the smooth gurgle of something poured from a bottle. And now he was standing in the doorway, blocking out the light so she could not see his features. She recognized his hard, muscled body. She knew it well.

There was the tingle of fine champagne on her tongue, the muted laughter they shared over a toast, the soft gasp she gave as his lips claimed hers. The rock-solid feeling of his body as they slipped together, sweaty and not caring, on the cool sheets.

And then there was rapture, the feel of his lips touching her, exploring her body, the sweet saltiness of his skin against her tongue, the probing, heady hunger that made her wild, crying out for more, welcoming the fantasies of a thousand dreams.

She was more than ready, craving his love, eager to taste all the familiar pleasures that had been denied her lately. She opened her eyes and looked up, loving the lean, long look of him. Her fingers played along his cheekbone, tracing the fine lines at the corners of his mouth. Laugh lines, as her grandmother had called them. The tips of her fingers brushed against his skin, stroking, loving. They were lost in an eternity of passion.

Now the room was growing brighter, the morning sun was peeping over the edge of the pines. She could smell the clean, fresh air and feel the exhilaration of being awake, together, before another living soul. The stereo was on. She knew it was her favorite song, but she couldn't quite make out the melody. And now it was playing the same note over and over, stuck on a groove, the same note again and again and again. . . .

"Oh, God!" Marian sat up and turned off the electronic alarm. The sun was vainly trying to enter the cracks in the venetian blinds, and morning was here. She had to hurry, or they'd be late.

She slipped out of bed silently. Dan was still asleep. She'd get ready and then wake him. He needed his rest. She just hoped that today would be easier than yesterday.

She was dressing when she thought of it. Laura was getting behind on her classwork. She'd bring home some books tonight and a copy of the assignments.

"Would you like that, baby?" Marian whispered the words. "I could help you right here at home."

She stood still for a moment, and then she smiled. Yes. Laura was here. She could feel her baby's presence. And she was right. Laura wanted to keep up with the rest of her class.

CHAPTER 8

"I got the call last night, and I still can't believe it. I went in to interview over three years ago!"

Drew sat facing them in the teachers' lunchroom. His tray was barely touched, and he was obviously too excited to eat.

"The Knicks?" Dan's tone was awed. "Go for it, Drew. That's what you've wanted all along, isn't it?"

Drew nodded. "Harvey said there'd be no trouble getting out of my contract. Butch Johnson's just waiting for the chance to take over the team."

"When are you leaving?" Marian managed a smile. Of course, she was happy for Drew, but she would miss him. He'd been a good friend.

"I'll wind up everything this week and give Butch a head start. Then I'll move during Christmas vacation. I feel kind of bad, leaving the basketball team right before the play-offs, but Butch'll do a good job. I'd be a fool to pass up a chance like this."

Marian stared at him across the cluttered table. Assistant coach of the New York Knickerbockers! Most high school coaches dreamed of a chance like this. It meant more money than a high school teacher could ever hope of earning and the chance to step up into the big spot someday. Drew would be a fool to stay here in Nisswa when the big leagues wanted him.

"We'll hit you up for a couple of tickets if we ever get to New York." Dan's grin was friendly. "I'm really happy for you, Drew. You deserve a break like this."

Of course Dan was happy, Marian thought. Now he didn't have to worry about Drew anymore.

Dan glanced at the clock and set down his coffee cup. "Well . . . I've got to get back. How about a push from the most famous member of the faculty?"

Marian stared after them as the door closed. First Laura had left them and now their friend Drew was leaving, too. She felt as if her whole life were unraveling, thread by thread.

The elementary wing was silent as she walked down the hall to her classroom. There were papers to correct before her class came in from lunch. She'd just have time for math class, and then there was a practice for the Christmas program. Perhaps the busy schedule would keep her from thinking.

The room seemed empty without the children. Marian switched on the lights and sat down at her desk. She needed something to cheer her up. She had never felt so all alone.

"Are you there, Laura?" She closed her eyes and tried to picture her daughter's smiling face. "I need you, baby!"

"Hi, Marian." Sally stood in the doorway. "Were you talking to me?"

"Oh, no . . ." Marian opened her eyes with a start, and her face grew hot. Had Sally heard her talking to Laura? "I guess I was just mumbling to myself. Are your kids coming to the practice, Sally?"

"You bet!" Sally grinned cheerfully. "We've been rehearsing all morning. My kids are singing 'Silent Night.' I just hope Margie Kujawa's got the words right this time!"

Marian looked puzzled, and Sally laughed. "I had the kids color a Nativity scene today. You know . . . Mary, Joseph, and Baby Jesus in the manger? Margie said there was someone missing. She wanted to color Round John Virgin!"

Dan was in a good mood. He chatted and laughed as they drove home. He didn't even complain when she stopped at the post office for stamps. Marian couldn't believe what a difference Drew's news had made. Now Dan was happy again. Today he was Drew's best buddy. But only because Drew was leaving town.

The line at the post office was long. The lady ahead of her was mailing Christmas packages, and Marian waited impatiently for the clerk to weigh each one. She had to buy stamps for her Christmas cards. If she didn't get them out this week, there would be no sense in sending them at all.

She was going to miss Drew. Marian stared at the large sign on the wall, reading it over and over without comprehension. THE POSTAL SERVICE WILL NO LONGER ACCEPT PACKAGES TIED WITH STRING. MAIL EARLY FOR DELIVERY BEFORE CHRISTMAS. Drew was a good friend. He'd certainly never been improper with her.

Marian gave a quick, impatient sigh and shifted from foot to foot. Her main concern now was being a good wife to Dan, and she'd make him her only male friend. Marian moved up to the head of the line and reached in her purse for her money. Dan was working now, and he appeared to be coping with his infirmity. She should be grateful that he was pulling out of his depression, taking an active interest in his classes and the hockey team.

At last it was her turn. Marian picked up her stamps and headed back to the van. She should be happy, but she wasn't. The only time she was happy was when Laura was with her.

There was a knock on the door as they were finishing supper. Marian left the room, and in a minute she was back with Ronnie Powell in tow.

"Ronnie needs to see you, Dan. I'll leave you two alone."

"Hey, Dan." Ronnie looked uncomfortable. "I've got some bad news, and Sally roped me into telling you."

A wry expression flickered across Dan's face. More bad news? This had certainly been the year for it. One more catastrophe couldn't hurt. Pile them on. . . . He could take it. What could be worse than losing Laura and turning into a cripple?

"Well, spit it out." Dan gave Ronnie an encouraging nod. The poor guy really looked uncomfortable.

"It's Muffy." Ronnie shook his head. "She's a lot worse, Dan. Sally thinks she's starving to death. We tried to get her to eat, but she won't touch anything. It's like Muffy doesn't want to live anymore. Do you know what I mean?"

Dan nodded. Poor Muffy. He had been afraid of this.

"We're taking her down to the clinic right now. Roy's waiting for us. I just thought I should tell you, that's all."

"We'll meet you down there." Dan gave a weary sigh. "Marian will want to hear what Roy has to say. She's going to be pretty broken up over this."

Marian's hands were trembling as she loaded Dan's wheelchair in the back of the van and drove through town to Roy McHenry's clinic. Ronnie's station wagon was parked in front. Roy's small clinic was immaculate, but she could still smell a blend of antiseptic and animal sickness as she pushed Dan through the door. Ronnie and Sally were waiting, sitting uneasily on the plastic-covered furniture.

"We dropped Jenny off at the Fischers'," Ronnie explained. "She's spending the night with Becky. Sally thought it would get her mind off Muffy."

Sally dabbed at her eyes with a handkerchief. "Roy's got Muffy in the back."

They heard footsteps, and Roy opened the waiting room door. "Marian? Dan?" He nodded a greeting.

"How is she?" Marian was the first to speak.

"Not good." Roy shook his head and sighed. "I don't know what to tell you, Marian. I really thought a visit with Jenny would do the trick, but

Muffy's much worse. She's literally starving to death, and there's nothing I can do."

"We tried every kind of dog food on the market." Sally was perched on the edge of her chair. "Jenny gave her scraps off her own plate, but Muffy wouldn't touch them. Ronnie even brought home liver from the butcher shop, but we still couldn't get her to eat. I feel so bad about this!"

Sally's voice was shaking. Marian reached out and patted her friend's hand.

"She wouldn't eat for us, either," Dan said softly. "You did everything you could, Sally."

Roy nodded. He took a deep breath and cleared his throat. It was plain to see he didn't like what he was about to say.

"I ran some blood work, and it doesn't look good. Muffy's body heat is at a dangerous low, and her muscles are beginning to cramp. I'm afraid she's terminal. She might live for another week or so, but it'll be very painful for her." Roy swallowed hard. "If Muffy were mine, I'd put her to sleep. She's suffering, and she's not going to recover."

"Oh, no!" Sally was crying now, tears streaming down her cheeks. "I'm so sorry! Are you sure you can't do something, Roy?"

The young vet shook his head. "You know me, Sally. I love animals. I certainly wouldn't advise it if there were any other way."

Dan reached out for Marian's hand. "I think Roy's right, honey, but you decide. I know you want to do what's best for Muffy."

Marian stared into his earnest eyes and dipped her head in a nod. Her mind was whirling, and she couldn't seem to think clearly. She had been so sure Laura's puppy would recover. But Roy was a good vet. If he couldn't save Muffy, no one could.

"Will . . . will it hurt?" Marian's voice was almost inaudible. "I don't want her to suffer, Roy."

"No. She'll go to sleep, a nice peaceful sleep. And there won't be any more pain."

Roy walked over and patted Marian on the shoulder. "I know it's hard, Marian, but you're doing the right thing for poor Muffy."

Now it was past midnight, and Marian was still awake. Dan had gone to sleep hours ago. She was tired, but she couldn't sleep. All she could think about was Muffy. She should have had the courage to sit with her, to pet her before she died.

"Oh, God!" Marian sat up with a sob. She had to find some comfort somewhere. She'd never felt so lonely and frightened. Dan had held her close when they got home. There had been comfort and love in his arms. But now he was sleeping, and she was alone again.

Marian slipped out of bed and walked through the silent house. Her mind was in turmoil. What should she do?

She climbed the stairs and opened the door to Laura's room. Yes, it was much better in here. A faint smell of roses still hung in the air. Laura was very fond of roses. Her dresser drawers were filled with rose sachets.

Marian curled up on Laura's bed. She would just close her eyes for a minute. The feeling of Laura was strong in this room.

"You're so close, baby. You're so close, I can almost touch you."

Marian's whispered words were comforting. There was a small, secret smile on her face as sleep came at last. Laura was here. And she could hear her baby talking, just to her.

Laura was laughing, her long, blond hair shining like a halo. They were outside in the backyard, making a snowman. Muffy was dashing and chasing at Laura's heels, frolicking in the snow. The little dog slid comically as she tried to go through a snow-drift, and Laura rescued her with a happy squeal. Muffy was licking her face now as Laura picked her up and held her close.

She was looking through a window at the happy scene outside. Marian tried to open the door to join them in their play.

"Come on, Mommy!" Laura called out. "Come out and play with us!"

But the door was stuck fast. Marian stared at it in horror. She couldn't go outside.

Laura called to her again, and tears ran down Marian's face. She tugged at the door with all her strength, but it would not open. She could see them through the window, but she couldn't get to Laura.

Marian sat up, tears running down her cheeks. It had been so real! This was the first time she had dreamed about Laura. And she couldn't join her, not even in a dream!

The minute she turned on the light, she saw it, Laura's diary, open to today's date. The blue-lined page was filled with childish printing.

Muffy is here. Thank you, Mommy. Now I'm not so lonesome anymore.

Was she still dreaming? Marian shut her eyes tightly and opened them again. The words were still there. She had to show Dan right away!

"Dan! Oh, God . . . Dan!" Marian rushed into the den and switched on the light. It was two in the morning, but Dan had to wake up. She wanted him to be happy, too.

"Oh, Dan, just look at this! It's another note from Laura!"

Dan's eyes snapped open, his sleep shattered. The room was filled with light, and Marian was shaking him. What was she saying? Another note from Laura?

"But that's impossible! I didn't . . ." Dan stopped, dismayed. He couldn't admit he'd written the last note. It would destroy Marian's happiness.

There was a tense moment as he struggled to think. Another note from Laura. And he hadn't written it. How was that possible?

He was puzzled for a moment, but then it was clear. Marian wrote it herself. Of course. She used to write things in her sleep all the time. He remembered how she kept a notepad by the bed. In the morning there would be lines of poetry or items for her grocery list. They used to laugh about it then. Should he remind her?

"Read it, Dan!" Marian thrust Laura's diary into his hands. "I'm so happy!"

As his eyes scanned the lines, Dan was sure he was right. Marian's subconscious was at work here. She was rationalizing Muffy's death. And she needed to believe that Laura was still with her in spirit.

He looked up into Marian's ecstatic face. There was just a small seed of worry as he stared at her. Hadn't Marian's delusion gone a little far?

No. She was happy now. He couldn't destroy that. All this would pass in time. Dan held out his arms, and she came to him, warm and loving and happy.

"Isn't it wonderful?" Her voice was a whisper as she snuggled up close. "Aren't you happy, darling?"

"Yes, I'm happy." As he spoke the words, he knew they were true. He was happy that Marian trusted him, confided in him. There was no reason to get upset over a harmless delusion. It really couldn't hurt her at all.

CHAPTER 9

Marian sat up and turned off the alarm. It was very early. The room was still dark.

Dan was sleeping soundly, the blankets snug around his body. Marian longed for that same comfort. The urge to cuddle up to Dan and go back to sleep was very strong. She wanted to wrap herself in warm covers and sleep the whole day away.

Even though it was torture, she pushed her feet out from under the blankets. The cold air shocked her into some semblance of a wakeful state. She crawled out of bed and got into her robe.

Marian stumbled slightly in the early morning grayness. The house was cold, chilled with the night, and she turned the thermostat up a bit. Heat was an extravagance in the far north, but she'd be damned if she'd freeze before she had her first cup of coffee.

The linoleum floor was cold on her bare feet as she hurried across the kitchen, walking on tiptoe to minimize the discomfort. She plugged in the coffeepot and took down a cup, shivering slightly.

Then she sat on a kitchen chair, feet tucked up under her robe, too uncomfortable to fall asleep but too sleepy to really wake.

The coffee was finally ready, scalding and aromatic in her cup. She took a cautious sip and grimaced as she burned her tongue. It was Friday, the last day before Christmas vacation. And she was supposed to arrive early to organize the children's Christmas party.

She dressed in front of the register, letting the warm, musty furnace air blow over her body. No time for a shower. No time to do her hair. Everything had to go smoothly now, or they'd be late. Make breakfast, help Dan dress, gather up the presents for her class that she'd wrapped last night, pick up her books, find Dan's books, remember to take the sheet music for Christmas carols, and pack the cookies she'd baked for the faculty lounge.

Marian took a moment, one precious moment, to do absolutely nothing. She opened the back door and stood there in the frosty cold, breathing deeply. Her breath puffed out in little white clouds as she stood silent and watched the sun lengthening over the banks of plowed snow. A dog barked somewhere in the stillness. A truck rumbled by on Main Street. There was the sound of a door slamming somewhere in the distance. Everywhere in town, people were rising, getting ready for work, making breakfast and straightening bedcovers, exchanging morning greetings over cups of strong coffee. Life was good here . . . or it had once been good.

* * *

"You'll come, won't you, Mrs. Larsen?" Jenny stood at the classroom door, her new pencils clutched tightly in her hand. JENNY FROM MRS. LARSEN, they proclaimed in gold lettering. Every student had five, a special Christmas present from their teacher.

"I'll try, honey," Marian promised. "It all depends on how Dan feels."

"Mom said to make you come," Jenny announced. "She said my daddy'd come in and carry Dan if he had to. Christmas Eve won't be any fun without you. You always come on Christmas Eve!"

"All right, I'll come." Marian couldn't resist Jenny's pleading. She'd talk Dan into it somehow. And if he wouldn't be budged, she'd go by herself for a few minutes.

"Merry Christmas!" Jenny called out, scampering down the hall. "I'm taking the bus today. My mom said it was good for me to be independent. She's in the teachers' lounge, waiting for you."

"A pack of Christmas dish towels." Sally was stacking up her gifts, displaying them for Midge and Edith. "And here's another pair of red and green Christmas-tree earrings. Say . . . do you gals know anyone with pierced ears?"

"I got handkerchiefs this year," Marian announced brightly, setting down her coffee to unfold a hideous poinsettia-printed square. "And oodles of talcum powder. I wonder if my kids are trying to give me some sort of hint."

"It's the mothers." Edith spoke with authority. "They give you whatever they got last year and didn't want to keep."

Midge Carlson, the only first-year teacher in the bunch, spoke up. "I think it's sweet. Mrs. Barnes gave me a fruitcake. There was a little note saying it was wrapped in brandy. She hoped I wouldn't mind."

Marian and Sally looked at each other and laughed.

"Keep it in your top closet for a month," Sally advised. "Then, when things get rough around the end of January, cut off a little piece during recess. Edith and I know. Mrs. Barnes's fruitcakes actually make teaching bearable."

"Oh, Marian?" Sally looked perturbed as she turned to Marian. "I'm afraid I have to renege on the party tonight. Jenny was supposed to spend the night with Ginger, but that fell through and I can't get a baby-sitter. It looks like I'll have to stay home."

"How about Ronnie?" Edith suggested. "Put him to work as a baby-sitter."

"Ronnie's tied up in a poker game with Dan." Sally rolled her eyes. "By the time he gets home, the party will be over. But you shouldn't miss the party, Marian. Why don't you go without me?"

"You can go with us," Midge offered. "Edith and I are going to stay until it gets rowdy."

"I'll let you know." Marian glanced at the clock and gathered up her things. "I've got to run now. Dan's last class is out in ten minutes."

Marian walked out to the deserted parking lot and started the heater in the van. The elementary-school teachers were already gone, and high-school classes were in session for another five minutes. Marian had developed the habit of leaving a little early and warming the van before Dan came out.

Cliff Heller always brought him to the parking lot and helped to get the wheelchair in the van. With the hydraulic lift Jim had installed, it was a simple matter to disembark at home.

Crowds of happy students streamed out of the school, throwing snowballs and shouting. School was out for two weeks. No homework and no studying. Christmas vacation was here.

Marian had a bad feeling about this particular Christmas vacation. It seemed Sally's news was an omen of disappointments to come. She had been looking forward to the teachers' party, the laughter and the noise, the good-natured ribbing and fellowship. She supposed she could go with Edith and Midge, but it wouldn't be the same without Sally. They had been together at every teachers' Christmas party for the past nine years.

He was coming now. Marian backed the van out a little so Cliff would have a nice flat place to wheel Dan. Connie Bergstrom was with him, and she waved at Marian. Connie was a sweet girl, the best teacher's aide Marian had ever had. They were a good-looking couple, Cliff and Connie. Laura loved to have them for baby-sitters. Marian wondered if she and Dan had ever looked that young and that in love.

Dan looked tired as he waved at her. He must have had a hard day. Perhaps he'd want to take a nap until Ronnie and the guys arrived.

Of course, she wouldn't be able to relax until later. Marian's shoulders slumped slightly in resignation. She had to clean up the house and buy some snacks for the poker party tonight. That meant dropping off Dan at home and going to the crowded supermarket for cheese and pretzels. They'd want pizza, too. She'd have to remember that.

Marian yawned. Now that she thought about it, she was tired, too. It had been a hectic day. Her class had been rambunctious, but that was normal for a party day. Actually, the Christmas party had gone very well. Three mothers had shown up as chaperones, and they had all brought refreshments. Everyone had had a good time except Marian.

She had managed to hide her sadness when they opened their presents. She had smiled and taken part in the games. But throughout the party, she had thought of Laura. Laura loved Christmas. Parties were no fun without her baby.

The guys arrived at seven. Ronnie carried in two cases of beer and found room for them in the refrigerator.

Gus Olson was already shuffling the cards when she went into the den. He had on a green eyeshade, and one of Ronnie's awful cigars was clamped in his mouth.

"Shall we deal you in, Marian? Dan says you're a mean poker player."

Marian grinned. "Thanks, but I'll pass. Edith just called. She wants me to come to the teachers' party."

"It'll do you good to go out." Ronnie nodded sagely. "You want her to go, don't you, Dan?"

"Well . . . sure! Of course I do."

There was a hesitation in his voice, and Marian turned to look at him sharply.

"I won't go if you want me to stay here, honey. The party doesn't really matter to me."

"No, you should go," Jim Sorensen said. "If you leave, we don't have to watch our language."

"Go ahead, Marian. I don't mind. Just don't kiss anyone under the mistletoe."

He was joking, but there was a warning in his voice. Marian heard it and knew what it meant. Drew would be at the party. Dan was still a little worried about Drew.

"Are you sure?" Marian bent over his wheelchair and whispered softly in his ear. "Really, Dan. I don't want to go if you'll be upset."

Dan reached out and patted her on the fanny. He winked at the guys and spoke loud enough for them to hear.

"Put on a pretty dress and get out of here, Marian. We've got poker to play. Just make sure you're home by one so you can bail me out if I get short of money."

They were kidding back and forth as she went upstairs to dress. Their loud voices and laughter sounded good in the house. It was wonderful to see Dan having a good time, and she felt a surge of excitement as she thought about the party. Maybe it would be fun, after all.

Marian drove up in back of the Elks Lodge and parked in the lot. Quite a few people were here. She recognized Edith's yellow Honda and Harvey Woodruff's green VW bug. She'd put in a token appearance and go right back home. It made her feel strange to go to a party without Dan.

The parking lot was slippery, and Marian picked her way across the ruts of packed snow, a bit unsure of her footing in high heels. She had thought there'd be a place nearer to the entrance. The sounds of the traffic on the highway a block away were muted by the snow. It was falling again, in lazy, heavy, white flakes. The snowplows would be out tomorrow.

As she opened the door, a blast of heated air and loud music rolled out to greet her. Harvey had hired Fred Norby's band again this year, and they were even louder than she remembered. Fred seemed to make up for a lack of talent with sheer volume, but he knew every piece on request. The band wasn't good, but they were fun. Fred could liven up any party after he'd downed a couple of drinks.

"Nice job of decorations!" Marian shouted over the din. Edith rushed up, beaming. She was the head of the decoration committee, and Marian had to admit the Elks Lodge had never looked so festive. Branches of evergreen hung from the rafters, interspersed with strings of lights and Christmas ornaments. There was a red candle at each table, surrounded by pinecones and a sprig of holly. And in the center of the dance floor, an enormous bunch of mistletoe hung suspended from the center beam.

"I think the lights make this big old place look much cozier." Edith was shouting, too, trying to compete with Fred's music. "I'm glad you came, Marian. Go up to the bar and get yourself some eggnog. It's very good this year."

The eggnog *was* good. Marian walked from table to table, chatting. Everyone seemed glad to see her, replenishing her eggnog glass every time it was partially empty. Without quite meaning to, Marian was beginning to get a little tipsy. They must have made the eggnog a lot stronger this year.

She was sitting with Edith and Midge when Harvey came to claim his yearly dance. Marian smiled and suffered through the ordeal. She was absolutely sure the principal's story about being a dance teacher in his youth was pure fabrication. Harvey whirled her around the floor with no discernible rhythm until Marian thought she would surely slip and fall. At least Fred Norby was on her side. The number was short, and her duty was done for another year.

"My turn." Marian turned to find Drew standing behind her. "Come on, Marian. It's the last chance I'll have to dance with you."

The moment was sad, but Fred's music sounded unusually mellow and Marian smiled as Drew led her in a slow waltz. Her head was spinning from the eggnog, and the bright little Christmas-tree lights seemed to dim, enclosing them in an intimate glow.

"Kiss that pretty lady! You're right under the mistletoe." Fred spoke into the microphone. Several teachers nearby cheered him on, and Drew planted a quick kiss on her cheek. Even though the kiss was perfectly innocent, Marian was very glad when they started dancing again.

"I'll open for a nickel." Ronnie grinned at Dan and winked. "Big spender, huh?"

"I'm in." Gus Olson tossed a nickel to the center

of the table. "How about you, Dan? Is that a little smile I see?"

"Just trying to fake you guys out." Dan tossed in a nickel and laughed.

"Sure . . . I know that expression." Jim Sorensen leaned back in his chair and rubbed his blond beard. "Okay, I'm in, but the next cards had better be good. Louise'll kill me if I lose too much tonight."

The bidding got all the way up to a dollar and a half before they folded. Dan flashed his four kings and raked in the pile of money.

"Some guys have all the luck!" Gus grumbled, opening another beer. "It's my deal, boys. And the luck's about to change!"

Dan grinned, but the words rang in his ears. *Some guys have all the luck.* Sure. Right now he'd trade places with anyone at this table. They didn't know how lucky they were.

Marian was thinking about heading home. The party was getting a little loud now, and she had a slight headache. She took three aspirins out of her purse and washed them down with the rest of her eggnog.

"Here's another glass, Marian." Harvey came up to her table with a drink in hand. "I've been meaning to ask you. What do you think of moving grade six to junior high? Will it disrupt the system?"

Marian almost groaned aloud. She'd be trapped for at least twenty minutes now, discussing the pros and cons of the proposed change. She picked up her glass and took a big swallow. Harvey always liked to talk education at these parties, and he had a habit of going on and on. It might be more interesting if she weren't quite sober.

"I'm not sure, Harvey." Marian smiled sweetly. "What do *you* think?"

Half an hour later, Marian managed to excuse herself to use the ladies' room. She had worked her way through four glasses of eggnog, and her head was whirling. She wanted to leave for home now, but she wasn't sure she could navigate the icy streets. It might be better to stay for a few minutes, until her head cleared.

She sat down in front of the long mirror and stared at her reflection. She looked good tonight. The blue knit dress clung to her figure, and her hair was sleek and glossy. She wasn't really beauty-queen material, but several men had been eyeing her all evening. It was a good thing Dan wasn't here. He'd certainly be jealous tonight.

Midge poked her head in the door. "So that's where you're hiding out! I must say I don't blame you. We saw you sitting there, stuck with Harvey. I just wanted to tell you we're leaving now. Edith wants to get home before her driveway's snowed in."

"Is it that bad out there?" Marian stood up and patted her hair. "Maybe I'd better think about leaving, too."

"You won't have any trouble." Midge laughed. "You know Edith and her driveway. She worries if there's half an inch of snow. Stay and enjoy yourself, Marian. I think this party's doing you a world of good."

"Just the person I wanted to see." Drew grabbed her arm as she walked across the dance floor. "How about another dance before Harvey catches me? He's got Mary's husband cornered right now, but I can tell he's looking for a new target."

"Where were you when I needed you?" Marian asked, grinning. "You didn't come to my rescue."

"Aw, come on, Marian . . . have a heart!" Drew glanced over his shoulder and winced. "And hurry up. He's looking right at me."

Marian giggled slightly. She had half a notion to refuse, but Drew's hand on her arm was compelling.

"All right, but consider it your going-away present." She laughed. "One rescue, all gift wrapped and tied with a pretty bow."

Marian stumbled slightly as they started to dance. She couldn't seem to keep her balance.

"I think you had one eggnog too many, Marian." Drew looked down at her and grinned. "If I didn't know you better, I'd swear you were smashed."

"Not me." Marian shook her head. "I'm as sober as a lawyer. No. A judge. And I think I need another little drink."

"You're going to have a hangover in the morning, Marian. Are you sure you want another drink?"

"Assotively, possilutely." Marian giggled again, her hand to her mouth. "I guess I am a little drunk. But I'm having so much fun!"

"It's your head, kid." Drew pulled her off the dance floor and found a place for them at the bar. "Eggnog, right?"

"I think the lady will switch to vodka now." Marian perched on a stool and smiled regally. "Vodka on the rocks, with a twist of . . . something."

Drew raised his eyebrows, but he poured the

drink. Marian took a sip and coughed. The vodka was harsh, but it felt like hot velvet in her throat. She felt loose and carefree, relaxed at last after a month of grueling tension. She could understand why people drank now; she had never really understood before. Everything was nice. There were no worries. This was turning out to be the best party of her life.

"Hey, Dan? Wake up, buddy. It's your turn to deal."

Dan gave a sheepish grin as he gathered in the cards and started to shuffle. He sure didn't want the guys to start asking him what was on his mind. He'd have to pay more attention to the game from now on.

As he shuffled, he imagined her dancing with Drew, their bodies pressed closely together. She'd probably had a couple of drinks by now. They always drank a lot at teachers' parties. Drew would be holding her a little too close, but she wouldn't mind. She'd be having a wonderful time, laughing up at him as she whirled around the floor.

"Don't you think they're mixed up enough yet?"

"Oh, yeah. Just trying to make sure there're five aces in your hand, Gus." Dan passed the deck over for the cut. He had to stop thinking about her. She was probably discussing teaching methods with Midge and Edith. His imagination was getting the best of him. Christ, he wished she'd get home soon!

* * *

His hands were warm, and Marian cried out softly. For some strange reason her hair was wet. Vaguely, she remembered a silly snowball fight in the parking lot. They really should go home now. It must be dreadfully late. Or were they already home? No, the curtains were striped. Her house didn't have striped curtains.

At least she wasn't drunk. Marian giggled softly. Look at how neatly she had solved that problem. Striped curtains, no striped curtains. She was not at home.

Her dress was folded carefully over the couch so it wouldn't wrinkle. That proved her sobriety. Had she folded it? She couldn't remember taking it off.

Marian opened her eyes wide and looked down at herself. She was wearing . . . nothing. That was funny. The best-dressed teacher at the party was wearing nothing.

There was a sensation of heat and wetness. It felt wonderful. The fingers of her right hand moved down to stroke his hair. The delicious feeling seemed to last for hours, and then she was weightless, watching the curtains recede as she traveled through the doorway and down the hall. Another doorway. Count them. One. Two. It was almost like flying. And then there was a warm, soothing rocking as she sank down on the bed.

A water bed. Her mind was working clearly now. She was on a heated water bed, and the sheets were warm and smooth. She turned to look at the floor and smiled happily. A pile of clothing was growing there. Shirt, pants, socks . . . She was tired of counting.

"Mmmm, it's just like swimming." Her voice was filled with laughter. "This is the first time, you know. I've never been on a water bed before."

There was answering laughter, deeper, more resonant. She tried to sit up to smile at him, but it was difficult to keep her balance. Gentle waves lapped under her, and she was floating, hanging on to the only solid bulwark, arms tightening around his body, pulling him close.

His body was smooth, heat generating under the surface of his skin. His tongue streaked like fire from one aching side to the other. She was caught in the cross fire. The heat was raging. Pleasure streaked through her body in a dizzying circle.

"Don't move." She heard him through a foggy filter. "Just enjoy, honey."

She heard herself laugh. She *was* enjoying and she made a sound, a low moan of animal pleasure. The room was whirling and she was in the center, drowning in a whirlpool of sensation. Faster she raged, whirling and dipping in heart-stopping ecstasy, almost lost in the bursting of this unexpected delight.

Her eyes opened wide and she looked up at him. The man she loved. Her husband. Wonderful Dan. But it wasn't Dan! Drew's face had taken his place!

Suddenly her thoughts turned cold, her mind icy with shock. She looked down to observe her flushed, heated body on the bed. Mind and body were separated fully. She felt nothing but disdain for the very sensations she had loved only a short moment before.

Bad, she thought from her post as unwilling

observer. *Don't. Now, don't. Stop it. Why are you doing this? Wrong. No. No!*

Shame flew from her mind to her body. And then panic so deep, she pushed him back and opened her mouth to scream.

"Marian! Jesus!"

She was quiet now. Calm. "I can't," she stated flatly. "I have to go home. I can't."

"Sure, Marian." He was looking at her with something like fear. "I'll take you back to the van."

She dressed calmly, efficiently, moving like an automaton. Her clear, rational mind gave the orders. And she felt nothing as she rode in silence to the cold parking lot, started the icy engine of the van, and drove off alone. She had not bothered to erase the fear on his face. It didn't matter. The only thing that mattered was Dan.

CHAPTER 10

"Are you sure you don't want me to wait until Marian gets home?"

"No, I'm fine." Dan watched as Ronnie carried the last of the dirty dishes into the kitchen. "Thanks for cleaning up, Ronnie. And thanks for playing such lousy poker."

Ronnie laughed good-naturedly. "How much did you stick us for, Dan?"

"Four dollars and thirty-five cents. That's almost as much as teachers' wages. Maybe I ought to quit working and move to Vegas."

Ronnie laughed. He'd heard this complaint about teachers' salaries before. They were all underpaid. He made more working for the resorts in a week than Dan made in a whole month.

"Well, I'll get going then. See you in a couple of days, Dan."

It was twelve thirty, and Dan switched on the television. *Kind Hearts and Coronets* was running on the movie channel. He'd seen it before, but it was still good diversion until Marian got home. She ought to be here any minute now.

Alec Guinness had been murdered for the fifth time before he started to worry. It was one fifteen, and Marian still wasn't home. If she wasn't home by the end of the film, he'd call the lodge. Maybe the party was running late this year.

They were running the credits now. Robert Hamer was one hell of a director! They didn't make comedies like this anymore. Dan reached for the phone as the last of the credits rolled. He really *was* worried about Marian. The streets were icy tonight.

There was no answer at the Elks Lodge. Either the party was over or they weren't answering the phone. Dan debated for a minute, and then he called Butch Johnson.

Butch answered the phone on the first ring. Dan could hear his stereo playing punk rock in the background.

"Isn't she home yet?" Butch sounded very drunk. "She left the same time I did. It was about twelve thirty, I think. We had a snowball fight in the parking lot, and Marian was blotto. Drew said he'd drive her home."

Dan clenched his fist as he thanked Butch politely and hung up the phone. She left with Drew! And it took only five minutes to get here from the Elks Lodge. He had known something like this would happen!

Maybe Butch was wrong about the time. He was pretty drunk. Or maybe Drew and Marian had stopped off for a cup of coffee. They might even be stuck in a snowdrift a couple of blocks from here.

Dan did his best to give her the benefit of

the doubt, but his mind was filled with horrible pictures. Marian in Drew's apartment. Marian in Drew's bed. Marian lifting her arms and pulling Drew down to her naked body. He felt a mixture of rage and despair as the minutes dragged on and on.

At 2:20 a.m. he heard her key in the lock. Then she was standing in the doorway, her hair disheveled, clothes disarranged, as if she'd dressed in a hurry. There was no doubt in his mind now. Icy rage took the place of worry.

"You were with *him,* weren't you!"

The tears that fell from her eyes were an affirmation. Then she was stumbling toward him, lipstick smeared in a red gash on her white face.

"Oh, God! I never meant to! Dan . . . please! I was so drunk, I . . . I thought it was you!"

Getting drunk was a sophomoric excuse. Dan trembled with anger. Oh, she was drunk, all right. Any fool could see that. But she had known exactly what she was doing!

He wanted to hit her, to rise from his bed and beat the living shit out of her!

Dan gave a bitter snort. That would be pretty hard to do. Marian had the odds in her favor. She could sleep with anyone she wanted, even bring them right into the house, and he wouldn't be able to do a thing about it. Damn these useless legs!

Dan turned his face to the wall. He wouldn't say another word to her. There was nothing to say. She had betrayed him by her own admission.

"Please, Dan, I swear it'll never happen again!" Her voice was shaking and desperate. "I never meant to hurt you. You've got to believe me. Please, Dan! Tell me you forgive me!"

Her guilty tears were wet against his cheek, but there was no way she could reach him now. He was isolated by his anger. He was a rock, a cold, untouchable shape in the bed as she cried out her useless pleas for forgiveness over and over again.

At last it stopped, and she was quiet. Dan was alone in his cocoon of pain. He heard her rise and get ready for bed, felt her slip under the covers beside him. Her skin was warm as she cuddled up against him, but he felt no closeness. She was a stranger now. The Marian he had loved was dead.

Marian had cried for hours, but he wouldn't forgive her. He was like a block of ice in the bed, frozen and still. Just being close to him made the cold creep into her heart. She was alone in her pain, alone in her guilt, totally and irrevocably alone.

Laura's room. She was out of bed the moment she thought of it. She would go to Laura's room and sleep. She would be alone there, but no more so than here. And Laura might come to her and comfort her.

She switched on the Snoopy night-light and opened the heat vent. It was better up here, away from Dan. There was comfort in the shape of Laura's toys in the dim light. Marian turned back the covers and slipped into the narrow bed. She was so tired. In no time at all she was warm and asleep.

* * *

Dan stared out the window. It was starting to get light. He couldn't make out the numbers on his watch yet, but it must be between five and six in the morning.

He was alone in the bed. Marian had left him, and he had heard her go up the stairs to Laura's room. Dan had felt relief. With Marian gone, he could sleep at last. Just having her beside him, sharing his bed, was a constant pain.

It seemed he had just dropped off to sleep when the dream came. It was another walking dream, the kind he had experienced before. This time he walked to the kitchen. The moon was shining in the window, casting pale blue shadows over the linoleum floor. He opened the refrigerator and poured himself a glass of orange juice, then stood at the window and drank it. The moon was cold and full over Heidelberg Hill. He rinsed out his glass and came back to bed, the floor icy under his bare feet. Then he pulled up the covers and went back to sleep, only to wake again with a strange sensation in his legs.

It was hard to believe it was only a dream. Dan reached down to feel his legs, grabbing the flesh between his thumb and finger, pinching hard. Nothing. There was no feeling at all. Not now. But they had tingled before, and there was a soreness in the muscles of his thighs. It was the same sensation he used to get when he skated too long or hiked up a long, steep hill. Now it was gone, but he remembered the dream. He had walked again, and it felt so real!

He stared out the window, eyes bleak, and

watched the daylight come. His mind was filled with memories, and his heart was filled with hate. Damn Marian for taking what he couldn't give her!

For a moment she was disoriented, unfamiliar with the shape of the room. Then she knew where she was. She was sleeping in Laura's bed. Marian sat up and blinked against the sun streaming in the window. It was late, eleven o'clock in the morning. Her head hurt.

Marian padded across the hall to the bathroom and took three aspirins. Her face looked back at her from the mirror over the medicine cabinet. Nothing had changed. She still looked exactly the same.

Perhaps it was all a dream? For a moment, Marian tried to believe that. But it wasn't a dream, even though her dreams of late were remarkably vivid. The borders were blurred between dreams and reality. It was much harder now to tell the difference.

Then she remembered, and the pain was back. Yes, it had really happened. Dan would never forgive her.

It was over. Drew was leaving for New York tomorrow. She would never have to face him again. But how could she face Dan!

There was no sound from the den as she passed the door. Dan was still sleeping. Marian plugged in the coffee and forced herself to drink a glass of orange juice. There was a terrible taste in her mouth. Then she sat at the table and sipped her coffee, wishing she could turn time back to early November. They had been so happy then.

She could hear the television go on in the den. Dan must be awake. She'd take him a cup of coffee and start his breakfast. She had to act normally, as if nothing had happened. It was the only way she could cope.

"Do you want coffee?" She winced at the dark circles under his eyes. She had caused them. What if he refused to talk to her? What would she do then?

"Yes, thank you."

His tone was civil, inflections neutral, as if he were talking to a stranger. Guilt stabbed through her as she set the coffee down on the bedside table.

"Oh, I forgot to tell you. I scheduled hockey practice for three this afternoon."

"During vacation?"

"It's not for the whole team." He was explaining so politely that Marian felt like a visitor in her own home. "Cliff and I arranged to get together a couple of times over the holidays. He wants some extra practice so he won't stiffen up. That ankle of his is still giving him trouble."

"I'll drive you to the school. I have to do some shopping, anyway. And now I'd better start your breakfast, or we'll never get out of here in time."

At least they were talking! Marian drew a relieved breath. It was a start.

Marian put some bacon in the pan and took out a carton of eggs. The phone rang, and she picked it up in the kitchen.

"Did you have a good time at the teachers' party?" It was Sally. "Tell me all about it."

"It was the usual thing, Sally . . . drinking,

dancing, and trying to avoid Harvey. Last night he wanted to discuss moving the sixth grade up to junior high."

"Did you see Drew? Somebody said he was leaving tomorrow."

Marian shuddered. Even hearing his name filled her with remorse.

"I danced with him a couple of times. Nothing much happened at the party, Sally."

At least that much was true. Everything had happened *after* the party. Marian pressed the bacon down with her spatula and put on the eggs.

"I just wanted to check in with you." Sally laughed easily. "Ronnie lost a buck and a half to Dan last night. How does it feel being married to a winner?"

Somehow Marian managed to finish the conversation. Her hands were shaking as she drained the bacon and set it on the plate. She was very glad this was Christmas vacation. There would be no rehashes of the party in the faculty lounge. Perhaps everyone would forget about it before school started again.

"I'll meet you here at four." Dan waved as Cliff pushed him off toward the rink. He was pretending everything was normal between them, and Marian was grateful. Nisswa was a small town, and people would talk if they thought anything was wrong.

Marian backed the van out of the lot and drove through town to the Red Owl. She had a grocery list a mile long, and the store would be crowded today. Most people did their weekly shopping on Saturday afternoon.

A red pickup truck was just backing out, and Marian found a spot next to the entrance. There was an empty shopping cart outside, and she pushed it through the door. It didn't take long to learn why it had been abandoned. Three wheels pulled for the meat case, while the other headed in the direction of the parking lot. She had half a notion to leave it in the middle of the aisle, but the store was crowded and there was a shortage of carts.

Pork chops for dinner. Marian picked up a package and tried to see the meat under the top layer. She hated these Styrofoam trays. Meat packaged in clear plastic was easy. All you had to do was tip it over to see the bottom. Now it was a guessing game. And they always put the best cuts on top. She should have gone to the butcher in Brainerd.

Chicken was safe. She put a whole fryer in her basket. And bacon. They had used the last this morning.

"Marian?" Dorothy Pepin barreled out of the paper-products aisle. "I'm glad I caught up with you. Did you have a good time at the teachers' party last night?"

For a second Marian was nonplussed. How did Dorothy know! But of course she didn't know. Dorothy was just asking a friendly question.

"It was fine," Marian answered, picking up two rolls of paper towels. "Noisy, crowded, the usual stuff. It looks like you're stocking up for vacation."

"Oh, my, yes!" Dorothy smiled. "I'm experimenting with tofu this week at home. I decided we should have a Chinese unit for the seniors. It's the *in* food right now. I'm asking the school board for a wok."

Marian glanced down at Dorothy's basket. It was filled with Chinese cabbage, water chestnuts, and a variety of sprouts. Some of the greens weren't green, and the sprouts looked limp and wilted. It was just like Dorothy to schedule a Chinese unit in the middle of the winter. Produce was expensive this time of year, and the quality was terrible.

"Oh, there's Drew!" Dorothy pointed toward the front of the store. "I have to catch up with him to say good-bye. He's leaving tomorrow, you know."

Yes, she knew. Marian watched Dorothy hurry down the aisle. She pushed her own cart around a display of Wheat Thins and stood there, shaking. She couldn't bear to face him. She'd stand right here and read her grocery list until he left.

The floor was muddy, and her boots were dripping. Marian hated the Red Owl in the winter. There was no way they could keep the floor clean. Customers tramped in dirt and snow, and the wheels of the shopping carts left streaks of grime on the ivory tiled floor. Why didn't they have a brown floor? At least it wouldn't look so bad.

She peeked out once while Betty was cashing Drew's check. A few moments later he left, a six-pack of Coke tucked under his arm. Marian pushed her cart back out into the aisle and took a deep breath. She was acting like a child, hiding this way, but he probably didn't want to face her, either. Thank goodness he was gone!

Snow was blowing against the plate-glass windows

as she finished her shopping and pushed her cart to the front of the store. There were six people in front of her, and Marian stood impatiently, glancing at her watch. There was only one checker, and this was a busy time of year. Someone really should complain about the service. Poor Dan was probably waiting in the parking lot by now.

The new electronic price sensor was out again. Marian heard Betty call out for a price check. Computerized checking might be a wave of the future, but Marian thought it took longer than the old way.

"Hi, Mrs. Larsen. How are you today?" Betty reached in the cart and slid the items over the glass sensor. "Oh, no! There it goes again. Ralph? I need a price check on Schilling garlic salt, small size!"

Marian didn't see him come in. She felt a hand on her arm and turned to see Sheriff Bates. He was puffing hard, as if he'd been running.

"Do me a favor, Betty. Ring up Mrs. Larsen's groceries, and send them over to the house. Marian, I need you to come with me for a minute."

Marian felt a cold chill as she looked up into the sheriff's eyes. Something had happened! Was it Dan?

Her legs were shaking as he led her to the door. She wanted to ask what was wrong, but she couldn't speak.

"I just got a call from the hospital, Marian." Sheriff Bates held her arm. "There was an accident at the hockey rink."

"No!" She had found her voice at last. Not another accident! She staggered slightly as the sheriff helped her into his car. "Is Dan all right?"

"I don't know, Marian." Sheriff Bates sounded sorry. "I got the call over my radio, and Tina didn't have the details. I just know that the ambulance came and took Dan and Cliff to the hospital."

Marian turned to stare out the window as Sheriff Bates hit the siren and raced through town. It was a nightmare. It was all happening again. The snow was pelting against the glass exactly the way it had on the day Laura was killed!

CHAPTER 11

"Lower, Cliff . . . close to the ice!" Dan yelled at the top of his lungs. "If you want speed, keep your body low!"

Cliff made another pass, and it was better. Dan shouted out encouragement from the sidelines. At first he'd dreaded the idea of getting all dressed up to come out here, but watching Cliff practice was pure pleasure. The kid was good, the best player he'd ever coached. If Cliff skated this well in the championship game, they had it made.

Dan blew a sharp blast on his whistle, and Cliff stopped near the end of the rink.

"We'd better start back now!" Dan hollered. "It's almost four!"

"Just one more run!" Cliff grinned at him. "Come on, Coach. . . . I'm just getting warmed up!"

Dan nodded. He knew how Cliff felt. He used to plead for one more minute on the ice when he was a kid, too.

The wind was rising now. Only moments ago the sun had streaked across the ice in patches of brilliance. Now storm clouds were building, and he could smell the snow. The inside of his nose tingled with the clean, cold scent, and Dan shook his head ruefully. No one from the South could ever understand how it was possible to smell snow in the air.

Dan rubbed his hands together briskly and leaned forward, squinting across the rink. Cliff was coming now, low and fast, just as he had taught him.

He was almost at the goal line when he went down. Cliff's left leg seemed to crumple, and then he was flat on the ice, hockey stick flying across the rink.

"Jesus!" Dan yelled out. "What happened!"

He expected Cliff to get up and grin, make some smart retort, brush the snow from his uniform, and try it again. But Cliff didn't move.

"Cliff!" Dan hollered out at the top of his lungs. "Are you all right?"

There was no answer. Cliff was as still as death.

Dan didn't stop to consider. He knew he had to get out there. He grasped the wheels of his chair and shoved with all his might, trying to get over the mound of snow that lined the rink.

There was a moment when the chair teetered, and he thought it would right itself, plow through the bank of snow and out onto the ice. But the snow was heavy, filled with chunks of ice. One wheel was hung up on the hard-packed snow. Dan gave a strong push with his arms, but his balance was gone. The wheelchair toppled, and he fell awkwardly, sprawling out on the frozen rink.

He gave a groan as his head hit the ice. For one

dreadful moment he thought he would pass out from the pain. He was dizzy, the trees swimming around him in a tilting circle, but at last his head cleared. He had to get to Cliff!

Dan prayed that his legs would work, that suddenly he would be able to walk. He tried to pull himself forward across the slick, frozen surface, twisting his body in an awkward crab-like motion. His legs hung as useless ballast behind him, dragging and scraping as he attempted to inch his way closer. There were agonized moments when he made no forward motion at all.

It was no use. Dan felt panic set in, and he pushed it away. He had to use his head. Cliff had fallen like a rock. The boy could be bleeding. He had to get there somehow!

He had it now. Dan raised himself on his arms, his palms flat on the ice. He lunged forward and slid, flopping down on the hard surface. He hit his chin in the process, but he was a foot closer to Cliff.

Dan took a deep breath and did it again. Damn his useless legs! He felt as helpless as a baby, and Cliff needed him.

His progress was slow but steady. Again and again, he used his arms for leverage, punishing his body cruelly for each inch he gained, until his arms were trembling with fatigue.

"Once more . . . gotta make it!" He listened to the sound of his own words for courage. The rink was spinning now, tilting and fading in front of his eyes, but at last he reached the still boy on the ice.

There was no blood. Dan held his breath as he felt for a pulse. He thought he could make out a faint heartbeat. Cliff's arm was twisted at a crazy angle, and he didn't have the nerve to touch it. Somehow he had to get help!

It was after four. Dan gritted his teeth and lifted himself to his arms again. There was no telling what had happened to Marian. She might be stuck in line at the grocery store. He'd have to go for help himself.

His teeth were chattering by the time he propelled himself to the edge of the rink. By sheer determination he inched his way to the top of the bank and plunged down the other side. The snow was trampled here, and it would be easier than trying to crawl through unbroken snow. He had to get back to the school and holler for help.

Up. Forward. Up. Forward. Dan forced his body to obey the rhythm of his mind. The wind had picked up again. Snow stung his face, and his lungs were aching from the frigid air. His hands were so cold, he could no longer feel them at the ends of his arms. Looking down, he realized that he had lost one of his gloves. No matter. He couldn't go back for it. He had to get to the school just as fast as he could.

The huge pine trees in front of him were blurring, and there was a rushing noise in his ears. Still, he dragged himself forward, digging in with his elbows. He couldn't pass out. He had to do it. There was no one else. He had never been so alone in his life.

They sure threw away a lot of paper at the school! Lars Engstrom picked up a nearly empty notebook and tossed it into the cab. One of Lucy's kids would be tickled pink to get it. He found lots of good stuff when he picked up the school's trash. Last week there had been a box of pencils, red ones. And a whole bunch of old books.

Lars chuckled as he picked up a barrel and dumped it in the back of his truck. They thought he went straight to the dump, but he took the stuff home first and sorted through it. Over the last ten years he'd come up with some real treasures. There was a broken desk that needed a little fixing, a couple of shades that now hung in his living room, and a slab of blackboard that he cut down for the kids. Collecting trash was good work at a place like this.

He stopped for a moment, an empty barrel balanced against the tailgate. He could swear he heard someone hollering. The wind was blowing hard now, and he could've been mistaken, but it sure sounded like it was coming from the hockey rink. Maybe he should take a look.

Lars turned his face to the wind and nodded. Yep, that was somebody hollering. Kids weren't supposed to be on the hockey rink during vacation. Someone could get hurt on the ice.

He spotted them as he climbed up the crest of the hill. Cliff Heller was down on the ice. And Mr. Larsen! That poor, crippled Mr. Larsen was crawling through the snow on his elbows, legs dragging out behind him. There was a bleeding cut on his face, and his wheelchair was tipped on its side by the edge of the rink.

"I'm coming! Hold on there! I'm coming!" The wind whipped the words from his mouth as he broke into a run. "Are you hurt?"

"Call an ambulance!" Mr. Larsen saw him at last. "I'm all right, but Cliff needs help. Hurry!"

Lars turned and ran back toward the school. Seeing a pitiful thing like that made him glad he had two strong legs. There was a phone on the corner, and he dialed the clinic. He sure hoped they'd be all right. Cliff was a nice boy, and he liked poor Mr. Larsen. What a bitch of a thing to crawl through the snow that way!

The nurse said Dr. Hinkley would be right in to see her. Marian sat in the green plastic chair and shivered. She didn't want to be here. Every time she was in the doctor's chair, he had something dreadful to tell her. Dan had to be all right. He had to. Everything was her fault for letting him go to the hockey practice without her!

Marian clasped her hands together and tried to stop shaking. Dan was in a regular room, and that meant he couldn't be hurt too badly. The nurse had said room eleven. It was the same room he had been in before. Perhaps they were leaving it vacant, just for him.

Don't admit anyone to room eleven. That's Dan Larsen's room.

Didn't he go home?

Yes, but he's back. We're saving it for him. There's bad luck in that family, you know.

Her mind was wandering. Marian sat up straighter and tried to pull herself together. It was too much, that was all. The snowstorm, the cold afternoon, the same time of day as when Laura had died.

She had to stop thinking like this, or she'd go

crazy. Marian took a deep breath and turned to the window. Curtains of snow blew against the plate glass.

"Marian?" Dr. Hinkley called her name twice before she dared to turn around. She masked the fear in her eyes and faced him.

"He's going to be fine, Marian, but I think we'd better keep him overnight." Dr. Hinkley pushed some forms across the desk toward her. "As far as I can tell, it's minor lacerations coupled with a case of exhaustion. His hands will be painful for a while, but there's no evidence of frostbite. I'd say he's a pretty lucky guy."

Yes, lucky. Marian managed to hold the pen without shaking. His daughter was dead, his wife was unfaithful, and he was injured and paralyzed. How lucky could one man get?

"He's got a lot of courage, that husband of yours." Dr. Hinkley was talking again, and Marian forced herself to listen. "Lars Engstrom said he crawled almost fifty yards through the snow to get help. He's in surprisingly good shape for what he's been through. We'll keep him under observation tonight, and he can probably go home with you tomorrow."

"And Cliff?" Marian was almost afraid to ask. Dan would never forgive himself if Cliff was badly hurt.

"He's a little worse for the wear." Dr. Hinkley sighed. "His wrist is badly sprained, and there's the possibility of a concussion. Cliff won't be playing any hockey this season, but he's going to be all right."

"Have you told Dan?"

"He knows. I'm afraid he blames himself for the

accident, Marian. He thinks Cliff was pushing too hard, just to please him. And he's convinced that Cliff's injuries would be less severe if he'd gotten help sooner. Of course, that isn't true, but you know how stubborn Dan can be."

"I'd better go to him." Marian stood up and handed the papers to the doctor. "Room eleven?"

"You can peek in on him if you want." Dr. Hinkley joined her at the door. "I gave him a sedative so he won't wake up until tomorrow. It was quite an ordeal for him, and he felt so bad about Cliff. I thought he could use a good night's sleep."

Her heels clicked down the hospital corridor, keeping rhythm with her thoughts. Poor Laura. Poor Dan. Poor Cliff. And poor her. Too many bad things had happened, and there were more to come. She could feel the pall that hung heavy over her life, and she was so tired of fighting. She wanted to give in and sink into despair. If it weren't for Laura, she'd have no reason for trying to cope with it all.

He was sleeping, just as Dr. Hinkley said. The lines of fatigue were deep on his face, and he looked like an old, tired man. Marian had thought she was incapable of more pain, but she was wrong. Her heart broke as she stood with her hand on the door.

CHAPTER 12

Marian got into her nightgown and turned down the covers of Laura's bed. She had slept up here every night since the teachers' party. Dan didn't want her downstairs with him. He said she needed her rest and the television would keep her awake, but Marian knew the truth. She should have been upset, but she wasn't. She was much happier sleeping up here in her baby's room.

There might be another note from Laura tonight. Marian smiled as she slipped into bed. Laura's room was so comforting.

Dan had been home for three days now, and Marian was tired from the strain of being so carefully polite. He was a stranger to her, friendly but distant. It was like having a roommate in college.

Her eyes were closing now. Marian felt a warm glow as she slipped into her dream. Laura was calling to her, trying to tell her something. It was something very important, but Marian couldn't make out the words. She listened intently, but

Laura's voice grew fainter. Now it was no more than a whisper.

She called out, but her baby was leaving. Laura was walking backward, holding out her hands. Her mouth was moving, but Marian was too far away to hear. The space that separated them was growing wider and wider. What was it that Laura was trying to tell her? What did her baby want?

Marian awoke with a start. It was daylight, and the sun was peeking in the yellow curtains. Laura's diary was on the little table, where she'd placed it last night. It was blank.

"What's wrong, baby?" Tears came to Marian's eyes. "Tell Mommy, and she'll make it better."

"I'm going to run in and see Dan today." Ronnie sipped his morning coffee and watched Sally make pancakes. "I just can't believe the bad luck he's having. That poor guy's going to go crazy if things don't look up."

"I talked to Marian last night." Sally turned a pancake and poured another on the griddle. "Do you think she's all right, Ronnie? I'm more worried about her than I am about Dan."

Ronnie shrugged. "You know her better than anyone, honey. What do you think?"

"I think something's wrong. It's just a combination of little things, but Marian's changed."

Ronnie was looking at her questioningly, and Sally tried to explain. "Last Wednesday I walked past her classroom. The kids were at lunch, and Marian was all alone. She was sitting at her desk with her eyes closed, sort of concentrating, you know? I wasn't going to bother her, but then I heard her talking. At first I thought she was talking to me, but she didn't know I was there. Then I realized she was talking to Laura!"

Ronnie looked doubtful. "Are you sure, Sal? Maybe she was just talking to herself."

"That's what she said when I asked her. But there're other things, too, like her roll book. Laura's name is still there, Ronnie. I can understand that. Maybe Marian can't bear to erase it. But Marian marks her *present*! There's a little red *P* right next to her name. I checked again, right before vacation. According to Marian's attendance records, Laura's been in school every day since she died!"

"That's pretty strange." Ronnie nodded. "Do you think . . . ?" He stopped in mid-question as Jenny came into the kitchen.

"Pancakes!" Jenny grinned, showing the gap where she'd lost her baby teeth. She plopped down in a chair and put her elbows on the table. "I heard what you said about Mrs. Larsen, Mom. I'm worried about her, too."

Sally bit back her automatic comment about eavesdropping. Maybe Jenny had noticed something in the classroom.

"Why are you worried, Jenny?" Sally carried a stack of pancakes to the table and set out the butter and syrup. "We want to know."

Jenny forked three pancakes and poured syrup on them before she answered. Sally could tell she was thinking.

"It's hard to explain," Jenny said at last. "I'm in the Bluebirds. That's a reading group, Dad. There's the Bluebirds and the Robins and the Sparrows. Laura was a Bluebird before she got killed. Now there's just five of us Bluebirds, but Mrs. Larsen passes out six workbooks. At first we passed the extra one back, but she got so sad! Now we keep it and hand it in later. She does it every morning. There's always one too many workbooks. It's like Mrs. Larsen doesn't know Laura's gone. I think she's trying to fool herself so she won't be sad."

Sally raised her eyebrows and looked at Ronnie. It was an astute comment for a seven-year-old.

"You mean she's pretending?" Sally encouraged her.

"Sort of." Jenny took a bite and chewed. There was a long silence while they waited for her to swallow. "It's like Mrs. Larsen's playing a game with us, only she doesn't know it."

Ronnie and Sally exchanged glances over Jenny's head. "Anything else?" Ronnie asked.

"There's the folder." Jenny chewed again. "Mrs. Larsen's got a blue folder on her desk with Laura's name on it. Every time she passes out homework, she puts one in there. I asked her what it was for. She said everyone should keep up with their homework. I don't understand how Laura can keep up with us kids when she's dead. Is there any blueberry syrup, Mom?"

Sally nodded and got the blueberry syrup down from the shelf. Jenny had a disgusting habit of mixing blueberry and maple in puddles on her plate. But she was right about Marian. The homework folder proved it. It tied in perfectly with the attendance records. Marian had never accepted

Laura's death. She was living in a dreamworld where Laura was still alive.

"Why don't we ask Mrs. Larsen to come to the sledding party? She should have fun. Mrs. Larsen forgot how to have fun."

"That's a good idea, Jenny." Sally beamed at her daughter. "I'll call her right now and ask her. Or better yet, why don't you call?"

Sally didn't say a word as Jenny ran for the phone. There was a rule about leaving the table in the middle of a meal, but this was an exception.

"That was Jenny on the phone." Marian set Dan's breakfast tray on the bed. "She said Ronnie was coming in this afternoon to see you. And she invited me to the children's sledding party on New Year's Day. I think Sally put her up to it. She probably thinks I need some diversion."

Diversion? Dan almost laughed. She had gotten plenty of diversion the night of the teachers' party!

Marian walked to the Christmas tree and turned on the lights. "That looks better! How about the presents, Dan? Do you think it's too early to put them under the tree?"

For a moment he didn't know what she was talking about. Then it hit him, and he winced slightly. Laura's presents. They were hidden in the hall closet upstairs.

"There's no sense putting Laura's presents under the tree, Marian. If they bother you, get rid of them."

"Yes, of course." Marian shivered slightly. "I just forgot for a minute, that's all. I'll send them home with Ronnie. Jenny can have them."

"No!"

For a moment, his rage got the best of him. Those were Laura's presents! He had bought them for her. Jenny didn't deserve them. If Laura couldn't have them, no one could!

"What's the matter, Dan?" Marian was staring at him in surprise.

"Oh, nothing." Dan managed a smile. "I wasn't thinking clearly, that's all. Of course you should retag them for Jenny. That's the sensible thing to do."

Marian stood on tiptoe to get the presents out of the closet. She always hid them on the top shelf so Laura couldn't peek. She carried them to the bedroom and made new tags. "To Jenny from Santa," she wrote.

There were quite a few packages. Marian tore off the old tags and replaced them automatically. When she got to the large red and silver one, she stopped.

This was Laura's Pretty Patty, the doll she had begged for. She couldn't give it to Jenny. Laura had to have something for Christmas!

Marian picked up the box and carried it across the hall. She put it on Laura's little table. "To Laura from Mommy," the tag read. "Do not open until Christmas." It gave Laura's whole room a festive air.

She was doing the right thing, Marian was convinced. Dan might think she was crazy, but she knew she was right. Every little girl needed a new doll at Christmas. And Laura would have her Pretty Patty.

Some noise had awakened him. Dan listened. There were footsteps above his head. Marian was in Laura's room again.

He was worried about Marian. She had lost weight, and there were dark circles under her eyes. Dan knew she was sleeping in Laura's room every night, waiting for another note. At first he thought the notes were good for her, but now he knew better. Marian's delusion had gone too far.

At least she was coping. Dan supposed he ought to be grateful. Marian had been a model wife for the past few days. She took good care of the house and made wonderful meals. If only she'd let go of this crazy note business.

Now it was quiet again. Marian must have gone to sleep. Dan sighed and closed his eyes. He really should be nicer to Marian. They needed each other.

She was finished now. Marian put Laura's present under the tree and stood back to admire her work. The small plastic Christmas tree was all decorated, and the lights twinkled brightly. She had almost forgotten, and that made her feel bad. Now Laura had her own little Christmas tree for a nice cheery night-light.

All the miniature balls and decorations had been stored in the attic. It had been a task getting them down. She had to work quietly. Dan was asleep. He wouldn't like the idea of putting up Laura's Christmas tree this year. Dan still thought Laura was dead.

CHAPTER 13

"Surprise!" Marian was wearing a red and green holiday apron. She carried in Dan's breakfast tray and set it down with a flourish. She had made eggs Benedict just for Dan. It was Julia Child's recipe, and everything had turned out right. Of course, she couldn't buy truffles in Nisswa, but a slice of ripe olive looked almost as nice.

Marian was determined to make this holiday a cheerful occasion. Laura was watching. They had to pretend to be happy for her. Laura would be sad if they didn't have a special breakfast on the day before Christmas.

He was surprised when he saw her smiling. Marian hadn't smiled in a long time. And she was all decked out in a Christmas apron. He had to admit she was trying.

Dan managed to smile back at her. He guessed he could try to match her holiday spirits. He hadn't forgotten, and he wasn't going to forgive her, but this *was* Christmas.

"Say!" Dan raised his eyebrows as he looked at

the tray. "You're getting pretty fancy, aren't you? It's too bad we don't have a bottle of champagne to go with this."

"We do." Marian ran to the refrigerator and came back with the bottle. "It's just a domestic from California, but Gus said it was good."

"Look in my center desk drawer, Marian. There's a package in there with your name on it. You can wear it to the Powells' tonight."

"Oh, Dan!" Marian opened it carefully, saving the paper. "But how did you . . . ?"

"How did I get out to buy it?" Dan finished the sentence for her. "I rented a pair of legs. Sally picked it out for me. She said she knew exactly what you wanted."

"She did!" Marian smiled as she pulled out the tiny gold chain. "I've wanted one like this ever since I saw hers."

There was a long moment as they looked at each other. Even though they were trying to be cheerful, this holiday was different. In other years, she would have thrown her arms around Dan and kissed him. Now she couldn't. He wouldn't want her to.

"Thank you, Dan. It'll look lovely with my red dress. Let me run and get yours."

Dan smiled. Marian had liked the chain. Sally had picked it up two weeks ago. Now he was glad he'd shopped early. If he'd waited until last week, he might have decided not to get her anything. That would have been petty. She was still his wife.

There was a moment of suspense as Dan unwrapped his package. Marian winced as he tore off the paper, but she bit her tongue and kept silent. She'd always been a paper and bow saver, but this wasn't the time to be picky. They were getting along for the first time in a week.

"They're beautiful!" Dan pulled out the gloves and shook his head when he saw the tag. "Brooks Brothers? These are expensive, Marian! It says the lining's mink."

"I ordered them from New York." Marian smiled in satisfaction. "Your old ones are wearing out. Now you have new, classy gloves to wear to school."

"Oh, no. These gloves are too good." Dan shook his head. "Put them in my bottom desk drawer, will you, Marian? I'll save them for a special occasion."

"You could wear them at the championship game." Marian spoke without thinking. She winced as she saw the expression of pain cross his face.

"Sure." Dan's tone was bitter. "That'll be a special occasion!"

He had deliberately avoided thinking about the championship. There was no way the team could win without Cliff. And Cliff's accident had been *his* fault. He never should have gone back to coaching. He was no good for the team. He was no good for anyone now.

Marian saw his mood blacken. The tender moment was ruined. Dan picked listlessly at his breakfast. He was depressed now, and Marian knew there was no way to regain their earlier cheerfulness. She wished she could take back her thoughtless comment, but it was too late. The damage was done. All the joy of the morning was gone.

The winter wind howled around the eaves, and Marian shivered as she looked out the living-room window. The storm had come up around noon, and the weather reports were not encouraging. The highway patrol predicted another three inches before morning. Travelers' advisories were out. There was no way they could drive to Sally's tonight.

The phone rang, and she heard Dan answer. Marian stared out at the four-foot snowdrift blocking the street. She had been looking forward to the celebration at Sally's, and now it was impossible. The van couldn't even make it out of the driveway.

"Marian?" Dan was calling her. She turned from the window and walked slowly to the den. She felt caged and helpless in this white prison. If only she could get out!

Dan relayed the message. "Ronnie's coming in to pick you up at five. He's got the Snow-Cat running, and you're supposed to wear plenty of warm clothes. He'll bring you back later tonight."

"But how about you?" Marian felt guilty at the surge of excitement she felt. "I can't go with Ronnie and leave you home alone."

"I didn't want to go in the first place." Dan looked at her coldly. "It's no fun to sit in a wheelchair and get stared at all night."

"But it's Christmas Eve!"

"So what?" Dan gave a rueful laugh.

"You'll be all alone!"

"Actually, I thought I'd sneak out the minute you leave. I'll call up one of my old girlfriends and take her dancing. I understand there's a new nightclub in Brainerd. I ought to be really good at that sort of thing."

"Dan!" Marian stared at him in amazement. She'd never heard him this bitter and sarcastic.

"Just kidding, Marian. At least you don't have to worry about me. I'm like your favorite household plant. Set me down somewhere and I'll still be in the same place when you come back."

"I'd better not go. I don't think this is the time to leave you alone."

"Oh, for Christ's sake! Can't you take a joke? Go, Marian. Go out to Sally's!"

Marian stared down at him, indecision written on her face. Dan knew he had her worried. He was really being a bastard.

He softened his voice. "Sorry, Marian. I'll be fine by myself, really. Make me some Tom and Jerry batter before you go, and I'll watch the specials on television. You know how disappointed Jenny will be if you don't show up."

That got to her. Dan could see her weakening. He was making a conscious effort to be nice now. It wasn't fair to coop her up in the house with a cripple.

"If you're sure you don't mind . . ." Marian wavered. Dan was right. Jenny would be terribly upset if she couldn't come. Maybe Laura would come, too. Laura might be with her at the Powells', watching Jenny open her presents. This Christmas Eve could be fun, after all!

He was lonely. Dan put a big spoonful of Tom and Jerry batter into a mug and filled it with hot water from the thermos. The bottle of booze was sitting on the bedside table. He added a generous portion.

He'd been fine when she left. It was late afternoon, and he had Omar Bradley's autobiography to finish. Then night closed in, shutting him off from the world outside. He looked out the window, but all he could see was the reflection of his reading lamp and his bedridden image in the glass. For the first time he understood why shut-ins called the "time" operator just to hear the sound of another human voice.

The phone by the bed rang sharply. Dan pulled himself up straighter and reached to answer it. Maybe it was the "time" operator calling him?

"Mr. Larsen? Thank you for all the super presents! I like the cowgirl outfit best of all. Mom says I can wear it to school! I'm sending your present back with Daddy. You're gonna love it. I made it myself!"

There was a long pause, and Sally came on the line. "Dan? I hope Jenny didn't wake you. The presents were really wonderful. She's never had a Christmas like this before!"

"I wasn't sleeping, Sally." Dan made his voice cheerful. It had been a shock hearing Jenny's voice. She sounded so much like Laura.

"Oh, Dan?" Sally lowered her voice. "You can feel perfectly safe eating Jenny's present. It's fudge, and I supervised the whole thing. She got the recipe out of the *Muppets Magazine*."

"Hi, Dan!" This time it was Ronnie. "I just wanted to say Merry Christmas. We'll leave here about ten or so, so expect us at a little after eleven."

"How are you, honey?" There was a lilt in Marian's voice as she took the phone. "Sally baked the best turkey I ever had. She covered the whole thing with mayonnaise so it wouldn't dry out. I'm bringing you some. Just a second. I'm going to drag this phone around the corner."

There was a pause and a cracking noise. The Powells' phone was in the hallway. Dan remembered that it had a twenty-five-foot cord. Marian must be taking it into the kitchen so she could talk privately.

"Are you really all right? I've been worried about you. If you're lonesome, I'll tell Ronnie I have to leave right away."

"I'm fine, Marian." Dan gave a bitter smile. "Just enjoy yourself and come home when you planned. There's no hurry."

It was a relief to hang up the phone. Of course, it was very nice of them to call him, but it was tiring to pretend to be cheerful when he wasn't. Hearing their happy voices with laughter and conversation in the background made him feel that much more alone.

Dan turned on the television. There was no sense sitting here moping. He'd make the best of it. There was bound to be something interesting on the tube.

A Charlie Brown Christmas was on Channel 3. Dan watched for a minute, sipping his drink. Charlie Brown was choosing a Christmas tree. The one he picked looked comically pathetic. Laura had loved this cartoon. Dan switched the channel with a sharp jab of the remote control.

Another one of Laura's favorites was playing on Channel 6. *How the Grinch Stole Christmas!* They had watched it together last year. The Grinch began to blur, and Dan blinked his eyes fiercely. This wasn't a good one to watch, either.

They were showing *It's a Wonderful Life* on the movie channel. At least that was safe. Dan mixed himself another Tom and Jerry and settled down to watch. It was one of his favorite films. Jimmy Stewart was just getting ready to jump off the bridge.

Dan sat up with a jolt. He must have fallen asleep. His legs tingled, and for a moment he was filled with excitement. Then he remembered. He'd had another of those walking dreams.

The movie was still playing, but it was almost over. It was the Christmas scene. Jimmy Stewart's happy family was gathered around him, under the huge Christmas tree. His littlest daughter looked just like Laura.

Everything reminded him of Laura tonight! Dan gave up trying to escape. He had lied to Marian. Christmas Eve was a terrible time to be alone. He didn't know how much longer he could take it. Why hadn't she seen through his bravado and stayed home with him!

It wouldn't have made a difference. Dan leaned back and closed his eyes. Having Marian in the same room was no comfort to him now. She didn't understand how he felt.

Maybe he should have gone to the Powells'. The van might have made it. Then he would have been surrounded by people instead of being alone.

He played the scenario out in his mind. Marian had said the dinner was wonderful. He would have enjoyed that. And right after dinner, they'd opened their presents. He could picture Jenny opening Laura's packages, squealing over each new treasure. Could he hide how he felt about Jenny?

Dan shivered. It was a good thing he'd stayed at

home. He couldn't stand the sight of Jenny. It was crazy to resent her, but he did. Jenny wasn't the only one. He hated to see any of Laura's friends. They were alive, and Laura was dead. It was too painful. He wished he never had to see any of them again.

A hard, choking sob tore from his throat. He closed his eyes against the pain and fought for control. There was no purpose in crying. Laura was dead, and no one could bring her back. At times like this he wished he'd died with her.

Marian called out when she came in the door, but there was no answer. She took off Dan's parka and hung it next to the heat vent to dry. Her boots were full of snow, and she brushed them off with the broom. She was nearly frozen, but it had been worth it. At least she had made Jenny happy.

Dan was asleep. Marian tiptoed over and turned off the Christmas-tree lights. There was a dim bulb in the lamp on the television, and she turned that on, just in case he awoke. Jenny's present went on the bedside table. Now he'd know that she'd gotten home safely.

It had been an exhausting evening. Marian climbed the stairs and went into Laura's room. The miniature Christmas tree was glowing softly, and Laura's package was untouched under it. Somehow she'd expected some sign from her baby.

Laura was gone. She had tried to find her all evening. Marian had been so sure that Laura would be with her, watching Jenny open her presents.

There was no sign, no feeling of Laura's presence at the Powells'.

Marian put on her nightgown and crawled into the small bed. Laura was not here, either. Christmas was so lonely without her. She had to come tonight. Marian was beginning to worry. Where was her baby?

CHAPTER 14

Marian rolled over and pushed the blanket back. Every muscle in her body ached, and her head was throbbing. It was a result of her ride on the Snow-Cat. Miles of holding on tightly over bumpy roads had taken its toll. She had to get up and take some aspirin.

She'd slept restlessly, dreaming of Laura. It was the same dream she had had before. Laura was trying to tell her something, and she couldn't make out the words. Laura wanted something, that much was clear. If only she knew what it was!

Laura's diary lay open on the dresser. Marian felt frustrated and helpless as she stared at the blank page. No note this morning. No note for a week. It was so hard to wait. She was beginning to lose hope.

It was an ordinary morning, cold and still. The sky was gray with lingering snow clouds. Marian ran water into a glass and took three aspirins. Christmas morning would be a time of joy in other houses, but not here. Here it was just another cold winter morning.

Marian put on a pair of Dan's woolen socks and wrapped herself in his old army jacket. She sat huddled at the table, waiting for the coffee to perk. Steam rolled up in a cloud as she took the first cup, cheating a little and pouring before it had finished. She held her face close to the coffee-scented warmth and breathed in deeply.

She caught sight of herself in the mirror as she paced between the doorway and the window, waiting for Dan to awaken. She looked like a refugee from a surplus store. It would have been comical if her face were less tragic.

How long would he sleep? She really wanted some company. It didn't matter that Dan was silent most mornings. Just knowing he was awake would make her less lonely.

He started to stir as the sun cast its first shadows over Heidelberg Hill. She went in with his coffee, but he was silent, as usual. Then she made breakfast and kept him company as he ate. Her feeling of despair stuck with her all morning.

In the afternoon, Midge and Edith dropped by. They were full of Christmas cheer. If she was a bit quiet, they made no mention of it. Sally called to chat for a while, and the Ringstroms from next door arrived with a plate of Christmas cookies. Marian made polite conversation, her mind on other things. In the evening they heard the children playing on the far side of Heidelberg Hill. It was all rather sad, Marian thought. She could see other people's lives going on about her, but she was separated and alone.

The night dragged on slowly. Dan was reading a new book on the Civil War. She brought in her own book, a popular exposé of high government officials, but she couldn't seem to get involved with the story. The book was well written and lived up to its jacket blurb, but she kept staring at the page, reading the same paragraph over and over, her thoughts wandering. She and Dan were strangers, sitting in the same room, each separated by little pools of yellow light falling on meaningless pages.

"I'm tired." Marian stood up and stretched, yawning widely. "I think I'll go to bed now."

"Good idea." Dan didn't even look up from the page he was reading. "Get some sleep, Marian. You'll feel a lot better in the morning."

So he had noticed her quiet mood all day! Marian turned to look at him, but he was engrossed in his book again. It was better this way. She didn't want to answer a lot of questions on how she was feeling. She would take a couple of aspirins and sleep. Dan was probably right. She would feel better in the morning.

There was a winter bird on the windowsill when Marian opened her eyes. The tiny, brown sparrow cocked its head and stared at her, beady eyes bright. It hopped the length of the window ledge and flew away when she moved to get out of bed. Poor little sparrow. She had frightened it.

Marian glanced at the clock. It was barely six. Why had she awakened so early?

Then she saw it, and her heart pounded alarmingly. There was an empty box with crumpled wrapping paper under Laura's Christmas tree, and the Pretty Patty doll was sitting in a place of honor on the bookshelf. Laura's diary lay open beside it. Her baby had opened her Christmas present!

I love you, Mommy. Thank you for Pretty Patty. I'm trying so hard not to be lonesome.

Suddenly tears stung Marian's eyes as she read the note. Laura was lonely. She had to do something to help!

Dan would know what to do. Marian raced down the stairs with the book in her hands. She had to ask Dan how they could help Laura.

Dan groaned. It was an effort to open his eyes. He had read late into the night, and now Marian was shaking him awake at the crack of dawn, insisting that he look at another fake note from Laura. She said Laura was lonely. That was crazy! He was just too tired to take part in Marian's little charade. Why didn't she go away and leave him alone?

"Cut it out, Marian!" Dan shook her arm off roughly. "I don't want to see any notes. Just leave me alone, and let me sleep!"

Marian backed away from the bed. Dan was angry. He wouldn't even look at Laura's note. How could he help her decide what to do if he wouldn't even read it?

Tears ran down her cheeks as she fled to the kitchen. Dan had yelled at her. He didn't care. She was the only one who cared about her baby!

Marian's hands were shaking as she made the coffee. She sat down in a kitchen chair and waited for the carafe to fill. There was anguish on her face as she stared down at the book in her hands. Poor Laura! She was so lonely. She missed all her friends and playmates. It hurt to think of Laura so alone and unhappy. If only she knew how to help!

It was ten o'clock when Dan opened his eyes. The house was quiet, but he could smell coffee. Marian was awake.

"Marian? Is there any more coffee?"

"I'll be there in a minute."

Her voice sounded thick, as if she'd been crying. Dan sighed as he remembered. There was something about another note from Laura. Marian had tried to wake him, and he had snapped at her. Now he felt guilty for being so insensitive. This note business was getting to him. Perhaps he should bring it up, try to convince her that she had written the notes herself.

By the time Marian arrived with his coffee, Dan had changed his mind. It was a mistake to discuss her delusion. That would only lend credence to the whole thing. It was wiser to wait and see if she mentioned it.

It was mid-afternoon, and Marian was restless. She couldn't show Laura's note to Dan. Not after his rejection this morning. She'd have to deal with the problem herself. There must be a way to make her baby happy again.

The Ringstroms' cat was scampering over the

snowdrifts. *Anywhere else,* Marian thought, *a sensible cat would stay indoors.* But Zuzu was a true Minnesotan, frolicking at twenty degrees, as if it were spring.

Marian decided to go for a walk. The exercise would be good for her, and the fresh air might clear her head. She took her coat out of the closet and pulled on her boots.

When Marian peeked in the den, Dan was asleep again. The Broncos were getting the best of the Raiders, but it was only a minute into the second quarter. She stood in the doorway and watched one play.

There was a notepad by the bed, and Marian wrote a quick message. *Gone for a walk. Back soon.* She propped it up where he'd be sure to see it. She could hardly wait to get out of the house!

The cold air was bracing. Marian walked down the sidewalk, swinging her arms. She'd walk until she was tired. It would be a relief to let her mind relax and think of nothing at all.

CHAPTER 15

It was a boring afternoon. Becky Fischer walked down Main Street, kicking up clouds of snow with the toes of her new fur-lined red boots. She hated vacations. There was no one to play with. She stopped in front of Heino's Our Own Hardware and admired her reflection in the plate-glass window. Her curly, black ponytail was tucked up inside the hood of her brand-new red parka. With her red boots and brown snow pants, her mom said she looked like Santa's helper.

It was cold just standing still, and Becky ran on down the sidewalk, boots squeaking against the snow. Rexall Drugs was her next stop. She hoped Ginger was home. The Allens lived in an apartment up over the drugstore.

Becky rang the bell outside, her mitten pressed tightly against the cold metal button. She could see all the way up the stairs, right through the lace curtains, but no one was coming down. Becky shifted from foot to foot and glanced in the drugstore window. LET REXALL BE YOUR SANTA THIS YEAR, a sign read. She hoped Ginger's dad had made a lot of money over Christmas. Her mom said the drugstore might be the next business to close down in the winter. Then the Allens would move away or go somewhere warmer until spring. Becky didn't like Ginger all that much, but she was the only other girl who lived in town, now that Laura was dead and Jenny had moved.

Why didn't they come? Becky pressed the buzzer again, three sharp pokes. Maybe the doorbell wasn't working. She couldn't hear it ringing upstairs. There was another door up there, but Ginger's mom kept it closed in the winter. She said there was a bad draft from the street.

Maybe they weren't home. Becky frowned grumpily. No one was home today. She wanted to show Ginger her new Fascinatin' Lady Makeup Kit, and now she wasn't home!

"They ain't home, Becky!" big Jake Campbell called out from across the street. "I seen 'em leave in the car. They was goin' over to Pequot Lakes to visit relations."

"You want to see my Fascinatin' Lady Makeup Kit, Jake?" Becky asked, running across the plowed street to where he was standing. "I got it for Christmas. Look, it's got lipstick and everything!"

"Mighty nice, Becky." Jake grinned down at her. Becky could smell liquor on his breath, and she turned her face slightly. Mom didn't like her to talk too much to Jake. He was the town drunk, and sometimes he said things that didn't make sense. Her dad said Jake was a war casualty. Becky liked him, though. He was always nice to her. He was big and strong, and one time he'd fixed her bicycle wheel when it was bent.

"Well, I gotta go, Jake. I'm going over to the school to see if anyone's there."

Becky waved and took off down the center of the street. It was easier walking here than on the sidewalk. Some people hadn't shoveled, and the snow was deep. Maybe they were all gone for Christmas. Or else they thought they didn't have to shovel on a holiday.

The playground was deserted. The swings hung down lifelessly on their metal chains, creaking slightly in the wind. The slide was covered with snow, and Becky brushed off some and sat at the bottom, staring off at the trees. This was no fun at all!

She supposed she could go to see Mrs. Larsen, but that was no fun, either, now that Laura was dead. It wasn't fair that Laura was dead. Laura was her best friend ever!

Becky sniffed and wiped her nose on the sleeve of her new parka. She used to have fun with Jenny and Laura. It was great having two best friends, but now Jenny lived way out on that farm, and she never saw her, either, except for school. Vacations were awful. There was nothing to do!

She could see the old icehouse in the distance, way out past the Northlakes Creamery. Becky shuffled her feet in the snow and dug ruts with her toes. They were all going to sneak in there last summer, but Laura and Jenny chickened out. Laura was scared, and Jenny said her mother would skin her alive if anyone found out. Becky still wanted to go. It was dark and black inside, and there might be lots of stuff people had put there and forgotten. There could be diamonds or money or anything!

She didn't consciously decide to go, but her feet moved, and then she was walking toward the old icehouse by the river. It was getting colder, and she curled up her fingers inside her mittens to make her hands warmer. The snow was higher here, and she jumped across the ditch to the other side. It sure was a long walk to the icehouse, but it would be worth it. This time she was going in, all by herself. Well, maybe she wouldn't really go inside, but she'd peek through the cracks to see what was there. Jenny would be green when she told her about it.

The closer she got, the more she decided she'd just peek in. The icehouse looked scary and black against the gray sky. Jenny would think she was really brave for coming here all by herself.

What was that! Becky heard a noise, faint and high, carried by the wind. She stopped and listened, tipping her head to one side. There was no sound now. Whatever it was, was gone.

There it was again! Becky moved up to the door and pressed her ear to the crack. Yes, there was someone inside the icehouse.

She wanted to run for home. There wasn't supposed to be anyone inside. Thinking of someone in that shadowy, gloomy place scared her. But what if it was a kitten that had slipped through a crack in the wall? It would die in there if somebody didn't go in and get it.

The thought of a kitten alone in the dark made tears come to Becky's eyes. She loved kittens. She should go in and get it, even though she was scared. Her mother might let her keep it.

"I'm coming, kitty." Becky's voice was no louder than a whisper. She tugged at the door, but it was stuck. Finally, she got her boot in the crack and pried it open.

"Here, kitty, kitty!" Becky stood in the doorway, squinting into the shadows. "Where are you?"

Becky took a hesitant step inside. She didn't see the kitten anywhere. She moved forward another couple of steps and called out again.

There was a scraping noise from the back of the building. A large shape loomed in the darkness. There was someone here!

Becky froze in fear. Her knees started to shake, and her breath caught in her throat. She was afraid to take her eyes off the shape in the shadows.

Panic made her awkward as she backed toward the door. She stumbled against the wall and cried out in terror.

There was a deafening roar as the huge old saw whirled into life. It made so much noise that no one heard her horrified screams.

"I was beginning to get worried." Dan frowned slightly as she came back to the den. "Where were you, Marian? I thought you were going for a short walk."

For a moment the question startled her. She *had* gone for a short walk. Then she caught sight of the clock by Dan's bed. Four fifteen. She had been gone almost two hours!

"It was nice outside," Marian tried to explain.

"I . . . Well, I guess I just poked around, Dan. I didn't realize it was getting so late."

"That's okay." Dan nodded. "You look better, Marian. There's color in your cheeks now. Were you cold?"

"No . . ." She tried to think. "At least, I wasn't cold until I came in. Now I'm freezing. I guess I'd better have some coffee to warm up."

It was strange. Marian stood by the sink while the coffee heated. It seemed as if she'd been outside only a few minutes. And she couldn't seem to remember where she'd walked. She had rounded the corner by the Lutheran church and then . . . nothing. Marian shivered slightly. It was almost frightening. Time had passed, and she had no idea where it had gone. She hoped she hadn't met anyone she knew and had failed to speak.

The phone rang while she was preparing supper. Marian answered in the kitchen. The cord stretched as far as the stove, and she flipped the potatoes with one hand and held the phone in the other.

"Marian? It's Donna Fischer. I was just wondering if Becky might be over there. She was supposed to be home an hour ago."

"No, she's not here, Donna." Marian turned the potatoes again. "Did you check the school? Sometimes the town kids meet at the playground during the vacation."

Marian felt sad as she hung up the phone. Donna hadn't called in a long time. Not since Laura died. Before that, the three girls had been inseparable. Laura, Jenny, and Becky. The Terrible Trio, Marian had called them. They were always at one place or another, getting into mischief together.

She hoped Becky was home by now. Marian glanced out the window. Shadows were lengthening over Heidelberg Hill. Surely, Becky would head for home the moment she realized it was getting dark.

The phone rang again. This time it was Sally.

"Is Becky at your house? Donna just called here, and she's fit to be tied. She called me on the off chance that Becky got a ride out with Ronnie."

"I haven't seen her." Marian turned off the burner under the potatoes. She had a terrible feeling that something was wrong.

"How about the places where the girls used to play?" Sally suggested. "I know she's not at the drugstore. I called there. How about the icehouse? Weren't they fascinated by that place?"

"Yes. They always wanted to go there, but it was off-limits. Dan said it was so run-down, it might be dangerous."

Marian stopped speaking and took a deep breath. The abandoned icehouse was no place for a child to go alone. Becky certainly wouldn't have gone there! Or would she? There was no telling what a bored seven-year-old would do for excitement.

"I'd better run over and check, Sally. If Becky's there, she could be hurt."

"Wait for me." Sally hollered out something to Jenny in the background. "I can be there in ten minutes. That darned place hasn't been used in years. Maybe a board fell in or something."

Marian carried a tray in to Dan, but she was too

nervous to eat. She kept thinking of Donna and how worried she must be.

"Sally's coming in," she told Dan. "Becky Fischer hasn't come home yet, and Donna's worried. We're going to go out looking for her."

"She's probably down at the gas station, conning someone out of a Coke." Dan shrugged. "I'm sure she's all right, Marian. But if it makes you feel better, go ahead. I'll watch the news while you're gone."

Sally honked, and Marian grabbed her warmest jacket. It was turning cold as darkness fell. Donna said Becky was warmly dressed, but even an insulated snowsuit was no match for subzero temperatures. They would go straight to the icehouse.

Marian's heart was pounding as they drove up in front of the sagging wooden structure. It was two stories high, bare and black against the darkening skyline. Becky certainly wouldn't have gone in there alone. Laura used to have nightmares about the place!

"There's a big flashlight under the dash on your side." Sally pointed. "Grab it and let's go."

They heard the noise as they got out of the car. Marian gasped as she recognized it. "The saw's running! We've got to hurry, Sally!"

The wooden door groaned on its hinges as they pulled it open. The noise of the saw was earsplitting. Sally found a switch by the side of the door and pressed it. The saw stopped with a screech.

"I wonder how long that's been running." Sally's voice was loud in the stillness. "I'm surprised it still works."

The silence was almost more deafening than the noise. A smell of old sawdust and dampness came from the dark inside. Marian turned on the flashlight, but it cast a feeble yellow circle against the vastness of black. It was scary. Yes, she admitted it. It frightened her even to think of going inside in the dark. But Becky could be here, hurt, injured, even . . . ! No, she couldn't think of that! Becky was probably safe at home by now, but they still had to make sure.

Marian shivered as they walked into the darkness. Her mind screamed out a warning. Something was here, something hideous. She didn't know if she could bear to face it.

CHAPTER 16

"Sally? I don't like this. . . ." Marian stepped into the blackness and stopped, sweeping the light in an arc. "Wait! Over there!"

Something pink had glittered in the beam of the flashlight. Marian spotlighted it again, against a pile of boards in the corner.

"I'll get it." Sally crossed the old creaking floor to retrieve the pink case. "Fascinatin' Lady Makeup Kit. Becky got it for Christmas. She called Jenny this morning to tell her about it.

"Becky?" Sally called out her name, and they listened to the dark silence. *"Becky?"*

"She was here." Marian's voice was shaking. "Do you think we ought to call the sheriff, Sally? I've got a bad feeling."

"Shine the light on the far wall, and work your way around." Sally gave Marian's arm a firm pat. "She might still be here. We've got to find her!"

As Marian started to sweep the beam of light over the back wall, Sally grabbed her arm.

"Wait! Shine it back in that corner, by the saw!"

The flashlight moved slowly, fearfully, in Marian's hand. It caught the old saw in its beam, blade gleaming dangerously, wet with blood.

Marian drew her breath in sharply. There was a red boot, brown snow pants, a red parka, and Becky's face, white and grotesque in death. She was lying in a pool of glistening blood.

Before Marian could stop, the beam of light moved on. Becky's arm was tossed in the corner. It was no longer attached to her body.

For a moment the two women stared, stiffly frozen with horror. There was a watch on Becky's small wrist, a red plastic band with Mickey Mouse on the face.

"Oh . . . dear . . . God . . . !" The words hung heavy in the air. Neither Marian nor Sally knew who had spoken them. Then everything went black as the flashlight dropped with a crash from Marian's nerveless fingers.

"The sheriff!" Sally grabbed Marian's arm and pulled her to the doorway. "Come on, Marian . . . move! We have to get the sheriff right away!"

It was an accident, the sheriff decided. Becky had been playing in the icehouse, playing with the huge old saw. And her game had turned into tragedy. There were editorials in the paper about old, condemned buildings. The Lions Club offered to help tear the place down. The Fischers could sue, a leading lawyer said. The building was a community menace. But it was too late. Becky was dead.

Marian had slept restlessly for the past two nights,

reliving that terrible scene in the icehouse. When her thoughts were too frightening, she would sit in the kitchen, drinking cup after cup of coffee. Dan was kind. He offered to help, but Marian knew there was nothing he could do for her. She was numbed, but her mind would not be still. She had seen Becky's face over and over again in her dreams.

"You need to be around people." Dan faced her over their breakfast coffee. It was two days since Becky died, and Marian still felt divorced from reality. She was living in slow motion, cooking the meals, doing the housework, but nothing was quite real.

"Why don't you call Sally? Ask her if they want to come in and play cards tonight?"

"All right." Agreeing was easier than trying to explain why it didn't matter one way or the other. Maybe it would be good playing cards with Ronnie and Sally.

At least she hadn't said no to cards tonight. That was a good sign. Dan watched the listless way Marian walked to the phone. Seeing Ronnie and Sally should cheer her up. Sure, it was a terrible thing finding Becky that way, but Marian had to snap out of it.

Marian looked over at Ronnie and began to smile. He was humming "I Left My Heart in San Francisco" under his breath. And it was her turn to declare trump!

"Oh well." Marian looked down at her cards and

hid a smile. "I suppose it should be something black. . . ."

Ronnie was really squirming now. It served him right for being so blatant!

"I guess I'll go with hearts." Marian almost laughed out loud as Ronnie gave her a big grin. Wait until he saw her hand. She didn't have a single heart!

"What did the first-grade teacher say when she got a flat tire?" Sara looked over at her and laughed. "Oh, oh, oh. Look, look, look. Damn, damn, damn."

Marian couldn't help it. The joke really wasn't *that* funny, but it felt so good to laugh. She hadn't laughed like this in days. She poured herself another drink and picked up the cards to deal.

They played until midnight. Marian was in good spirits when she said good night at the door. For the first night since they had found Becky, she wasn't afraid to go to sleep.

She got Dan settled in bed and went upstairs. It was cold tonight. The outdoor thermometer was stuck at fifteen below. Marian opened Laura's heat register all the way and got into her warmest nightgown. She wasn't really sleepy. Perhaps she'd read for a while. Laura would like to hear a story.

Marian picked up the copy of *Charlotte's Web*. Her students loved the book. She read a chapter a day, right after lunch. Was it fair to read it to Laura first? Laura would be ahead of the rest of the class.

"What do you think, baby?" Marian opened the book and stood quietly listening. "Do you want to hear it first?"

The light was good in the chair by the bed. Marian sat down and smiled to herself. Laura deserved a few extra chapters. She was eager to hear what happened to Wilbur.

Her voice filled the room, soft and melodic. Marian loved to read aloud to her baby. She finished the chapter and placed the book on Laura's small table. She left it open on purpose. Laura wanted to look at the picture. It showed Wilbur posing under the web Charlotte had spun. TERRIFIC, it said, in an intricate design.

Marian stretched out on Laura's bed. She yawned and rubbed her eyes. Now she was really tired. She covered herself with Laura's quilt and snuggled into the warmth. She felt peaceful and restored here in Laura's bed. There was a soft smile on her face as she went to sleep.

Marian was happy. There was a feeling of joyous expectation as she opened her eyes and blinked against the morning light. The sun was out for the first time in days, and her baby had been here. She didn't have to look. She knew it.

Laura's diary was next to the bed. Marian reached for it with eager fingers. The smile on her face spread to rapture as she saw the big, childlike printing.

She's here. I'm so happy, Mommy. Becky came to play with me.

Laura was happy again! Marian was so relieved, she laughed out loud. Now Laura wasn't all alone.

This time she had to show Dan. Marian ran down the stairs with the diary in her hands. Dan had to read it. Laura had a playmate now, and she was happy.

"Dan! Wake up, honey! You have to read this! It's another note from Laura!"

He groaned as he struggled to sit up in bed. Marian thrust the book into his hands, and he glanced down to read the lines. She was doing it again, right when he thought everything was all right.

"Isn't it wonderful, Dan?" Marian's face was bright with excitement. "Laura's not alone anymore! Look! She says she's happy!"

It was the same thing all over again. Dan felt a surge of anger and helplessness. Marian was writing these crazy notes in her sleep. Somehow he had to force her back to reality. This whole thing was completely insane!

"Marian, I want you to listen to me." Dan faced her with a determined expression. Her delusion had gone too far. He had to take a hard line with her now, even at the risk of being cruel. Nothing else would be effective.

"Laura is not writing these notes. You are. Laura is dead."

For a moment he thought he had gotten through to her. Her joyful expression wavered, but then it was back again, in full force.

"I know Laura's dead, Dan. We both know that's true. But she's writing these notes. That's what makes it so wonderful. She's telling us that dying isn't the end. Don't you see? She's still there, somewhere, loving us and watching over us."

"No, Marian. Laura's not writing these notes. You are. Don't you understand what's happening here? You're upset over Becky's death, and writing these notes makes you feel better."

She was frowning now, trying to puzzle it out. "You think *I* wrote this note?" she asked at last.

"I know you did, Marian. Remember how you used to write things in your sleep? The poetry? The grocery lists? You kept a notepad right by the bed, and sometimes you wrote something in the middle of the night. You couldn't remember doing that, either. Laura's dead. She's gone. You'll never hear from her again. Dead people can't write notes."

"That's not true!"

She grabbed the diary from his hands and ran from the room. He was being mean, trying to get even with her for the teachers' party. Dan was lying about the notes, lying about Laura. He wanted to hurt her, but she wouldn't let him. No one could take her baby away from her!

She didn't calm down until she got to Laura's room. Then she sat in the rocker and drew a deep breath. What should she do now? Dan didn't believe this was a note from Laura.

It *was* hard to believe. Marian nodded. She would be the first to admit that it sounded crazy. Perhaps Dan hadn't been trying to hurt her. He just didn't have enough faith to believe.

She looked down at the diary and read it again. She knew Laura had written it. It didn't really matter about Dan. It would be foolish to try to convince him.

She's here. I'm so happy, Mommy. Becky came to play with me.

As she reread the words, peace stole into her heart. Laura was happy. That was the important thing. Laura was happy because Becky was there.

Was it right to feel joy over the death of a child? The thought sobered Marian. Perhaps it was not in good taste, or however you defined those nebulous things. And she certainly wasn't rejoicing over Becky's awful accident! She would have done anything to prevent it from happening.

But it *had* happened. It must be God's will. And now Laura had a friend to play with.

Suddenly Marian felt better. It was all explained now. Grief was tempered with joy, and everything was changed. Becky had not died in vain. That would be a great comfort to Donna, if she could tell her. But Marian knew better than that. She had learned an important lesson from Dan this morning. Dan thought she was crazy. Donna would think she was crazy, too, for believing such a thing. No one could understand . . . no one but her. It was Laura's secret she had to keep.

She opened the diary to the next page and stacked Laura's books neatly on the table. She would buy a flower today to put in a vase on Laura's table. Her baby loved flowers. And right after the funeral, she'd stop at the drugstore for the new

issue of *Jack and Jill*. They could read it together up
here in Laura's room.

In a way, it was best that Dan was paralyzed.
Marian paused thoughtfully as she brushed her curly
hair. He couldn't come up here to see all the wonderful little changes she would make in Laura's
room. Dan would be sure she was losing her mind if
he saw fresh flowers on Laura's table and the new
books she was planning to buy. She pushed thoughts
of Dan to the back of her head. This was for Laura
and for her, a little secret between mother and
daughter. What Dan didn't know wouldn't hurt him
in the slightest.

Dan was still horrified. He had tried to be calm
and reasonable, to present the facts in a no-nonsense
way. But Marian would not face reality. She still believed Laura was writing her notes. And nothing he
could say would change her mind. She had dashed
from the room like a madwoman, clutching the
diary in her hands. What could he do to snap her
out of it?

He expected her to be angry when she came
back downstairs. He thought she would scream or
cry. He was ready for anything but the serene smile
she gave him when she came in to say good-bye.

Mood changes were a sign of mental illness. Dan
thought he remembered reading that somewhere.
Marian's mood had gone from rage to serenity in
the space of ten minutes. Didn't that prove that
something was wrong?

He would have to do something soon. Dan sat up

a little straighter and sighed. He'd keep a close eye on Marian. If things got worse, he'd have to ask someone for help.

Marian sat with Sally on the hard wooden bench that served as a pew. The Congregational church was plain, no stained-glass windows, no rubbed oaken pews, no fancy altar cloths or statues. It was rather like a converted storefront, Marian thought, except it was up here on a hill, set apart from the business section, painted white, with a metal cross on top. It had been the Bible church before this, and the Church of Christ a few years back. The congregation was the same, but the ministers had changed. It seemed no clergyman wanted to stay in Nisswa for long.

There were no flowers. The small pink coffin stood alone and bare at the front of the church. Donna had asked that the money be given to the church instead. Marian guessed they could use it. The young minister looked to be barely twenty, with a black, threadbare suit and a tentative voice. There were three churches in Nisswa. Redeemer Lutheran, St. Paul's Catholic, and this church, the poor country cousin.

Erik Wahlstrom got up to read the eulogy. He was a teller at the First State Bank and an elder in the congregation. Marian wished she could smile at him. Erik looked nervous.

It was over very quickly. There wasn't much to say about a seven-year-old child. Donna was weeping as the young minister led her from the church. Marian ached to say something to comfort her. She wanted to pull Donna to the side, show her Laura's note, give her hope again. But then the moment was past. She took Donna's hand and murmured something appropriate. Then she followed Sally down the steep concrete steps.

CHAPTER 17

They decided to have the sledding party as scheduled. It would take everyone's mind off the tragedy. Marian bundled up warmly and left the house at seven thirty. She took the shortcut through the woods, climbing up the back of Heidelberg Hill. The moon was bright tonight, and it was cold and clear. It was a good feeling being up here all alone, the snow crunching under her boots. The moon threw blue-black shadows of trees all around her, and Marian took a deep, gulping breath of the fresh cold air.

She could hear the shouts of the children long before she reached the top of the hill. There was a sled track just over the crest, two parallel lines that swerved their way down the slope to disappear in the distance below.

She could see the bonfire now, and Marian hurried toward it, ducking under pine branches that hung low and heavy with snow. There were already skaters on the pond, gliding in circles across the smooth surface, laughing and calling out to each other.

"Look out below!" a man shouted. Marian stopped to watch a toboggan hurtle down the gentle slope. Jim Sorensen was in the front, steering, his face a laughing flash as he whooshed past in a cloud of powdery snow.

The chaperones were sitting on logs around the bonfire. They were drinking coffee out of Styrofoam cups. Sally saw her and waved, patting the log next to her.

"You walked through the woods alone? It's dark up there!" Sally sounded shocked, and Marian laughed.

"The moon's bright tonight." Marian accepted a cup of coffee and took a sip. Then she coughed and drank again. "This tastes like brandy!"

"Shh!" Sally put a finger to her lips. "Ronnie filled the thermos. He made it half-and-half because it's so cold."

"Mom? Can I ride on Mr. Sorensen's toboggan?" Jenny came racing up and dropped her skates at Sally's feet. "Oh, hi, Mrs. Larsen! Do you want a ride, too?"

"I think I'll wait a little while, Jenny." Marian reached down to tuck in Jenny's long, ribbed scarf. "I'll just stay here and talk to your mom."

"She's been waiting for this all day." Sally shook her head. "The minute Jim got that toboggan, the news spread like wildfire. I bet every kid in school called him to see if he'd bring it tonight."

"At least she's not depressed." Marian smiled. "I thought maybe . . . with Becky and all . . ."

"She took it pretty hard at first," Sally admitted.

"But she seems to be all right now. Come on, Marian. Let's walk over there and watch them come down."

Marian thought Jenny still looked a little depressed. It had been a terrible year for her, losing two of her favorite friends. The Terrible Trio was gone now. Jenny was the only one left. It was sad for Jenny to be separated from her friends. The three girls had been so close.

Jenny was right behind Jim, wedged in by the older kids. There was no way she could fall off. Marian heard her excited squeal as the toboggan shoved off. Jenny was hanging on tightly, her laughing face a blur as she streaked past. When they came to a stop at the base of the hill, Jenny rolled off and tugged at the rope. She was ready to go all over again.

"Okay. Once more." Jim let himself be persuaded. "Who's the strongest? We need the strongest and quickest to shove off."

Marian felt a rush of love as she watched Jenny trudge back up the slope, sturdy legs churning through the snow. Her scarf had come loose again, and Marian wished she could tuck it in. Jenny was a dear little girl. She had been Laura's very best friend.

There were numerous spills and scrapes, but none of them were serious. Some of the younger children were so well padded, it was an effort for them to walk. They tramped through the snow, puffing and laughing, not feeling the cold in the slightest. They reminded Marian of stuffed toys, legs and arms no longer bending in the proper

places with twenty extra pounds of kapok sewn in
their clothes.

There was one advantage to wearing snow
pants, Marian thought as she saw Ricky Owens
slide across the ice on his bottom. Ricky didn't
even wince. He just got up, grinning, and skated
off again.

"Evenin', Miz Larsen."

Jake Campbell stood by the edge of the pond,
watching the children skate. There was a wide,
happy grin on his face, and Marian could tell he
was half drunk on whatever he was carrying in his
brown paper bag. She waved but avoided him
neatly, hurrying off toward the crowd around the
bonfire. When Jake was drunk, he'd talk your ear
off about his days in the army. He lived in a corrugated tin shack on the edge of town, subsisting entirely on the small check he got from the VA each
month. Jake had come back to town after being injured in combat and had just stayed. He seemed
perfectly harmless, even though he said some
strange things now and then. The children liked
him, and Marian supposed he had just as much
right to be there as anyone else in town.

Sally was off supervising a group of younger
children, helping them slide down a small slope
in cardboard boxes from the Red Owl. Connie
Bergstrom was with her. Marian looked around for
Cliff. If Connie was here, Cliff couldn't be far away.

There he was, building a snowman with four
younger children. Marian grinned as she saw him
using his cast as a lever to lift the heavy balls of
snow. She'd have to remember to tell Dan about

that. It seemed that no injury would keep Cliff down for long.

Midge had brought three huge saucers of bright orange plastic with handles on the inside. She was attempting to organize a lineup of kids. The disks were a novelty, and they all wanted a turn to slide and spin down the hill.

Jenny sat down on a log by the bonfire. She missed Laura and Becky! This party would be fun if they were here.

The toboggan ride was over. Mr. Sorensen said she had to wait until everyone had a turn before she could go again. Jenny understood about taking turns, but now she was bored. Her mom was with the kindergarten kids, and Jenny didn't want to join them. She was too old to slide down a snowbank in a box. And she didn't feel like riding on a saucer, either. There was nothing to do.

She pulled her sled over to the baby hill and went down once. That was no fun, either. It was such a little hill. When she played with Laura and Becky, they went down much bigger hills than this.

Jenny stood alone, away from her laughing classmates, and stared up at the big hill. She remembered what they had decided last summer. They had all made a promise, Laura, Becky, and her. This year they'd slide down the big hill at night. Should she do it alone? Becky and Laura were dead. They couldn't keep their promise, but she could keep hers. It wasn't right to break a promise.

Mom would be mad. Jenny frowned in concentration. Dad wouldn't like it, either. She'd probably get a spanking for breaking the rule. Was it worth a spanking to keep her promise?

Marian wandered from group to group, returning to the bonfire a couple of times for a refill from the thermos. She spotted Jim Sorensen leaving with the toboggan and waved at him. Then she looked around for Jenny. Her skates were still by the log, so she wasn't out on the pond. Now that she thought about it, she hadn't seen Jenny for quite some time.

She wasn't in Midge's group, and Sally was still with the younger children. Ronnie was on the far side of the bonfire. Jenny wasn't with him, either. Her sled was gone, though, and there were tracks where she'd dragged it away.

Marian walked to the edge of the clearing and peered up through the trees. She wasn't sure, but she thought she saw a small figure disappearing around a pine tree near the path. Surely, Jenny wouldn't be foolish enough to go down the big hill in the dark. It had been declared off-limits for this party.

Should she get Ronnie? Marian stood, undecided. Perhaps it wasn't even Jenny up there. Jenny could be anywhere in this crowd of children. She should still go up and check, though. A child could get hurt up there, and they'd never know until noses were counted to go home.

Marian climbed up part of the way and stopped, listening. She was sure she heard someone ahead of her on the path. If Jenny was up here, she'd scold her and bring her down. Rules were rules, and Jenny was no exception. She had to hurry and catch up with whoever it was. Heidelberg Hill at night was no place for a child!

It took a long time to climb up the big hill. Jenny stopped halfway and caught her breath. The woods were dark now. Dense pine branches blocked the moonlight. It was quiet and lonely up here by herself.

She wanted to turn around and go back. This was no fun without Laura and Becky. But that would be a chicken thing to do.

The big hill was almost up to the sky. Maybe it was so high that Laura and Becky could see her from heaven. She had to do it for them. They'd be glad she'd kept her promise.

At last she was there! Jenny turned at the top of the hill. She could see the bonfire flickering faintly on the snow below her. The dark shapes down there were her friends, laughing and having a good time. Her mom was there, and so was her dad. It was scary up here all alone.

There was a noise behind her, and Jenny froze. It sounded like someone was walking through the trees.

"Who is it?" Jenny's voice was high and a little frightened. It wasn't nice being scared in the dark. She didn't like it one bit!

Someone was coming! Jenny whirled and ran for the slope. She threw her sled down and jumped on top of it. She pushed as hard as she could, but the sled wouldn't budge. She was stuck!

She looked back, frightened. The last thing she saw was a bulky shape blocking out the moon. And something heavy covered her mouth before she could even think to scream.

"Jenny!" Sally cupped her hands around her mouth and called out loudly, "*Jenny!*"

Where *was* that child! Midge had saved her turn in line all this time, and now Jenny had wandered off somewhere else.

"Have you seen Jenny?" Sally warmed her hands at the bonfire. But no one there had seen her. Maybe she was out on the pond with Ronnie.

There was a sled coming down the big hill. Sally put a hand to her mouth as it swerved dangerously. The kids weren't supposed to be up there. This was the very thing they were trying to avoid!

"Is that Jenny?" Ronnie walked over to join her. "Sure it is! That's her Red Flyer!"

"Just wait until I—" The threat caught in Sally's throat as the sled crashed into a tree at the bottom of the slope. She was running now, and Ronnie passed her with his long strides in the snow. They were all running toward the still form on the sled.

She screamed once, a high wail of anguish. Then someone stopped her from coming any closer. Strong arms shielded her, led her away, but Sally had seen. Jenny's neck was twisted at an impossible angle. Her baby's eyes were open, seeing nothing. And there was an expression of terror on her beautiful dead face.

* * *

Sheriff Bates was already there, red lights flashing brightly against the snow. Marian rushed out of the woods, panting with exertion.

"There was someone up there!" she managed to gasp. Then she saw the stretcher with Jenny's body. The sheet was pulled up, hiding Jenny's face. Marian couldn't help it. She broke into sobs.

"Marian, over here." Sheriff Bates pulled her over to the side, away from the small body on the stretcher. "Where were you? Did you see anyone?"

"I heard him!" Marian took a deep breath and swallowed hard. "I heard someone on the path, and I ran after him. He got away, but I found this jacket at the top of the hill!"

She held out the jacket with shaking hands. Then she gasped as she recognized it in the light from the bonfire.

"It's Dan's! That's Dan's old army jacket, Sheriff! We always kept it hanging on a hook in the garage."

Sheriff Bates took the jacket and examined it. Dan's name was sewn on the olive-drab strip over the right breast pocket.

"Was your garage locked, Marian?"

"No, of course not."

"Did you notice the jacket was missing before tonight? Think, Marian. It might be important."

"No . . . I don't know, Sheriff! It could have been missing. I . . . I don't think I would have noticed!"

Marian stumbled heavily, and Sheriff Bates supported her. Midge was standing nearby, and he motioned for her.

"Will you and Edith get Marian home and stay

with her until I get there? She needs some help. I'll come to the house just as soon as I can."

Marian looked really bad. Sheriff Bates leaned closer to peer into her wide, startled eyes. He'd seen that same desperate look in the eyes of a deer trapped by a spotlight.

"And, Midge? Catch Dr. Hinkley before he leaves for the hospital. I think Marian's in shock."

CHAPTER 18

Sheriff Bates closed the door to the den when he came in. There was a serious expression on his face.

"Sit down, Sheriff." Dan motioned to a chair. "What happened out there? Edith said Jenny's dead! Something about a terrible accident?"

"That's right." The sheriff nodded. "I need your help, Dan. Would you mind answering a few questions?"

"Of course not."

"You were here all night. Is that right?" Sheriff Bates took out his notebook. He winced at the bitter look that crossed Dan's face. Of course Dan had been here. Where else could he go? He wished he hadn't asked that stupid question.

"Did you hear anyone outside your window? Anyone messing around in your garage? Any noise that sounded suspicious?"

"No. I had the television on, and I dozed off a couple times. I didn't hear a thing, Sheriff."

Dozed off weren't exactly the words for what had happened to him tonight. Dan sighed as the sheriff made notes in his little plastic-covered book. His walking dream had been especially vivid tonight. His legs were still shaking, even though they had no feeling. It was more like muscle fatigue than anything else. Of course, it was all a dream. He had to remember that. The sensation of climbing had been merely a figment of his subconscious.

"You're positive you didn't hear anything? Think hard, Dan. It's important."

"No, not a thing. What's all this about, Sheriff?"

"I just finished questioning Marian." Sheriff Bates looked up and sighed. "She's really upset, Dan. Marian thinks she chased a man through the woods tonight, but she couldn't give me a description. She says she never actually saw him. She just heard him running on the path ahead of her. And she found your old army jacket at the top of Heidelberg Hill."

"My jacket?" Dan frowned. "Jesus, Sheriff! Do you think the man Marian chased might have something to do with Jenny's accident?"

"I'm not sure, Dan. It was dark in the woods, and Marian was distraught. She may have been chasing an animal, for all we know. The jacket may not have any significance at all. Marian said you kept it in the garage. Anyone could have taken it. It might have been lying up there for weeks, though it looks fairly clean."

Dan nodded slowly. He supposed the sheriff was right. Still, something about the man in the woods and his army jacket was vaguely unsettling.

"Well, thanks for the help, Dan." Sheriff Bates stood and snapped shut his notebook. "Just as a precaution, I'd make sure your house and your garage were locked from now on. Don't forget you're alone up here at the edge of the woods."

"Sure . . . I'll do that, Sheriff." Dan stared at the door long after Sheriff Bates had left. The sheriff obviously didn't believe that Marian had chased a man in the woods. What if she had? Was Jenny's death really an accident?

It had to be an accident. Dan closed his eyes and thought hard. Everyone loved Jenny. Surely, no one in Nisswa would want to harm her.

Another accident! Dan shivered. Now Jenny was dead. First Becky and then Jenny. One by one Laura's friends were dying. Now he felt guilty for resenting the girls. He hadn't really meant it. It'd been painful to see Becky and Jenny; he had hoped he wouldn't have to see them again. But he certainly hadn't wished for their deaths!

"I don't know, Pete." Dr. Hinkley shuffled through the stack of medical reports on his desk and sighed. "I've got the preliminary autopsy reports right here, but I can't say with any authority whether Jenny's neck was broken before she smashed into that tree. It could be a simple accident. Or it could be murder."

Sheriff Bates frowned. This was bad. "How about off the record, Doc? What do you think?"

Dr. Hinkley looked grim. His bushy eyebrows almost met as he frowned. "Those bruises on Jenny's neck bother me, Pete. There's absolutely no medical proof, but someone wearing heavy gloves *could* have broken Jenny's neck and then pushed her sled down the hill."

"Christ!" Sheriff Bates winced. "Maybe Marian *did* chase someone in the woods, Doc. It's cases like this that make me wish I'd been a plumber."

"Now, Pete. You're just tired. Let me get you a refill, and we'll hash this out together. You're the best sheriff we've ever had, but sometimes it helps to kick ideas around."

Sheriff Bates gave a tired smile. He just hoped the rest of the town felt the way Doc did. Doing a good job as sheriff was important to him.

By the time Doc was back with the coffee, Sheriff Bates was thinking clearly again. He had to treat this like a murder, even though it probably wasn't. Explore all possibilities. That was what they did on TV.

"Let's assume the worst." He took a gulp of his coffee and opened his notebook. "Can you think of anyone in Nisswa who's crazy enough to kill Jenny Powell?"

There was a long silence while Dr. Hinkley thought. Someone in Nisswa off balance enough to kill little Jenny?

"No, I can't think of anyone," he said at last. "The only person with a history of mental illness is Jake Campbell, but he's harmless. Jake's practically a big kid himself."

"No, it couldn't be Jake." Sheriff Bates tapped his pen against his notebook impatiently. "I can't think of anyone, either. It's just a pity that Dan Larsen was asleep. His room faces Heidelberg Hill. I talked to him earlier, but he didn't hear a thing."

Dan Larsen? Dr. Hinkley frowned. Dan had a whopper of a mental problem. Should he say anything to Pete about Dan's "walking dreams"?

No, it was clearly ridiculous. Dr. Hinkley discarded the idea. He wasn't even sure that Dan actually sleepwalked. He hadn't mentioned it lately.

"It can't be anyone from town, Pete." Dr. Hinkley looked serious. "If Jenny was murdered, it has to be a transient. How about checking the state hospital to see if anyone escaped?"

"I'll go down to the office and call right now." Sheriff Bates stood up. "Doc? You don't think we should say anything about the possibility of murder, do you?"

"Definitely not. It'll only upset poor Ronnie and Sally. And there's no sense alarming the town. I think a quiet little investigation would be wise, Pete. The less people know about this, the better."

Sheriff Bates nodded. Doc was right. If the people in Nisswa thought a murderer was on the loose, they'd panic. That was the last thing he needed right now.

"I'm ninety percent sure it was an accident." Dr. Hinkley walked the sheriff to the door. "This has been a bad winter in Nisswa. First poor Laura Larsen. And then little Becky. And now Jenny. It's frightening, Pete."

"Three little girls gone, just like that." Sheriff Bates sighed heavily. "It makes me sick, Doc. If I had a little girl, I'd watch her like a hawk!"

It was past two in the morning when Dr. Hinkley finished filling out the death certificate. He scribbled a few instructions for Mabel Kaun, the night nurse, and walked down the quiet hallway to the parking lot.

Dr. Hinkley unlocked his car and scraped the windshield free of ice. Then he got in and turned on the ignition. The late-model Buick started with no trouble. When he'd bought the car, Jim told him to warm it up for five minutes before driving it in the winter, but Dr. Hinkley was just too tired. He put the car in gear and pulled out onto the street.

Nothing was moving. Even Jerry Pietre's Siberian huskies were inside tonight. Dr. Hinkley turned the corner at the Conoco station and noticed that the streetlight in front of the drugstore was out again. His headlights were two tunnels of light in the darkness. The surrounding buildings were dark and deserted. Businesses were closed. The town was sleeping and peaceful, just as it always was this time of night. It seemed utterly inconceivable that there might be a murderer inside one of those friendly houses.

As he passed the street that led to Dan's house, Dr. Hinkley shivered. Something was bothering him, a strange, anxious feeling at the back of his mind. Marian had found Dan's jacket up there in the woods. If Dan wasn't confined to bed, he'd be Pete's prime suspect.

Was Dan Larsen capable of murder? Dr. Hinkley switched the defroster on high and squinted to see out of the windshield. Dan *could* be walking. It was medically possible. Dan's leg muscles were in remarkable shape for a man who'd been immobile for over a month.

The car fishtailed on the ice as Dr. Hinkley took the corner a little too fast. He straightened out and drove on a little slower. He'd heard and seen enough to think Dan had a motive for the murder. He found it painful to be around Laura's friends, and he was filled with rage about the injustice of Laura's death. He'd resented deeply the happiness of families whose young daughters were still alive, particularly Laura's little friends.

He must be really tired to think up such a ridiculous theory. Dr. Hinkley snorted as he got out of the car to open his garage door. It was absurd to suspect Dan of murder. There was absolutely no rational basis for his wild suspicions. Now he was glad he hadn't said anything to Pete. He would have looked like a first-class fool.

When Marian awoke, the house was quiet. She sat up carefully, reeling a bit from the shot Dr. Hinkley had given her. She remembered Edith and Midge helping her up the stairs, making her lie down on the bed and covering her with a blanket. They had offered to stay. And she had told them it wasn't necessary, just to make sure to lock the doors behind them.

Marian got out of bed and looked at the clock. It was five in the morning. She had slept all night. Soon the sun would be rising, and it would be another day.

Poor Jenny! Marian felt the hot tears behind her eyelids. She had been crying in her sleep. The pillow was wet.

Slowly, she moved toward the door. Her body felt leaden and awkward. It must be the aftereffects of Dr. Hinkley's shot. It took her a full minute to slip into her robe and fasten it. Where were her slippers? Groggily, she found them and pulled them on

over her chilled feet. Then she moved toward the
stairs, one foot in front of the other, like a half-
awake child.

Dan must still be sleeping. There was no sound
as she shuffled across the living room and stopped
at the door to the den. Yes. He was snoring softly.
She was glad he could sleep. Last night had been
awful.

She wanted coffee, but the noise might wake
him. Marian took a glass of orange juice instead.
There was a dry metallic taste in her mouth, and
the juice washed it away. It was difficult to move.
Even lifting the glass to her lips was an effort. Dr.
Hinkley's shot must have been very powerful.
Sleeping pills had never affected her quite this way.
She was so tired, she didn't know if she could make
it back up the stairs.

She counted the steps as she climbed, but even
thinking the numbers was too much effort. Finally,
she was at the top, and she paused at the door to
her room. No. She didn't want to go back in there.
She would nap on Laura's bed until the sun was up.
It always made her feel better to sleep in her baby's
room.

The sky was starting to lighten as she climbed
into Laura's narrow bed. It was warm here. Safe.
Now she would sleep. And when she woke up,
everything would be better.

Marian tried to brush it away, but the light was
still in her eyes. Why didn't they turn the lights off?
It was impossible to sleep with a light in her eyes.

She blinked and sat up. It must be late! The sun

was streaming in the window, and she could hear a snowplow on the street outside. She felt just fine now. Dr. Hinkley's shot had worn off at last.

Marian glanced at the clock. It was past ten. No wonder she felt better! She had slept a total of eleven hours.

As she got out of bed, Marian saw a lump under the covers. A fuzzy blue face with bright button eyes stared up at her. It was Laura's teddy bear. In the daytime the bear sat in the rocking chair, and at night it was Laura's bedtime companion. She must have taken it to bed with her last night, just like Laura used to do.

She picked up the bear to carry it back to the rocker. Then she saw the diary. Marian ran across the small room to seize it eagerly. There was another message from her baby!

Don't feel bad, Mommy. Jenny's here, and she likes it. She missed Becky and me.

Jenny was there! Marian smiled happily. It made her feel good to think of the three girls playing together. And Laura had been here again, watching her while she slept. Marian felt loved and comforted.

"Be happy, Laura." She whispered the words into the air. "Thank you for telling me. And say hello to Becky and Jenny. I'll save all their homework for them."

Marian made the bed and placed the bear back in the rocker. Then she put Laura's diary in the bear's lap. Her baby would laugh when she saw the bear reading it. It would be their own private joke.

Then she closed the door softly and hurried off to get dressed. Poor Dan would be wondering if she was going to sleep all day!

"You can only stay a minute, Marian." Dr. Hinkley opened the door to Sally's room and gestured toward the bed. "We have her sedated. She may not be able to talk very well."

"Sally . . . dear . . ." Marian's breath caught in her throat as she saw her friend's desolate face. "Oh, Sally . . . you don't know how sorry I am!"

Sally looked at her for a moment, and tears began to run down her cheeks. "I'll be all right, Marian. It's just . . . such a shock. One minute she's playing, and the next minute she's . . ."

"I know." Marian patted Sally's hand. "You've got to have courage, Sally. You have to go on. There's no other choice."

"How did you do it, Marian?" Sally's voice was trembling. "How did you stay so strong through it all?"

"I . . . I don't know." Marian dropped her eyes. She wanted to share her secret with Sally, but it wouldn't be right. Sally would have to find her own secret to keep her strong.

Dr. Hinkley was beckoning to her from the doorway. Marian knew she had to leave. She leaned down to kiss Sally's cheek and smooth back her friend's hair.

"You'll find your way, Sally," she whispered. "I know that somehow you'll find your way."

* * *

"How was she?" Dan was sitting up in bed when she got back home.

"Dr. Hinkley said they've been keeping her sedated, but she'll be all right." Marian crossed to the window and opened the drapes. "Did you talk to Ronnie?"

"I think he'll be fine once the funeral's over and Sally's back on her feet. What a horrible shock!"

"Yes, it seems that way at first." Marian turned, her face thoughtful. "There's some consolation, though, some reason for it all, if you stop to think about it. Laura missed Jenny so much. And now they're together."

"Marian! That's kind of gruesome, isn't it?"

"Not really." She moved toward him, her face earnest. "Remember that note from Laura right after Becky died? Laura said Becky was with her and she wasn't so lonesome anymore. Now it's even better. Laura has Becky *and* Jenny to play with. They're all happy, Dan. I know they are. Everyone is much better off now."

Dan stared at his wife, her eyes luminous and shining in the twilight. Marian looked insane. She had to be crazy to believe a thing like that. And she really did believe it, even though he'd tried his best to make her face reality. He felt a chill start in his mind and spread over his entire body. Marian was completely insane. She was carrying on just as normal and ordinary as you please, and she was completely mad!

She said something about supper, and he nodded, not really hearing her. His mind was racing, dread thoughts surfacing with chilling clarity. Marian believed Laura was lonely. She would do anything for Laura.

The first was Muffy. Dan shivered under the covers. He didn't think Marian had the little puppy killed deliberately. He knew Muffy really was ill. But it had happened, and the next morning there was the note from Laura, the note that *Marian* had written.

After Becky's death there was another note, another fabrication of Marian's sick mind. Sheriff Bates said it was an accident, but suddenly Dan remembered. Marian had gone for a long walk on the afternoon of Becky's death. And she came home dazed, unable to tell him where she'd been. What if she'd gone to the icehouse and waited for Becky there? Was Marian capable of cold-blooded murder?

He wanted to stop, but his mind kept on adding it up. Marian was there, on the hill, last night. She claimed she'd chased a man through the woods, and she'd found Dan's old army jacket up there. Everyone thought she was brave for chasing a stranger in the dark. But what if there was no fleeing stranger? What if Marian had killed Jenny herself and made it look like a tragic accident?

He shouldn't think this way. It was wrong. Marian couldn't be that crazy. She was the same rational, kind Marian who held slumber parties for the kids on rainy summer nights, the same normal Marian who taught second grade and baked cookies for Laura's best friends.

But she wasn't the same, and he knew it deep down inside. Marian was insane, and she had killed Laura's best friends. She was sending victims to

Laura one by one to keep her baby from being lonely.

He had to tell someone! Dan reached for the telephone and dialed the sheriff's office. They had to stop her!

"Sheriff Bates speaking."

Dan's fingers gripped the phone until his knuckles were white. Would the sheriff believe him? Marian certainly didn't look insane. She taught her class and acted normal most of the time. How could he tell Sheriff Bates that whenever Marian thought her baby was lonely, she killed off someone to keep Laura happy?

"This is the sheriff. Is someone on the line?"

Dan swallowed hard and replaced the phone in the cradle. He had no proof that Marian was the killer. The sheriff would think that *he* was the crazy one!

What could he do? Dan tried to think. He was a little afraid of Marian. She had killed Becky and Jenny. If she thought he suspected the truth, she might kill him, too!

He'd have to watch her and gather proof for the sheriff. He'd build an airtight case before he turned Marian in. It would help if he could follow her when she left the house, but that was impossible. He needed someone to help him, someone to be his legs. But who could he trust?

CHAPTER 19

Marian sat in the lily-scented church and dabbed at her eyes with her handkerchief. She had no tears, but it was the right thing to do. Everyone would think she was hard-hearted if she didn't make them think she was crying. She felt terrible about Jenny's death, and the funeral was an awful ordeal, but there were no tears. She was every bit as sorrowful as Midge and Edith, but the tears would not fall. Perhaps it was because she was the only one who knew the truth. She knew Jenny was happy playing with Laura. It was impossible to cry about a tragic thing like this when she knew it had all turned out right in the end.

It was a pretty funeral. Marian gazed at the banks of flowers surrounding the small bronze casket. Her flowers were there, lovely pink roses, Laura's favorites. Father McMahon was shaking something over the casket now, intoning a blessing, Marian surmised. She knew next to nothing about the Catholic ceremony. She stood and knelt when everyone else did, the prayer rail hard against her knees.

Ronnie and Sally were holding up very well. His arm was around her shoulders, protecting her from the world. They were lucky to have each other. Marian was a little surprised at Sally's strength. She had almost decided to share Laura's notes, but Sally didn't seem to need the secret.

"She's going back to work next week." They stood in a group on the church steps and watched the hearse drive off to the cemetery. "Sally's so brave, don't you think?"

Marian nodded. Edith was right. Sally was just as brave and strong as she had been. Did she have a secret of her own? Could Sally possibly know that Jenny was with Laura?

"Religion helps at a time like this," Midge said earnestly. "Father McMahon's been out there almost every night. I think Sally's strength comes from the Lord."

Yes, that was probably it. Marian smiled back. Somehow she felt relieved to learn that Sally's strength was not the same as her own.

"I think we should offer to take her playground duty for a while. I know how I appreciated those coffee breaks the first few days I was back."

"That's a good idea, Marian," Edith said. "I'll organize all the elementary teachers. We can take turns. At least we'll be doing something to help."

"And one of us should be with her that first week at lunch. I didn't feel like eating, but all of you urged me. We don't want Sally to get run down."

"You're so kind, Marian," Midge sighed. "I want to help, but half the time I don't know what to do. Sally's so lucky to have a friend like you."

It was the first day of school after the long vacation. Dan shifted the books in his lap and watched Marian carefully in the rearview mirror. She looked perfectly normal today.

Dan knew he was being paranoid. He couldn't help it. He had watched Marian's every move for the past four days, but nothing unusual had happened. It made him feel disloyal to spy on her, but there was no other choice. He'd be the happiest man alive if he could prove he was wrong about Marian.

"Oh, there's Cliff." Marian pulled into their parking spot and waved. "He looks rather dashing with his arm in that cast. Connie's there, too. I guess they're waiting for you, Dan."

"Hi, Mrs. Larsen." Connie came up to take Dan's briefcase. "I get to push today. I flipped Cliff for it, and I won."

"Thank you, Connie." Marian opened the back door of the van and positioned Dan's chair on the ramp. Cliff waited below, ready to help. A moment later Dan was borne away, already surrounded by a throng of students.

As Marian walked toward the entrance of the school, the buses began to pull up. Doors opened, and crowds of students streamed toward the front entrance. She would have to hurry. There would be a line of children waiting to get in her room.

The note came in the middle of her science class.

There will be a brief meeting of all teachers in the faculty lounge directly after fourth period.

"Is it something for us, Mrs. Larsen?" Joey Cracowski was curious.

"Just a notice for a teachers' meeting, Joey." Marian smiled at him. "Now, Joey, how would you classify a teacher? Mammal, reptile, fish, or bird?"

By the time Marian had dismissed her class for lunch, she was tired. The children were always restless the first day back after a vacation. She had been forced to spend an hour listening to a recital of Christmas presents they had received. At least she had managed to turn it into a spelling lesson. Ricky Owens had learned to spell *Parcheesi*. Marian wasn't sure if that knowledge would help him in later life, but at least he'd learned it.

"Oh, what a morning!" Sally rushed out to join her. She looked a little pale, but she seemed to be coping with her kindergarten class. "What's the teachers' meeting about, Marian? Have you heard?"

Marian shook her head and found places for both of them against the far wall. Harvey came in and called them to order.

"Mary's received a total of seventy-three calls this morning. Parents are demanding we take some security precautions."

Seventy-three calls was over one third of the total enrollment. Both Marian and Sally were shocked.

"The Nisswa school board held an emergency meeting, and we set three new criteria for student supervision."

Harvey cleared his throat and read from his list.

"Number one. When the final bell rings, all teachers will accompany their classes to the buses. Bus drivers will then assume the responsibility for student safety. Roll will be called before the bus departs, and parents will meet their children at all bus stops.

"Number two. Extracurricular activities will be held as usual, but no student is to be dismissed until a parent or responsible adult has arrived to act as escort.

"Number three. No student is allowed on the playground alone, and a teacher or responsible adult must accompany any student leaving the premises for any reason."

He glanced up over the rim of his glasses to grin at Dorothy Pepin. "I know this is an imposition, Dorothy, but that means no more student runs to the grocery store for cooking class." Harvey paused for effect. "Unless, of course, you can talk the Red Owl into sending a limousine. Actually, they should. Your food budget keeps them in business!"

There was a burst of laughter, and Dorothy's face turned red. Everyone knew she sent the senior girls to shop on school time.

"I think that's all. And, Sally? I know the whole staff joins me in offering our sincere sympathy.

Just let us know if there's anything we can do. We all love you."

The meeting broke up with a clatter of chairs. Marian and Sally walked into the lunchroom together.

"How are you doing, Sal?" Dan waved them over to a table. "Did Santa make them any smarter?"

"He brought them presents, not brains." Sally sank down into a chair gratefully. "Would you believe Gail Swensen forgot how to count over Christmas? And none of them remember what quiet time means. My kids have a real talent for forgetting everything I've ever taught them."

Marian caught sight of Sally's face as she brought their trays. Her friend looked tense and white. She supposed that was only natural. Sally's voice was a little too loud; her smile forced. But she was here, and she was able to teach her class. Marian was proud of her.

"Here we are. Three turkey surprises!" Marian set their trays on the table. "Now you know where everybody's leftover turkey went. They donated it to the school cafeteria."

"Hey, Pete! Over here!"

Sheriff Bates turned and headed toward the back booth where Gus Olson and Jim Sorensen were waiting. They always saved him a place. The Truck-stop Café got pretty crowded at lunchtime.

"Anything new on Jenny's accident?" Jim lowered

his voice and glanced around him. "Everybody knows about the guy Marian chased."

"Forget about the guy in the woods." Sheriff Bates sighed. "Marian didn't even see him. It was probably a rabbit, Jim. There's absolutely no reason for people to get upset. Jenny's death was an accident, nothing more."

Sheriff Bates stopped talking as Emma came rushing over to their booth. He gave her his best cheerful smile.

"A hamburger and coffee, Emma . . . and an order of onion rings. You're a sight for sore eyes, girl. I swear you get prettier every day!"

"Sheriff Bates!" Emma blushed fiercely. She set down his coffee and hurried off to fill his order. She was Charlie Bower's oldest girl, a large-boned dishwater blonde, and no one had ever called her pretty except the sheriff.

"Burger and rings!" she shouted out to Joe Paquette in the kitchen. "It's for the sheriff!"

Emma watched while Joe made a double patty, extra thick. She added an order of fries to the onion rings and took three slices of American cheese from the refrigerator. Joe flipped two crispy pieces of bacon and stacked them on top of the hamburger patty. The sheriff was a special customer. He brought a lot of business their way.

Emma loved to see Sheriff Bates come in. He teased her, and he always left a nice big tip. She made a special point to make sure his coffee cup was always full. The Truckstop Café was practically his second office. Sheriff Bates spent a lot of time in here talking to the truckers.

It was time for more coffee. Emma hurried over with a freshly brewed pot. She refilled all three cups and giggled as the sheriff made a pretense of pinching her rear. Then she dashed back to the kitchen to check on his burger.

Jim waited until Emma was out of earshot. "People are pretty upset, Pete. Louise is afraid to let Jamie walk to school by herself."

"Dora's the same way." Gus added cream to his coffee and lit a cigarette. "She's taking the car to pick up the twins. I don't know, Pete. Something's fishy about Jenny's accident. There's a rumor going around that it was murder!"

"There's absolutely no proof of murder!" Sheriff Bates scowled heavily. He'd heard it all before. A half dozen people had stopped him on the street this morning.

"Now, look, boys." The sheriff stared across the table at them. "Rumors don't do anybody any good. I'm investigating the accident, and that's all I can do. We've just had a bad winter here in Nisswa. You can't blame me if people have accidents!"

"Hey . . . we didn't mean to be critical, Pete." Gus pushed the sugar across the table for him. "We all know you're doing the best you can. People are just jumpy, that's all. And a jumpy town's not good, you know? It hurts business."

"Yeah, I suppose it does." Sheriff Bates sighed. "It'll all blow over in a couple of weeks. Gus, I bet business at the bar has dropped a lot, huh?"

"It sure has!" Gus looked unhappy. "Nobody goes out at night anymore. I hope things get back to normal soon. It's going to be a bad month for us."

It was a bad month for him, too. Sheriff Bates made a fake lunge at Emma as she set down his hamburger, but his heart wasn't in it. He tried to be tough like those law-enforcement people on TV, but he bet they never had troubles like this. He'd been faced with some real ugly things the last couple of weeks. The people in town never thought about it. They just took his job for granted. If there was trouble, they called him, and he had to face it. Sometimes it wasn't a pretty sight.

He picked up a french fry and chewed thoughtfully. First, there was little Laura Larsen, skewered on the harrowing machine. He had had to get her down. And Becky Fischer in the icehouse. He had had to pick her up and take her to Doc Hinkley. And now poor Jenny Powell. It was enough to make a grown man have nightmares. All those awful sights and they expected him to take care of everything. It was a wonder he had the stomach for his job.

That was another big worry. He might not have his job for long. This was an election year, and his back was to the wall. He liked being the sheriff of Nisswa. Usually, it was a pretty easy job, until something like this came along. Then he earned every cent of his pay. If Nisswa didn't get back to normal soon, he was in big trouble at the polls.

* * *

"Are we having hockey practice tomorrow, Coach?" Cliff cleared a path, and Connie pushed the wheelchair through a crowd of students. "I heard something about cutting down on after-school stuff."

Dan smiled. Cliff was eager, even though he was on the bench for the championship game. He took his new duties as assistant coach seriously. Cliff was a good kid.

"Practice as usual, Cliff. We'll all leave together because of the new rules. You spread the word tomorrow at school. We'll meet in the gym and go out in a group from there."

"It's because of the accident, isn't it, Mr. Larsen?" Connie sounded serious. "I heard someone say Jenny's accident might be a murder."

"I don't know, Connie." Dan turned back to look at her. "But the new rules are a good idea. It never hurts to be careful."

"Poor little Jenny!" Cliff shuddered. "If it was murder, I hope they catch him soon. I'd do anything to make sure nothing like this ever happens again!"

Dan looked at him sharply. Cliff's fists were clenched, and his expression was grim. Was Cliff the one to help him?

"Why don't you drop by if you've got some time tonight, Cliff?" Dan kept his voice carefully neutral. "There're a couple of plays we haven't gone over yet."

"Sure, Coach. Is seven too early? I have to pick up Connie at nine. She's filling in for Inga at the drugstore tonight."

"Seven's just fine." Dan smiled as they helped

him into the van. For the first time he felt hopeful. Cliff might just believe him. Between them they had to fix it so Marian would never kill anyone again!

It was still early, but no one was moving on the street. Marian stared out the living-room window and sighed. It felt like Nisswa was under siege. No one was venturing out tonight. People were locked up in the safety of their homes. Even though the sheriff wouldn't confirm or deny the rumor, everyone in town believed that Jenny had been murdered. Marian wasn't sure how she felt about it. She was certain she had chased something in the woods, but she didn't know whether it was an animal or a man. The whole frenzied episode was a confused blur when she tried to recall it. She was better off not thinking about it all.

Marian turned from the window and walked to the couch. She was at loose ends tonight. Cliff was still closed up with Dan in the den. They were talking hockey, she supposed. She really should do something useful until Dan was free.

There were no papers to correct. She had finished them during her break. Of course, there were always lesson plans, but they could wait. She was already three weeks ahead, and that was far enough.

She climbed up the stairs and went into her bedroom. There was plenty to do up here. She could always reorganize the closet, but that seemed like too much work. Perhaps she'd finish her book or just stretch out on the bed and relax.

Marian heard the front door close, and she watched from the window as Cliff left. He got into his bright green van and drove away. Cliff wasn't afraid to go out at night. Or was he? He had looked pretty nervous when he left the house.

It was nearly nine. She supposed she could go downstairs and watch a little television with Dan. She didn't want to leave him alone too much. He'd been so quiet the past few days. Then, after he was asleep, she'd help Laura with her homework. She had enough work sheets for Becky and Jenny, too. The girls had to keep up with their class, and there was a whole page of subtraction problems to do before school tomorrow.

CHAPTER 20

"Are you sure it's safe up here?" Connie shivered as Cliff turned the van around at the top of the hill. Usually, there were other cars; it was the place for teenagers to park. Tonight the hill was deserted. There weren't even any tire tracks in the snow.

"It's safe as long as we lock the doors." Cliff sounded surprised as he backed the van around and parked it. "Don't tell me you're turning chicken on me, Connie. We've been up here lots of times before."

"But not after Jenny!"

Her voice was so sharp that Cliff turned to stare at her. Connie was really freaked out tonight.

"They were all talking about it down at the drugstore. Mr. Allen said he went down to Our Own Hardware and ordered a gun. He's sure Jenny was murdered!"

"Aw, come on, Connie. . . ." Cliff reached out with his good arm and patted her shoulder. "People are just overreacting, that's all. Switch places with me, will you? This cast gets in the way."

"But aren't you scared?" Connie climbed over him and slid under the wheel. She settled her head against Cliff's chest. "I am. I get scared every time I think of Jenny. And Becky, too!"

"Relax. There's no one up here but us. Just don't think about it anymore. This is the first time we've been alone in two weeks."

"That's true." Connie cuddled a little closer and ran her fingers up under his jacket. "Why don't we turn the heater on, Cliff? Then we won't need our coats."

"Just for a minute. Go ahead and start the engine. We'll let the van warm up a little, but then we have to turn it off. Lots of people die from carbon monoxide poisoning in the winter."

He was so careful. That was one of the things she loved best about him. Connie started the engine and pushed the lever on the heater to high. Then she slipped out of her coat and draped it over both of us.

"We could always get in the back." Cliff's voice was shaking a little, and Connie knew what that meant. It had been a long time. For a while the weather had been too terrible to park. And then there were all those baby-sitting jobs. She wouldn't do anything in somebody else's house. It was one of her rules. Peggy Volker got in trouble last year, when Mrs. Bjornson caught her in the bedroom with Tommy. The kids were all sleeping, and they hadn't been really doing anything so awful, but Mrs. Bjornson told everyone in town not to hire Peggy again.

"I'd better set my watch. I have to be home at eleven. My parents are really cracking down now.

They said they wouldn't even let me go out if it was anyone but you."

"That's what I like. Loyalty." Cliff watched her set her new digital watch with the alarm feature. "Nice watch, Connie. Did you get it for Christmas?"

"My boyfriend gave it to me." Connie laughed. "It's the best present I ever got. I just love it, Cliff."

Cliff figured the watch was worth the forty-five dollars he'd spent, just to see the expression on her face when she opened it. Connie wasn't expecting anything so expensive. She was worth it, though. Connie was the prettiest girl in the senior class, and she was the nicest, too. Cliff felt very lucky she was in love with him.

"Come on, Romeo. Let's see what you can do in the cast." Connie switched off the engine and climbed in the back. Cliff had an old mattress back here, and it was almost like their own apartment. Of course, it was nicer in the summer, but Cliff couldn't do anything about that.

Connie shivered with anticipation as she heard Cliff taking off his clothes. She loved these wonderful private moments just between the two of them. She thought about it all the time. Right in the middle of algebra class she would catch her breath and remember the way his hard body fit into hers.

"Hurry up, Cliff." Connie pulled off her sweater and tossed her bra in the front seat. She couldn't get her clothes off fast enough. Her voice was low and kind of breathy. She always sounded like this when she knew they were going to do it. She loved to cover up under the blanket and touch him all over. He was so hard and strong and wonderful.

Right now, just thinking about it, she could hardly wait.

"You feel so good!" Cliff groaned as he slipped in under the blanket. She was toasty warm, and her skin felt like hot velvet under his fingertips. He propped himself on his elbow and slipped one hand up to touch her. There was no way he could get enough of her.

And she was just as crazy about making love as he was. It was amazing. Connie read all the books on technique, and they tried everything. He'd just about died when she licked him all over with her hot little tongue. Connie would try anything if she thought he'd like it. And he felt exactly the same way about her.

"You do it to me this time." Connie pulled him close and reached down to fondle him eagerly. "And tell me what it's like. I want to know."

"You got yourself a deal." Cliff lowered his head to kiss her. He'd been wanting to do this all week. It was impossible to think about anything except her responsive body and the moans of pleasure she gave when his tongue found the best places. Cliff forgot all about Mr. Larsen and his shocking suspicions for a long, wonderful time.

"Cliff Heller! I don't believe it!"

Connie pulled on her slacks and brushed back her long brown hair. "Here . . . snap my bra, will you? Mr. Larsen can't be serious! Are you sure it wasn't some kind of sick joke?"

"You should have seen his face, Connie." Cliff

propped his feet against the dashboard and put on his socks. Connie said that for some reason, it made her feel weird if he left them on. "Mr. Larsen was serious. I'm sure he was. He really thinks Mrs. Larsen murdered Jenny."

"But, Cliff . . . that's impossible, isn't it?" Connie stopped fixing her hair and stared at him. "You don't think she did it, do you?"

"I don't know. I'm not sure what to think. It all made sense the way he explained it. He says Mrs. Larsen hasn't been right in the head since Laura died. He thinks she flips out sometimes and acts normal the rest of the time. And when she's flipped out, she kills Laura's friends so Laura can have playmates."

"Ooh!" Connie wrinkled her face. "That's creepy!"

"I'm not saying it's true, but it could be." Cliff shrugged. "You know Mrs. Larsen, Connie. Does she ever act weird to you?"

Connie took time to think. "Well . . . she was kind of spaced out right after Laura was killed, but that's only natural. It was a shock. I don't know, Cliff. I never really noticed. When I work in her room, I spend most of my time with the kids."

"Watch her when you go down there tomorrow, will you? I'm just curious, that's all. It's probably not true, but the coach is a straight guy. I don't think he'd say anything like that if he didn't believe it."

There was a metallic beeping, and both of them jumped. Then Connie laughed and pushed the button on her watch.

"Time to go home," she announced. "Come on, Cliff. . . . I don't want to be late. I'll spy on Mrs. Larsen for you tomorrow. And I won't say a word to anybody about it. But I still think Mr. Larsen's playing some kind of sick joke on you."

"Wild honey." Cliff grinned at her as he started the van. Then he laughed at her puzzled expression. "You taste like wild honey. I never ate any before, but I know that's what it would taste like. It's really nice, Connie. I could get addicted to wild honey in a big hurry."

Connie blushed. Cliff said the sweetest things. She could feel the tingling start at her toes and work its way up to the rest of her body. Cliff had really done it to her tonight. He was wonderful!

Her house was on a side street, a block from the school. Cliff pulled up in front and shut off the engine. Then he pulled her close for one last kiss.

Connie noticed that the porch light was on. The drapes opened a crack and then closed again. Her mother was waiting. She mustn't stay out here too long. She had to be on her best behavior now so her parents would be pleased.

"Good night, Cliff. I had a wonderful time." Connie laughed out loud. She sounded so proper now. She wanted to throw her arms around him and give him a big, hot kiss, but she settled for a quick peck on the cheek at the door. Cliff understood. That little peck was just in case her parents were looking. Then she stood with the door partway open, watching him until he got back in the van.

They had to get more time alone. Maybe tomorrow night, if she could talk her parents into letting her out of the house. Cliff made her feel so good. She felt warm all over just thinking about what they had done tonight. And she wanted to do it all over again.

It was much too early to get up. It was still dark in Laura's room, and Marian tried to go back to sleep. She had at least another hour before she had to start getting ready for school.

No, it was no use. She was awake now. Marian flicked on the lamp next to the bed and blinked in the sudden flood of brightness. There was no sound from downstairs. Dan was still fast asleep. Something had awakened her long before her normal time to get up.

Marian shivered slightly and pulled Laura's blanket up around her shoulders. The house was always so cold right before dawn. She remembered hearing that most terminal patients in hospitals died in that dark, cold hour just before daybreak.

Why was she awake at this ungodly hour? Marian drew in her breath sharply. Laura. Had Laura been here?

She reached for her robe and struggled into it, looking frantically around the room for some sign that her baby had been here again. She was sure Laura's diary had been on the table, but now it was gone. Could Laura be teasing her by hiding the book?

Marian made a careful search of the room. There was nothing hidden among the books on the table, no diary in the toy box or on any of the shelves. She searched the closet thoroughly, but it wasn't there, either. The diary was gone, just like Laura.

Suddenly she remembered, and Marian rushed to the bed. Laura used to hide her favorite things under her pillow. Yes, there it was. She had been sleeping on Laura's diary.

Her hands trembled as she turned to the proper page. It was Tuesday, January tenth. The page was completely blank.

It was such a disappointment that Marian dropped to her knees by the side of the bed. There was no message, no word from her darling baby. Tears formed in her eyes and rolled down her cheeks as she knelt there, head bowed, shoulders quivering in despair.

"Please, baby!" Her voice was a whisper. "Send me a message, Laura. Please!"

Gradually the sobs diminished. Marian's shoulders straightened, and a look of rapture came over her face. Her eyes were closed. She was listening with every pore of her body. Her baby was calling to her, and only she could hear.

The room was lighter now. The muscles in her legs were cramped from sitting in one position for so long. Marian blinked and looked at the clock. It was nearly six thirty, and she had to put on the coffee. Dan would be awake soon, and Harvey wanted the teachers there early today. This was the morning the new safety procedures went into effect. And teachers were required to meet the buses and take immediate charge of their classes.

Marian took a shower and dressed quickly. She

gazed in the mirror as she brushed her hair. She looked different today. A smile was hiding behind her eyes, and her cheeks had a healthy, rosy glow. She looked happy. That was the difference. It was a wonderful day when her baby talked to her!

CHAPTER 21

"Don't forget now. Tell me everything that happens." Cliff walked with her as far as the landing. "I'll be waiting for you at the lockers."

Connie felt very alone as she went down the stairs into the elementary wing. She was a little nervous. What she had promised to do felt almost disloyal. Still, it couldn't hurt anything if Mrs. Larsen was innocent. After Cliff dropped her at home last night, Connie had thought about it. Reluctantly, she had reached a decision. And now here she was, standing in front of Mrs. Larsen's door, prepared to spy on a teacher she liked and respected.

"Here's Connie!" Ricky Owens pulled at Marian's sleeve. "Can we have art class now, Mrs. Larsen?"

"Hello, Connie." Marian turned and smiled. She was folding up squares of white paper at the front table. The children were clustered around her. There was a large six-sided figure drawn on the blackboard and several smaller, less perfect versions under it.

"We're making snowflakes today," Marian explained. "Who can tell Connie how many sides a snowflake has?"

Several children shouted out the answer. "Six!"

"And what is a six-sided shape called?" Marian nodded to Joey Cracowski, who was waving his hand in the air.

"A hexagon!" Joey beamed proudly. "We're making hexagons today, Connie. Mrs. Larsen's folding the paper, and we're gonna cut 'em out. Then we're gonna make a mogul."

"Mobile," Marian corrected. "We're going to have our own beautiful snowfall right here in the room."

"That sounds like fun." Connie watched as Marian folded another piece of paper. "What can I do to help, Mrs. Larsen?"

"Some of the children will need help cutting out their snowflakes. Why don't you go to my office and get the large art scissors? They should be hanging on the board over my desk."

Connie hurried to the small office at the rear of the room. It was a fairly recent renovation, a floor-to-ceiling partition that hid a small desk and one wall of shelves.

There was a door with a window in it. The little room could be locked during recess to keep any dangerous items away from the children. It had been one of Mr. Woodruff's first projects when he took over the school. Connie remembered when the small office was built. It was right after Susan

Rhinbolt ate a jar of paste when Miss Adams was out of the room.

Most teachers used this place for storage, and Marian was no exception. The shelves were filled with jars of tempera paint and reams of construction paper. The supply board was over the desk. It had been a gift from last year's class, a clever idea that the children had designed. It was simply a piece of plywood painted blue, with silhouettes of supplies painted on it in red. A nail held each item in place.

The board was nearly full. There was an extra stapler, a tape dispenser, a paper punch, and several sharp X-Acto knives. The red silhouette for the large art scissors was not covered by the scissors. Connie pulled out the desk drawers and searched through them, but she couldn't find the shears. Marian's tote bag was sitting on top of the desk. Perhaps she had taken them home with her last night.

Connie lifted out a pile of corrected homework papers and looked under it. No scissors. She was about to put the papers back when she noticed the name on the top sheet. Laura Larsen! There was a large red A next to her name.

She was almost afraid to look at the rest of the pile. Connie took a deep breath and paged through it quickly. Becky Fischer! Jenny Powell! Mrs. Larsen had filled in all three papers and then she had graded them. Connie recognized her handwriting. She had to tell Cliff about this!

Connie straightened the pile and replaced the papers with shaking fingers. When she turned around, Mrs. Larsen was standing in back of her.

"I . . . I'm sorry, Mrs. Larsen. I can't seem to find

your scissors." Connie pointed to the silhouette on the board. "I looked in your tote bag. I hope you don't mind. I . . . I just thought you might have taken them home with you last night."

"Oh, they're around here someplace, but we don't have time to look for them now." Marian smiled at Connie and glanced at the clock. "Run down to Mrs. Powell's room and borrow hers, will you, Connie?"

Connie hurried down the hall to the kindergarten room. Her heart was pounding so hard, she could barely breathe. Thank goodness Mrs. Larsen hadn't seen her going through the homework papers!

The kindergarten was at the end of the corridor. While Mrs. Powell went to look for her scissors, Connie held up some pictures for the kids. Poor Mrs. Powell looked tired. There were dark circles under her eyes. Connie didn't think she could go on if she were Mrs. Powell. It must be terrible to suspect your child was murdered!

She didn't think of it until she was out in the hall again, carrying the scissors carefully, point down. If Cliff was right, Mrs. Larsen had killed Jenny! How could she murder her best friend's child!

Connie stopped and leaned against the wall. Her knees were shaking. She didn't want to go back to the second grade. Finding those papers was creepy! Cliff just had to be wrong about Mrs. Larsen. She might be a little crazy, but she couldn't be a killer!

Cliff was counting on her. Connie took a deep breath and started up the hall again. It was best to pretend that nothing was wrong. She had to get through the hour somehow. Then she could tell Cliff everything.

Connie spent the rest of the period helping the children cut out their snowflakes. Even Ricky Owens managed to do a good job on his. Connie thought they all looked very nice when they were done. Mrs. Larsen might be crazy, but she was still a good teacher. Her class would never forget the definition of *hexagon*.

"We'll put them up tomorrow." Marian stacked the huge snowflakes in a pile on the table. "You'll help us, won't you, Connie? I think they'll look wonderful hanging in front of the window."

Marian walked Connie to the door. "Would you stop at the office and ask Mary if she has some fish line? The shop class is sending us a dowel for each window."

"Yes, Mrs. Larsen." Connie managed a smile. "That art project was really a math lesson, wasn't it?"

"In a way." Marian smiled back. "Learning is fun, and children remember when they take an active part. I used to cut out colored squares and triangles and pentagons when Laura was quite young. She still remembers. Laura knows all of her shapes now."

Connie couldn't help it. She shivered slightly. Mrs. Larsen talked as if Laura were still alive!

"You'd better hurry, Connie. There goes the bell. Drop the scissors off at the kindergarten, and don't forget to tell Mary about the fish line."

"It could have been a slip of the tongue." Cliff frowned slightly as they leaned against the lockers.

"Tell me about those homework papers again. Are you sure they weren't old ones?"

"I'm positive." Connie opened her locker and took out her chemistry book. Her hands were still shaking. "I passed out those papers myself. I know they're not old."

"It's just like the coach said." Cliff stared at Connie as she dropped her book. Her hands were shaking, and she looked scared to death. He put his arm around her and hugged her hard. "Let's cut the next class, Connie. We'll catch Mr. Larsen in his office. I think we'd better tell him about this right away."

"Oh, Connie's just wonderful with the kids." Marian poured herself a cup of coffee and sat down next to Sally. "How's Dianne Jacobs doing in your room?"

"I think she belongs with an older group." Sally sighed deeply. "You're really lucky having Connie. She's going to make a fine teacher someday."

"Why don't we work out an exchange?" Marian paused thoughtfully. "I could send Connie to your room on Tuesdays and Thursdays. And I'd take Dianne. I'll talk to Connie tomorrow and see what she thinks."

"Great idea! I really like Connie."

"I do too." Marian drank the rest of her coffee and headed for the door. "She seemed a little nervous today, but I heard they're having a big test in algebra. That must have been it. Well, back to the salt mines. Only an hour to go."

* * *

"It's okay with my parents." Connie hung up the phone and picked up her books. "They said to bring you home with me for supper. I told them we were going to the library to study."

"I don't like missing hockey practice, but this is more important. Mr. Larsen wants us to check the area at the top of Heidelberg Hill."

The wind was blowing, and Connie zipped her long parka and put up the hood. Cliff drove in as far as he could, and they left the van next to the pond.

"Sheriff Bates searched here already." Connie tramped through the snow, holding Cliff's gloved hand. "I don't think we're going to find anything, Cliff."

"He might have missed something. It can't hurt to look. Let's climb the path and split up at the top. You check one side, and I'll check the other."

Connie frowned, but she didn't say anything. She really didn't want to be in the woods at all, but Cliff thought it was important. She could feel her knees shaking, and it had nothing to do with the cold. It felt creepy up here, knowing what had happened. She wouldn't come up here at night for anything in the world!

"Hey, Connie. Would you rather stick together?" Cliff glanced down at her worried face.

"Uh . . . yes. I guess I'm a little nervous, Cliff."

Cliff held Connie's hand a little tighter. He knew exactly how she felt. It grew darker the higher they climbed. The big pine trees blocked

out the winter sun, and the woods were caught in
a sort of perpetual twilight. It was quiet up here.
They were all alone. Their boots crunched on the
crust of the snow, and the snapping of the twigs
underfoot was loud in the stillness.

They were near the top of the hill when Connie
slipped. Cliff caught her with his good arm, and she
laughed nervously.

"New boots," she explained. "They're still slick
on the bottom."

Cliff bent over to look at the snow. "No, you
slipped on something. See? It's a glove."

Connie watched as he brushed it off. It looked
like a brand-new glove.

"This couldn't belong to Mrs. Larsen." Cliff
slipped it on. "It's big enough to fit me. See if you
can find the other one."

Connie kicked at the snow with the toe of her
boots. They managed to clear a big area, but nothing turned up.

"Somebody has one cold hand." Cliff shrugged.
He turned the glove over and examined the lining.
"Brooks Brothers? That's expensive, Connie. I bet
somebody's upset about losing it."

"Cliff? You don't think it has anything to do
with . . . with Jenny, do you?"

"I doubt it." Cliff ran his fingers over the soft fur
inside. "Come on, Connie. We might as well take
this glove with us. We'll give it to Mr. Larsen tomorrow, and he can put it in the lost and found. If we'd
found both of them, I'd be tempted to keep them.
Just feel that lining!"

They were chilled by the time they got back to the van. Cliff dropped the glove behind the seat and turned on the heater full blast.

"We'll stop by my house for a second. I'll give the coach a quick call and tell him what we found. Then we'd better get over to your parents'. I sure hope your mom's making meat loaf for supper."

CHAPTER 22

Dan leaned back against the pillows and stared at the book that was open on his lap. He really should work up a lecture on the Spanish Civil War, but he couldn't seem to concentrate on his material. Maybe he could show a slide of *Guernica* and spend the whole period discussing it. The kids would enjoy that, and they'd be learning painlessly.

After a few more moments of staring at the page, Dan closed his book. It was no use trying to read. All he could think about was Cliff and Connie, and what they'd discovered today. Marian was bringing home class work for Laura and her dead friends. Connie said Marian filled in the answers and then graded the papers with the rest of the class. That ought to be proof that she was insane. Now, if they'd only find something on Heidelberg Hill . . .

The phone rang, and Dan reached over to answer it.

"Mr. Larsen? It's Cliff. Connie and I found a glove on the hill. It's black with mink lining. And it says Brooks Brothers on the label."

His glove! Marian must have worn his new gloves when she killed Jenny!

Dan gripped the phone tightly. "Bring it to school tomorrow and I'll . . ."

He stopped suddenly. Marian was standing in the doorway!

"I'll take care of it then. Nice of you to call, Cliff. I'm sure those hockey plays will be helpful. Marian's here now. I've got to run."

"More hockey plays?" Marian shook her head and smiled. "I swear, that's all Cliff thinks about. Are you hungry, Dan? I've got some chicken to fry."

She left him alone while she fried the chicken. Dan stealthily dialed Cliff's number, but no one was home. If he could walk, he'd go out and caution them. They shouldn't say anything about the glove. It was very important to keep it a secret until he had enough facts to incriminate Marian. If Marian heard they'd found it, she'd know he was spying on her!

Dan managed to make polite conversation through dinner, even though his mind was miles away. His glove! There had to be a reason. Was it easier to break Jenny's neck with his heavy gloves? Or did Marian take them simply because they were warmer than hers?

She was doing the dishes now. He heard the water spraying from the faucet as she rinsed them. Those little homey sounds were suddenly chilling. His wife was a murderer masquerading as an excellent cook and homemaker.

"Dan?" Marian stood in the doorway. "I have to run to the store before it closes. We're completely out of coffee."

"Fine." He smiled at her absentmindedly. Then his expression sobered abruptly as he heard the front door close behind her. He could have been smiling at Jenny's killer just then. The thought made him shudder. At least there hadn't been any more murders, but he was still uneasy. The wind howled past the window, and Marian was out there somewhere, alone.

At least it was a miserable night. Dan relaxed slightly. There would be no one out tonight. Perhaps there was no need to worry. Marian would just run to the store and come right home. She couldn't very well kill anyone standing in line at the Red Owl! Also, so far she'd murdered only Laura's friends.

Dan's eyes closed, and he settled back against the pillows. Maybe he'd take a little nap until Marian got home. He really didn't have to worry tonight. Nothing was going to happen.

"How did you manage to get out of the house?" Cliff opened the door of the van for her. "I thought your mother was going to make you stay home."

"She was." Connie grinned at him. "I told her the truth. I said we wanted to find somewhere to park and do illicit and immoral things to each other. She told me to stop kidding and be home at ten thirty."

Cliff shook his head and grinned. Thanks to Connie, they had three precious hours together. And she hadn't even lied about it to her mother.

The streets were icy, and Cliff put the van in low gear to drive up the hill by the Congregational church. Flurries of snow whipped against the window, and

Connie shivered. They were in for another two inches, at least. Maybe school would be closed tomorrow if the weather got worse. That thought did nothing to dampen Connie's spirits.

She reached over to snap on the radio. Cliff could get only one station, KTIG in Pequot Lakes. It was a religious station that went off the air at ten, but at least they had the news and weather.

"Time is eight-oh-four, temperature minus twelve on the KTIG thermometer. Wind chill brings that down to a frigid thirty-two below. Some roads are closed due to blowing snow, and travelers' advisories are in effect. Now some heartwarming music from the Christian Gospel Singers. . . ."

Connie reached out and turned the knob. She wasn't in the mood for gospel music. She wished Cliff would hurry and install the new radio his parents had given him for Christmas. Then they could listen to anything they wanted.

"We've got the whole place to ourselves again tonight." Cliff turned the van around and backed into the corrugated garage the church still owned. There had been a church bus once, but now it was gone. The garage had been empty for the past three years. "It's nasty out there. Listen to that wind."

"But it's nice in here." Connie gave him a quick kiss. "I guess I'd better set my alarm watch again. My mother's in a good mood, and I don't want to spoil it by getting home late."

It was their own private world in here. Connie turned on the dash lights and set her alarm. They were alone at last. The heater made a comfortable hissing sound, and she smiled as she slipped between the seats and climbed in the back. This was exactly where she wanted to be. Sometimes she wished she could stay with Cliff like this forever.

"Can we leave the heater on?" The air was cold on her bare arms as she took off her blouse. "It gets cold in here so fast, Cliff."

"You won't need the heater in a minute." Cliff laughed and shut off the engine. "I've got a new way to keep you warm tonight."

He did. Connie smiled in the darkness as his body covered hers. She was really warm now. Actually, she was hot, hot and ready for whatever he had on his mind.

"Oh, Cliff! What are you doing?" She giggled as he repositioned himself. Then she didn't have to ask anymore, and it was wonderful.

Later, she sat up with the blanket around her. "Listen to the wind blow, Cliff. It makes me feel cozy in here with you."

They were silent for a long moment, listening. Cliff touched her face. "Let's snuggle for a while, Connie. I'm really beat. I didn't get much sleep last night, thinking about what Mr. Larsen told me."

"Me neither."

Connie slid down beside him and gave a sigh of pure contentment. Her back was toward Cliff, and his body curved around hers. They fitted together like two spoons in a drawer. Connie smiled at the thought.

"Don't move," he whispered. "Just stay like that, Connie."

"I don't think . . . oh!" She gave a startled gasp as her doubts vanished. It just went to prove that anything was possible if you wanted it badly enough.

She must have dozed for a moment. When

Connie woke up, the van was cold. Even the blanket couldn't keep out the chill. Cliff was sound asleep, and she rolled off the mattress carefully, trying not to wake him. She'd let him sleep until her alarm went off.

The parka was cold against her bare skin. Connie almost gasped out loud as she slipped it on. She crawled in the front seat and braced herself for the unpleasant shock as she sat down on the icy vinyl.

The key was in the ignition, and the van started with no trouble. Connie revved the motor a couple of times and turned the heater up as high as it would go. A blast of warm air started to blow out of the vents almost immediately. Cliff's van was old, but it had a good heater.

Connie turned around to look in the back. Cliff was still sleeping. Not even the sound of the motor had awakened him. The windshield was steamed up, and she used the sleeve of her parka to wipe a clear spot. The wind was stronger now, and gusts of snow blew across the open garage door. If the radio was right, they wouldn't have school tomorrow. Then she could sleep in late.

Connie lifted her feet and propped them up right in front of the heater vent. Now her toes were toasty warm. She sat that way for a while, watching the snow flurries. She was almost ready to crawl in the back again. Now she was warm, and she missed Cliff.

She really should turn off the ignition and crawl back under the blankets with Cliff for the little time they had left together.

She hesitated as she reached for the key. She didn't want to shut off the heater. Then she'd be cold again, and soon it would be time to get dressed. There was nothing worse than dressing in the cold. Why turn it off! She wasn't going to go back to sleep. It would be perfectly safe to leave the van running for a little while. The garage door was wide open.

Cliff pulled her close as she got back under the blanket. She snuggled up to him and fitted her body to his. He was still sleeping, but he held her tightly. It made Connie feel safe to have him hold her like this.

She tried to keep her eyes open, but they fluttered closed a couple of times. It was warm inside the van now, and she yawned in contentment. Her head rested against Cliff's chest. She could hear his heart beating. Soon they wouldn't have to sneak around and sleep in the back of the van. When they started college, they could get an apartment and be together like this every night.

The soft sound of Cliff's breathing was rhythmic and deep. She felt herself falling into the same regular pattern, breathing the same air he was breathing, matching breath to sleepy breath. She was almost asleep when she thought she heard a noise. It sounded like heavy metal scraping and sliding. Connie's eyes closed, and she smiled slightly. She must be dreaming. She cuddled a little closer to Cliff and went back to sleep.

Cliff woke up once, and his head felt strange. The van was running, the heater going full blast. Connie must have gotten up and turned it on. He tried to sit up, but it was too much of an effort. The wind had died down now. It was still and quiet in the garage. Connie was sleeping so peacefully, he didn't want to risk waking her. They'd have to get up in a few minutes, anyhow.

Cliff's muscles felt like water, but he managed to raise his arm somehow and drape it over Connie's naked back. He loved her so much. His lips touched the warmth of her shoulder. There was just a moment, near the end, when his mind gave a dim warning. It was much too dark in the garage. The streetlight had been shining through the open door, but now it was pitch-black. There was something wrong. The garage door was closed. He had to get up and shut off the engine. He'd just close his eyes a minute and gather his strength for the effort. He was much too tired to move right now.

An hour later the engine coughed and died. The cold began to creep into the cracks of the windows, and the temperature lowered. The wind picked up velocity and whistled past the metal sides of the garage, rocking it slightly. Snow pelted against the closed door, and the hasp froze shut. The temperature dropped, and soon the inside of the van was frigid. Connie's Christmas watch glowed softly in the dark as the minutes clicked off. Ten eleven. Ten twelve. Ten thirteen. Ten fourteen. At last the time set matched the time on the display, and the watch started to beep. It made a rhythmic electronic sound over and over in the icy darkness. But there was no one to hear.

CHAPTER 23

The Truckstop Café was deserted. Sheriff Bates blew in on a flurry of snow and grinned as he caught Emma playing solitaire at the counter.

"Come on over here and give me a big warm hug, Emma," Sheriff Bates called out. "I'm frozen to the bone."

"Hi, Sheriff!" Emma hurried over to his reserved booth with a steaming hot cup of coffee. "You're early today. Jim and Gus aren't here yet. Say! I heard about Cliff and Connie. What an awful accident!"

"The gossips don't waste any time, do they?" Sheriff Bates cupped his hands around the mug of coffee to warm them. "It's a bad winter, Emma."

"Seems to me we've had a lot of accidents in Nisswa lately." Emma wiped off the already spotless table. "Hold on, Sheriff. I'll get you a bear claw to go with that coffee."

Mrs. Bergstrom had called at eleven thirty last night. Connie was late. Sheriff Bates had reassured her. The kids were probably stuck in the snow. He'd find them and bring Connie right home.

The hill in back of the Congregational church was a popular teenage parking spot, and the sheriff went there first. The moment he'd seen the closed garage door, he'd known there was trouble. The garage was always kept open, even in the worst snowstorms.

Poor Cliff and Connie! Sheriff Bates sighed as he spooned sugar into his coffee. There was something strange about the whole thing. He'd known Cliff pretty well, and the boy was a good, careful driver. It didn't seem likely that Cliff would leave the van running in a closed garage. Of course, if the kids fell asleep when the garage door was open, and someone came along and closed it . . . ? That would mean he'd have another possible murder on his hands. He hadn't found out a thing about Jenny Powell's accident, and now there was another one. And lately he'd been thinking hard about Becky Fischer. Of course, he'd assumed it was an accident, but someone could have pushed her into that saw. Five deaths in five weeks. Five kids dead in a town of a thousand!

"One of the truckers said he heard they were naked." Emma put down the bear claw and leaned closer. "Is that true, Sheriff?"

"That's how rumors get started, Emma." Sheriff Bates shook his head. "You tell everyone that they were fully dressed. Understand?"

"Sure, Sheriff." Emma looked up as the door opened. "There's Gus and Jim. I'll get two more cups."

Sheriff Bates sighed as Emma rushed away. The

gossip had started already. No matter how hard you tried to cover things up, they came out eventually. He hoped the Bergstroms and the Hellers wouldn't hear the rumor. Sure, it was true, but they didn't have to know. He'd swear on a stack of Bibles that both those kids had their clothes on.

Gus and Jim stomped the snow off their boots. They hung their parkas on the aluminum rack at the front of the café and spread out their gloves on the counter to dry.

"Want me to grill those for ya?" Joe poked his head out of the kitchen. "Bring 'em here, Emma. Five minutes on each side ought to dry 'em."

Gus laughed and tossed his gloves to Joe. Jim shook his head and grinned. "These are my Christmas present from Louise's mother. If you put them on the grill, they'll melt."

"Hello, Pete." Gus slid into the other side of the booth. "It's really bad out there. I never would have made it without Jim. He picked me up in the wrecker."

"We heard about Cliff and Connie on the radio." Jim slid in beside Gus. "It's a damn shame! You don't think there was foul play involved, do you, Pete?"

"No." Sheriff Bates sighed. He supposed everyone in town would speculate about Cliff and Connie, too. Then people would be even more nervous.

Emma rushed over to the booth, carrying three plates of pie. Sheriff Bates gave her a big grin. She was a lifesaver. He didn't want to talk about the accidents anymore.

"It's on the house." Emma set down the plates. "Joe heard they're closing the road on account of the storm. We're not going to get much business, so you might as well enjoy the pie before it gets stale."

Two more cups of coffee apiece, to wash down the pie, and they were fortified. Jim left a quarter tip and slid out of the booth.

"Guess I'd better get out there with the tow truck. There's going to be all sorts of people lining those ditches."

"I'll follow you. There's always somebody dumb enough to drive in snow like this." Sheriff Bates stood and grabbed his jacket. He discreetly added a dollar bill to Jim's quarter for the tip.

"Stop in on your way back!" Emma stood at the door and shouted after them. "Joe's putting up a kettle of soup. If there's anybody stranded, we'll feed 'em here. And they can sleep in the booths if the roads stay closed."

Sheriff Bates frowned. Nisswa had always been a nice, friendly town. The Truckstop Café took good care of stranded motorists. But if things didn't get back to normal soon, people would change. They wouldn't act friendly to strangers anymore. He had to put a stop to these awful accidents!

Marian was still sleeping. Dan switched the channel on the television and leaned back in bed. The wind was still blowing, and he could hear the snow flurries rattle against the windowpane. Harvey had called at eleven last night. School was closed for at least one day, perhaps two. That meant he wouldn't see Cliff and Connie until Thursday or Friday.

It was hard to wait. Dan felt like calling Cliff at home, but Marian had forgotten to plug in his phone last night. There was nothing to do but wait. He was waiting for the storm to be over, waiting for his legs to work again, waiting to see if his wife was an insane killer. But he wasn't waiting patiently. All this had to be over soon. He couldn't wait much longer.

He was still having those awful walking dreams. It was probably the strain he was under, but they only made matters worse. It had happened again while he was waiting for Marian to get back from the store last night. He had fallen asleep and walked. He'd testify to it in a court of law. When he woke up, his legs were shaking with fatigue, but they were dead and useless again. Then Marian had come home and Harvey had called and things got back to normal.

The News at Noon was coming on. Dan turned up the volume. There would be stories of stranded motorists and roofs caving in under the unusually heavy snowfall. Even though this was a Brainerd station, they occasionally had news from Nisswa.

"Tragedy in Nisswa last night claimed the lives of two teenagers. Constance Bergstrom, seventeen, and Clifford Heller, eighteen, died last evening in a parked vehicle in Nisswa. Authorities list the cause of death as carbon monoxide poisoning. The bodies were discovered near midnight in a closed garage."

For a moment, the news bulletin didn't register. Then Dan fell back against his pillow and groaned. Connie and Cliff! They were dead!

Marian went out alone last night. Dan drew his breath in sharply as he remembered. She had left about eight thirty and was gone for almost two hours. She'd said she had trouble starting the van, and he had believed her. And now Cliff and Connie were dead!

Marian stretched languidly and smiled. It was wonderful knowing she could sleep as late as she wanted. There was no school today, and it was like a vacation. She could stay up here all day if she liked.

The window was a solid sheet of frost. She could hear the wind howl around the eaves, but she was here, warm and cozy in Laura's little bed. She let her eyes close for a moment, reveling in the lazy moment. She had slept so soundly last night. She felt wonderful now. Every ache and pain had disappeared, and she was young and vital again.

There was a smile on her face as she sat up in bed. She really should get up and make coffee. It wasn't like her to stay in bed half the day. Dan would be waiting for breakfast, and now that she thought about it, she was hungry, too. She hadn't eaten much for supper last night.

Her robe and slippers were folded on the chair. Marian slipped them on and turned toward the door. Then she saw the diary on the table, and she gave a little sob of happiness. Her baby had been here again!

Cliff and Connie are here. I'm happy, and Becky's happy. But Jenny still cries for her mommy.

Cliff and Connie were there?! For a moment Marian was confused, and then she remembered the news bulletin she'd heard on Laura's little radio in the middle of the night. Two teenagers from Nisswa had died of carbon monoxide poisoning in a closed garage. It must have been Clifford and Connie!

Marian blinked back a tear. She was glad that Cliff and Connie were with Laura, but she felt so sorry for Jenny. Thank goodness Connie was so good with children. Perhaps she could make Jenny stop crying.

Marian put the diary back in its place and sighed. She felt better knowing that Laura had all her friends with her, but the part about Jenny disturbed her. It was a good thing Sally didn't know how unhappy Jenny was.

Jenny would get over it, Marian decided. And now she didn't have time to dwell on it any longer. She had to make a nice big breakfast for Dan. Waffles would be good, or French toast. She'd ask him which he preferred.

"Dan?" Marian called out his name as she came down the stairs. "Do you want waffles or French toast?"

"Come in here a minute, Marian. There's something you need to know."

Dan sounded upset, and Marian rushed to the den. The television was blaring, and she turned it down.

"What is it, honey?" she asked.

"I just heard some awful news, Marian." Dan pointed to a chair. "I think you'd better sit down before I tell you."

Marian knew what he was about to tell her, but

she sat down anyway. Dan was staring at her in a terribly unsettling way.

"It's Cliff and Connie. I just heard it on the news. They're dead, Marian. The newscaster said it was carbon monoxide poisoning."

She sat there quietly for a minute, but he was through. "I . . . I'm sorry, Dan. It must be terrible for their parents, but it's all for the best."

"Marian?" Dan was still staring at her. "Are you all right?"

"Oh, yes. I'm fine." Marian stood and started for the door. "Try not to be too sad, Dan. Remember how they used to baby-sit for Laura? At least they're with her now."

If Marian had turned to look back as she left the den, she would have seen the horrified expression on her husband's face. It took Dan at least a full minute to stop shaking. Marian hadn't been a bit shocked when he told her about Cliff and Connie. She must have known all along.

Now Dan knew the truth. Marian had killed Cliff and Connie. It might look like an accident, but Marian had killed them. First, she murdered Becky. And then Jenny. And now Cliff and Connie. When would this nightmare stop!

He had to get help. Someone had to believe him! Dan clenched his fists and thought hard. It was his fault that Cliff and Connie were dead. Somehow Marian must have guessed what they were doing. Or maybe she just killed them so Laura would have more company. There was no telling how her confused mind worked. She was insane, and she was a killer. Anyone in town could be her next victim.

He had to be calm now, calm and rational. Dan swallowed hard and forced himself to think. He would eat breakfast with Marian, just as if nothing had happened. And later, he'd ask her to plug in the phone. He'd tell her he wanted to call the Hellers, to offer his sympathies. It would be a perfectly reasonable thing for him to do. As Cliff's coach, he knew the family quite well. Marian would believe his excuse. She could even stay in the room when he called them. Then he'd say he was tired, but he'd call the Bergstroms later. She'd believe that. And when she was off doing something else, he'd put in a call to Sheriff Bates.

"Here it is, honey." Marian came in carrying a tray. The smell of French toast made him feel like retching, but Dan managed to smile at her.

"My favorite." He poured on some syrup and forced himself to eat. "You're a wonderful cook, Marian."

She was beaming at him, proud that she'd fixed something he liked. Her smile was beautiful; her eyes were clear and happy. She was so pretty, his hand started to shake. In that moment, he knew he still loved her. And he was the one who had to make the call, the call that would destroy her.

CHAPTER 24

When Sheriff Bates opened his door, Doc Hinkley
was already out with his shiny red snowblower. Doc
looked like a kid with a new toy, gleefully smiling as
he created a small blizzard on his front sidewalk.

"Hey, Pete!" Dr. Hinkley shouted loud enough to
be heard across the street. "You want a blow job?"

"Jesus, Doc! Shut up!"

Sheriff Bates's face turned bright red. Mrs. Heino
was just climbing into her station wagon.

Dr. Hinkley grinned and shut off the machine.
He pushed the snowblower across the street, chuck-
ling all the way. He'd really gotten Pete that time!

Sheriff Bates put his shovel back in the trunk of
his car and shook his head. "Whose healthy appen-
dix did you take out to pay for that?"

Dr. Hinkley just grinned and started up the machine. It took only a few minutes to clear out Pete's
driveway.

"I've wanted one of these for years," Dr. Hinkley
confessed. "If I get a call in the night, I have to

shovel for half an hour before I can go. Somebody could die in the time it takes me to get my car out."

"So you wrote it off your taxes as a business expense. Right, Doc?" Sheriff Bates laughed as the doctor nodded. "Seems reasonable to me. Well, thanks a lot for the help. Now I can get out to Madden's in time. I got a meeting of resort owners at eight o'clock sharp. Somebody's been dumping trash on their land. And then I have to be at the school at eleven to see Dan Larsen. He called yesterday and asked me to stop by."

"Dan Larsen?" Dr. Hinkley frowned. "I wonder what he wants."

"I don't know. Guess I'll find out soon enough."

Sheriff Bates watched Doc wheel his snowblower back across the street. He had to get in gear and drive out to Madden's. It wouldn't do to have the resort owners mad at him. Without them, Nisswa would go broke.

"Dan had a conference, so I guess it's just the two of us for lunch." Marian set her tray down at Sally's table. "How are you this morning, Sally?"

"The same as always. You try to teach, and they try not to learn."

Marian glanced sharply at her friend. Sally looked tired and discouraged. The energetic young woman who used to handle her kindergarten class with boundless enthusiasm was gone. Sally had aged. And she had lost weight. Marian wished there was something she could do.

"I guess I'm being gloomy." Sally tried to smile. She leaned closer to Marian. "Actually, I've been trying to talk Ronnie into moving away at the end of the school year. Nisswa's gone sour. You know what I mean, Marian? I just want to get out. Sometimes I get the feeling we're all sitting here waiting for the next catastrophe."

Marian nodded. "I know how you feel, Sally. It's been a hard winter for all of us, but it'll end soon. You just have to hang on."

"Sal?" The door to the lunchroom banged open, and Ronnie came in. "I have to go out to Pleasant Acres. Ray's put in a call for emergency help. The furnace went out in the big lodge last night, and all his pipes froze solid. Some of them burst, and we've got to get them all replaced and wrapped before tomorrow. He's got a party of thirty-five coming in from California in the morning."

"Will you be working late?" Sally looked worried.

"I'll knock off about eleven, honey. We could use the extra money, but I hate to leave you alone. Should I tell Ray to get someone else?"

"Don't be silly. I'll be just fine." Sally gave him a smile. "I've got tons of work to keep me busy, and eleven isn't so late."

"Call me out there if you need me, and I'll come home on the double." Ronnie leaned over and hugged Sally. "Promise?"

"Sure."

Marian noticed that Sally's smile wavered a bit. Her friend looked upset as Ronnie left.

"Would you like me to come over tonight, Sally?" Marian tried to be helpful. "We could find something to do."

"I've got something to do." Sally laughed slightly. "I still have to write all those progress reports for the parents. I'll just stay right here and work on them. I don't really want to go home all alone."

"Good idea. I've got some work to finish up, too. I'll take Dan home and fix supper. I'll bring you something to eat when I come back. You can stay overnight with me if you want, Sally. Make up your mind and let me know later."

Marian was rewarded by a smile from Sally. She didn't really have any work to finish in her classroom, but she was sure she could find plenty to do. New bulletin boards, perhaps, or some language sheets for next week's work. There was always work to be done if you were an elementary-school teacher. And if she came back to the school, Sally would have company. Dan would understand if she left him alone for a while tonight.

"Close the door, Sheriff." Dan sat behind his desk, looking serious. "I know who the murderer is!"

Sheriff Bates felt his heart race as he closed the door and sat down in the chair in front of Dan's desk.

"It's Marian!"

"What?"

"Let me explain. Marian's been crazy ever since Laura died. I didn't realize it at first. She acts perfectly normal most of the time. But then something sets her off, and she goes out and kills."

Jesus Christ! Sheriff Bates almost groaned right out loud. Was Dan playing some kind of weird joke on him?

"I've got it all down right here." Dan pointed to the sheet of paper on his desk. "December twenty-sixth, that's the day Becky was murdered. Marian was gone for two hours in the afternoon. I asked her where she'd been, but she didn't remember!"

"And you think Marian was in the icehouse?" Sheriff Bates drew a deep breath. "But why would Marian want to kill Becky?"

"It's so simple! Marian killed Becky because she thought Laura was lonely!"

Sheriff Bates knew he had to stay calm. Dan wasn't playing a joke. He was dead serious. He really thought Marian, sweet, kind Marian, was a murderer!

"Now, wait a minute. Why did Marian think Laura was lonely?"

"The notes! Oh . . . I forgot to tell you about the notes. Marian thinks Laura is writing her notes from the other side. I wrote the first one. I was just trying to cheer Marian up. But she wrote all the rest. She writes them in her sleep, and then she says they're from Laura. She really believes it."

"I see," Sheriff Bates said slowly. He kept his face carefully neutral. This whole conversation reminded him of a scene from *Alice in Wonderland*.

"Do you have the notes, Dan? I'd like to see them."

"No, I wish I did. You see, Sheriff, Marian knows I don't believe in the notes. I tried to convince her that she was writing them herself, but she wouldn't listen to reason. Now she hides them from me. They're probably up in Laura's room. That's where Marian goes when she talks to Laura."

"Let me see if I got this straight. Marian wrote a note to herself that she thinks is from Laura. The note said Laura was lonely. So Marian went out and killed Becky. Is that right?"

"Right!" Dan sighed deeply. "It's confusing at first, but then it all becomes clear. Now, let me check my dates. . . ."

Sheriff Bates raised his eyebrows as Dan looked down at the paper in front of him. Dan Larsen was sick. His mind had snapped. He really thought Marian was a killer!

"Oh, yes . . . January first. That's the day of the sledding party. Marian was there. You know that, Sheriff. She told you she chased someone through the woods."

Sheriff Bates sighed deeply. "I'm beginning to get the picture, Dan. And you think Marian was lying about the man in the woods?"

"Of course she was! That was just a cover story! She climbed up that hill and broke Jenny's neck. Then she made up that lie so you wouldn't suspect her."

Sheriff Bates took out his notebook and started to write. He had to take careful notes. Doc Hinkley would want to know exactly what Dan said. Dan was a real basket case.

"I see. And you think Marian killed Jenny because Laura wanted company. Is that right?"

"Precisely! Every time Marian thinks Laura is lonely, she kills someone else!"

"And Connie and Cliff?"

"Yes. They were next. I didn't see the note Marian wrote about them, but I'm sure she's got one. She shut that garage door and murdered them, too! I've got it down right here. Marian left the house at eight thirty, and she didn't come back until ten twenty. She said she was going to the store!"

Sheriff Bates had heard enough. It was painful to listen to this kind of crazy talk. He'd always liked Dan Larsen, and the poor man was totally insane.

"It may be my fault Cliff and Connie are dead." There was an agonized expression on Dan's face. "They were spying on Marian for me. If they were still alive, they'd back me up. Cliff and Connie knew Marian was the murderer!"

"Your fault?" Sheriff Bates jotted a line in his notebook.

"Yes. Marian may have murdered them because she suspected them of spying on her. I'm just not sure. Either that, or she thought Laura needed more company. Cliff and Connie used to baby-sit for Laura, you know. There's no telling what goes on in Marian's mind. I can't explain her motives, Sheriff. I just know you'd better arrest her right away! If Marian knows I talked to you, she'll kill me, too!"

The sheriff made another note in his book and closed it with a snap. He'd humor Dan, make him think he believed this crazy story. That ought to calm him down. Then he'd hightail it right over to Doc Hinkley's office.

"I've got it all now, Dan. Thank you for telling me. You did exactly the right thing."

Sheriff Bates stood up and managed to look Dan straight in the eye. "There's only one thing, and this is important. Don't mention this to anyone. Is that clear? Everything you've told me has to be kept under wraps."

Dan's eyes glittered feverishly, and Sheriff Bates swallowed hard. For the space of a second he was actually afraid of the man in the wheelchair. But that wasn't right. Poor Dan Larsen should be pitied. His mind was completely gone.

"Now remember, Dan." Sheriff Bates took a deep breath. "You'll only hinder my investigation if you tell anyone else. I'll take care of everything on my end, but it may take a little time. Mum's the word, right?"

"Right!" Dan smiled and nodded. "You can count on me, Sheriff Bates. I won't say a word."

At least he'd silenced the man for a while. Sheriff Bates got into his patrol car and pulled out of the school parking lot. His hands were shaking, and he reached into his pocket for a cigarette. All he found was a half package of Certs. He had quit smoking two years ago. This thing with Dan Larsen really had him rattled.

He popped a breath mint into his mouth and chewed hard. He'd go straight to the clinic. They'd have to lock Dan up. There was no choice. If this got out, it would just kill poor Marian!

Joyce Meiers was sitting at the reception desk. She gave Sheriff Bates a big smile as he came in.

"Dr. Hinkley's with a patient right now, but I'll tell him you're here. You can wait in his office."

Joyce was sure looking good. Sheriff Bates accepted a plastic cup filled with coffee and watched her as she walked away. It seemed only yesterday that Joyce was just another kid riding her bicycle through town. She had long braids then, and she was always skinning her knees. Now she was a nurse, all grown up and pretty as a picture in her white, starched uniform. The local boys had been after her for years, but Joyce wasn't interested. She went off to Duluth for nurse's training. Now she was dating the new dentist from Pequot Lakes. He was here half days at the clinic. There'd probably be wedding bells soon. Joyce was too pretty to stay single for long.

"Holy shit!" Dr. Hinkley sat down hard. "Dan thinks *Marian* is the murderer?"

"That's what he said. You should have heard him, Doc. He didn't make any sense at all."

"I'll call Judge Lawrence and set up a sanity hearing." Doc Hinkley reached for the phone. "From what you've told me, Dan's a sick man!"

Sheriff Bates nodded. Judge Lawrence had the power to commit Dan to the state hospital for thirty days' observation. They'd present all the facts, and the judge would decide.

"Eight o'clock tomorrow night at your office?" Doc Hinkley looked up at the sheriff. Pete nodded. The doctor scribbled a line in his appointment book and thanked the judge's secretary.

"Do you think we should tell Marian?" Sheriff Bates asked after Doc had hung up the phone.

Dr. Hinkley thought for a minute. Then he shook his head. "No, I think it's best to wait until Judge Lawrence makes his decision. Dan's calmed down now, isn't he?"

"I think so. I tried to act like I believed him. And I told him not to say anything about his suspicions. I said it would hinder my investigation."

"Then there's no sense in worrying Marian tonight. It's going to be hard enough for her when they take him away. We'll tell her after the hearing, Pete. I think it's kinder that way."

Sheriff Bates stood up and walked to the door. Then he stopped and frowned. "Say, Doc. You don't think there's any danger, do you? Dan can't do anything violent from that bed."

Dr. Hinkley looked uneasy. "I don't think so, but Dan's paralysis is hysterical, Pete. He could recover at any time. It's unlikely, but you can't rule him out as a suspect. He could be walking and not telling anyone. He *could* even be your murderer."

"Jesus, Mary, and Joseph!" Sheriff Bates shook his head. "I'll keep an eye on him, Doc. It's a damn good thing we're holding that sanity hearing right away!"

CHAPTER 25

"You gonna stay for long, Mrs. Powell?" Chet Turner stuck his head in her door. "I'm about ready to leave."

"Go ahead, Chet." Sally turned to smile at the young janitor. "Marian's coming in later to bring me something to eat. I'll probably be working for a couple of hours yet."

"Mr. Woodruff said teachers aren't supposed to be in here alone at night." Chet leaned on his broom and frowned. "I guess it'll be all right if I lock you in, though. Mrs. Larsen can use her key when she comes."

"Thanks, Chet." Sally gave him a smile. "I'll see you tomorrow."

The school felt empty when Chet left. Sally busied herself with her letters for a few minutes, and then she walked to the window and looked out. It was getting dark, and Marian should be here soon. She hoped so. She was hungry enough to eat a bear.

* * *

"Is anything wrong, Dan?" Marian was concerned as she watched him eat. "You've been so quiet all day."

"No, nothing's wrong."

"How do you like the broccoli and cheese sauce? It's Edith's recipe."

"Very good."

"You're not upset because I'm going back to the school, are you, Dan? I could always pack up Sally and bring her back here."

"No, that's all right, Marian. I'm just tired."

"Maybe you should rest while I'm gone. I won't stay out for too long. If it gets late, I'll call."

It was like trying to talk to a brick wall. Dan wasn't making any attempt to really communicate. Marian sighed and gave up the effort. Perhaps he really was tired. Today had been a long day, and the atmosphere was somber in school. Cliff and Connie had been the most popular kids in the senior class. Being around their grief-stricken friends all day was bound to be exhausting. Luckily, she had escaped most of that in the elementary wing.

"Well . . . I guess I'd better be going, then." Marian stood up and kissed him. "I'll be back just as soon as I can."

Dan tried not to shudder when Marian kissed him. He watched her walk from the room, and he listened to the familiar sounds as she got ready to go out. It was hard to pretend when he knew the truth.

The front door banged shut. She was gone. Dan pushed his plate aside the moment Marian left. He didn't feel like eating. Thinking about what he'd told Sheriff Bates had wiped out the little appetite he had left. When would the sheriff act? Dan wished he knew how long these things took. He imagined that by Sunday, at the latest, Sheriff Bates would come for Marian.

She was backing the van out now. He could hear the tires spinning in the driveway. He should have taught Marian more thoroughly how to drive in the snow, but now it was too late. He'd never teach her how to do anything again. She wouldn't need to know how to drive in a mental hospital. That was where they'd probably put her. Marian would spend the rest of her life in Brainerd State Hospital, and he'd visit her on the weekends, if he could find anyone to take him.

"Oh, God!" A moan of despair came from his throat. He was sentencing his own wife to a life behind locked doors, but what else could he do? He had to stop her from hurting someone else. In his heart, Dan knew he'd made the right decision. But that didn't make it any easier to accept.

It was dark now. Sally turned from the window and picked up her record book again. It was silly, but she was a little frightened here at school all by herself. Her room lights, the only ones on in the entire building, cast a reflection on the snow outside. The hallway was dark, and the light switch was at the very end. She wouldn't go out in that dark hall for anything!

Sally jumped as she heard the front door rattle. Then she smiled gratefully. Marian was back. The light switch flicked on, and suddenly the school was a friendly place again. She could hear Marian's heels click against the wooden floor. It was a commonplace, comforting sound.

"Meals on wheels, madam?" Marian laughed as she set the tray on Sally's little table. "I brought enough for both of us. I know it's no fun eating alone."

"Boy, am I glad to see you!" Sally laughed nervously. "This place is eerie at night. I kept thinking of werewolves and vampires and ghosts."

"You've been watching too many old movies." Marian spread out a cloth and unloaded the basket. "I've got pork chops and baked potatoes, broccoli and cheese sauce, and . . . blueberry pie!"

"No wonder it took you so long." Sally grinned. "When did you have time to bake a pie?"

"I had it in the freezer. I just popped it in the oven when I got home. As a matter of fact, these are the blueberries we picked at your place last summer."

"Now all we need is coffee." Sally headed for the door. "Sit down, Marian. I'll get it. You've outdone yourself."

The teachers' lounge was dark. The little light on the coffeepot was glowing like one red eye. It would have frightened her earlier, but now that Marian was here, her fears seemed silly and childish. The school was perfectly safe. No one could get in without a key. And only teachers had keys. It was just as safe as being alone at home.

"Here you are." Sally carried two steaming cups across the room and set them down on the table. "Let's eat, Marian. I'm really starved."

The meal was wonderful, and Sally was full of praise. Marian was a good friend to join her like this. After they had eaten, Marian went across the hall to her own room to work on her bulletin boards. It made Sally feel secure when she looked out her door and saw the light on in Marian's room. Actually, working late at the school was kind of fun. She was halfway through with her progress reports, and she'd been at it for only two hours. If she kept working, she could finish them tonight. Then she'd be all caught up, and the rest of the month would be easy.

"More coffee?" Marian called out from her room. "I'm getting some for myself!"

"Sure!" Sally hollered back. She heard Marian go into the lounge. There was a muffled exclamation. Then she was back at Sally's door with a puzzled expression on her face.

"The coffeepot conked out. It's stone cold. I can't work without coffee."

"Maybe we can go down to the cafeteria and heat it up," Sally suggested. "They don't lock up the kitchen at night, do they?"

"I don't think so." Marian shrugged. "Well, there's only one way to find out. Let's go."

The halls were dark and silent as they walked through the elementary wing. Sally was glad that Marian was with her. The eerie sensation had returned, but it wasn't as bad with Marian at her side.

Their footsteps made a hollow, echoing sound in the corridor as they went into the main building and passed the empty classrooms.

Sally shivered a little. There was a stretch of open space between the cafeteria and the classrooms that always seemed dark, even in the middle of the day. Harvey had turned it into a metal shop, and the tools and equipment were covered with plastic shrouds. It reminded Sally of a morgue, and her heart beat wildly in her chest as they hurried past.

Her fears vanished once they reached the cafeteria and turned on the lights. Now Sally felt foolish for being frightened. It wasn't like her to be afraid of the dark. She was so nervous lately.

Marian pushed open the kitchen door. The long metal counters gleamed under banks of fluorescent lights. Cookies were stacked high on enormous trays for tomorrow's dessert.

"I'll have to watch Joey Cracowski tomorrow." Marian grinned. "He loves peanut butter cookies. He always tries to snatch at least three of them."

"There must be a thousand of them," Sally said in awe. "That'd be almost enough for one afternoon at my house. You know how the girls go through cookies."

There was a long silence as the two women looked at each other. Sally's face fell as she remembered. The girls were gone. Jenny was dead, and so were her friends. There was no longer a reason to make a triple batch of peanut butter cookies.

"Don't think about it, Sally." Marian patted her shoulder. "It doesn't do any good to grieve. Just think happy thoughts."

"It's so hard." Sally sat down at the counter and waited for the coffee to heat. She could see herself in the gleaming stainless-steel surface. She looked tired and old.

"Things sneak up on me, Marian. Little things. I made butterscotch pudding last night because

Jenny loved it. I didn't remember until I poured it in the bowls. Ronnie hates butterscotch pudding. I'll never get over it, Marian. I'll never adjust!"

"Yes, you will, Sally." Marian smiled kindly. "I felt that way, too, at first. Then I discovered something that made me feel much better. Come on, let's carry this back to your room and I'll tell you."

The trip back wasn't as frightening. Sally concentrated on holding the pot steady so the coffee wouldn't spill. She was glad to see her own room, with the lights shining brightly. They sat down at her little table and shared the hot coffee.

"I couldn't stand it if I thought Laura was really gone," Marian confided, leaning close. "You see, Sally, I know that she's out there somewhere. And someday I'll be with her again. Until then, I just have to wait."

Sally froze with her cup midway to her mouth. Marian must be talking about heaven, but it sounded almost sinister.

"It's hard to understand, but I know Laura's really not gone. She sends me notes, Sally. Laura tells me she's happy. That's a great comfort to me."

Sally couldn't say anything. She hardly dared to breathe. Marian was crazy, but she didn't want to argue with her. Sally kept her face carefully impassive as Marian went right on talking.

"I wanted to tell you before, but I didn't think you were ready." Marian smiled. "Jenny's with Laura, you know. Jenny and Becky and Laura are together again. And now Cliff and Connie are there, too. That makes me feel so much better. Our little girls aren't lonely anymore, Sally. Isn't that wonderful?"

Sally nodded. She didn't know what else to do. Marian had lost her mind. Sally shivered slightly.

"Well, it's getting late." Marian glanced at her watch and smiled. "Do you have much more to do, Sally? I promised Dan I wouldn't stay too long."

"I'm nearly finished." Sally was proud of herself. Her voice was steady. "If you have to get back home, Marian, go ahead. I'll be just fine here. And . . . and I'll come over to your house when I'm done. How does that sound?"

"If you're sure you don't mind . . . ?" Marian hesitated, and then she stood up. "I'd like to check on Dan, Sally. You come soon, though, or I'll start to worry. I'll stop at the store for some snacks, and then I'll set up a card table. Maybe we can all play gin."

"Good idea. See you soon, Marian." Sally followed her to the door. "I guess I'd better lock this, just in case."

She turned the key in the lock the moment Marian was outside the door. Then she leaned against it weakly. Poor Marian. It was easy to slip over the edge when you'd lost a child. She had almost gone crazy those first few days after Jenny died.

Sally shivered again. She remembered her odd reactions in those first days. She'd stop suddenly and listen, sure that she'd heard Jenny in her room. Or she'd whirl around because there seemed to be someone behind her. She had confessed it all to Ronnie, and he said he felt the same way. It was difficult to adjust when someone you loved was suddenly gone. Poor Marian. She hadn't confided in anyone. Marian was trying so hard to have something to believe in, and now she was confused.

Sally blinked back tears. It was up to her to help Marian. She certainly wouldn't tell anyone else about it. Marian was doing fine in her classroom, and in all other respects she was normal. She just had some strange notions, that was all. Marian had lost a little corner of her reality, and someone had to help her get it back.

Sheriff Bates pulled to a stop in front of the school. Jake was huddled up against the front door, drunk again. One of these nights he was going to die of exposure.

"Hey, Jake! Come on over here!"

Jake wasn't moving. Sheriff Bates rolled up the window and got out of his warm car. There was snow coming again tonight, and he couldn't just leave Jake here. He'd have to bed him down in the jail again until he sobered up.

"Come on, Jake." Sheriff Bates hoisted him to his feet. "Steady, now. Let's walk to the nice warm car."

Sheriff Bates grabbed Jake under both arms and tried to drag him. He smelled like a brewery. Jake was really loaded tonight. It was like lifting a heavy rag doll, and the ice underfoot didn't help. It took awhile, but they reached the car at last.

He propped Jake up against the side of the car and turned back to look at the school. A light was shining in the elementary wing. And there was Sally Powell at the window, grinning at him.

"Hey, Sally! Want to take him home with you tonight?" Sheriff Bates shouted at the top of his lungs. He watched as Sally forced the window open.

"No, thanks." Sally leaned out, laughing. Jake had really tied on a good one this time. He was starting to slide down the side of Sheriff Bates's car, just like a wet noodle.

"Whoops! Hold on there, Jake!"

Sally laughed out loud as Sheriff Bates propped Jake up with a foot on his backside. It looked like an old Laurel and Hardy movie.

"I've been looking for Jake all over town. I knew he was out here someplace. There's another storm coming, so I'll bed him down in the jail, where it's warm and safe."

"Good idea, Sheriff!" Sally watched while Sheriff Bates tugged and wrestled Jake into the front seat of the car. She waved as he drove off. Jake would have frozen stiff as a board if Sheriff Bates hadn't found him.

Sally felt better as she closed the window and went back to her stack of papers. There was a parallel between Marian and Jake. Marian needed someone to lean on, just as Jake needed Sheriff Bates. She could help Marian through this difficult time. That was what friends were for.

CHAPTER 26

Jake was finally asleep. Sheriff Bates spread an extra blanket over Jake's cot and grinned. It had been a three-ring circus in here when he carried Jake into the cell. Jake was a noisy drunk. He had treated Tina and the sheriff to a medley of old Beatles songs until he finally curled up and went to sleep.

"I'm going to run over to the Red Owl and get us some snacks, Pete." Tina's voice was soft as she touched him on the arm. "I sure hope Jake doesn't wake up. If I have to hear 'Hey Jude' one more time, I'll scream!"

"Yeah!" Sheriff Bates grinned. Jake would never make it in the entertainment world. "Pick up some orange juice and doughnuts, will you, Tina? I'll make sure he has some kind of breakfast when he wakes up in the morning."

After Tina was gone, the sheriff transcribed his notes from his interview with Dan Larsen. They really should be typed, but he didn't want Tina to do it. The fewer people that knew about it, the better.

As he worked, he kept remembering his conversation with Doc. It was a ridiculous idea, but Doc seemed pretty serious when he said they had to treat Dan like a suspect. Just to set his mind at rest, he'd take a run past Dan's house when Tina came back. He wouldn't go in; just a quick run up the street would tell him if everything looked peaceful over there.

Now Jake was snoring. He sounded like a motorboat. Sheriff Bates chuckled to himself. Jake was the only person in town who wasn't concerned about the accidents. He was sleeping in there like a baby. Sheriff Bates wished he could sleep like that. He kept thinking about the kids who were dead, five of them. Nisswa was going to pieces around him. He was doing his job to the very best of his ability, but he wondered what terrible thing was going to happen next.

Now Sally wished that Marian had waited. The eerie feeling was with her again, and the thought of walking through the dark hallways made her shiver.

Putting it off wouldn't make it any easier. Sally buttoned her coat and picked up her purse. She was ready. Sally held her keys in her hand and forced herself to step out into the hall. She didn't want to turn off her room lights, but it was the responsible thing to do. Harvey was worried about the power bill again this month.

She took a deep breath and flicked off the switch. Her hand was trembling so badly, it was difficult to lock the door behind her. There. Now all she had to do was walk to the front door. Her car was parked directly outside, and she'd be at Marian's in no time at all.

Her footsteps were loud in the deserted building. Sally found that she was almost running as she hurried down the corridor. The school was different at night. Shapes that seemed quite ordinary in the daytime turned into frightening specters in the shadows. If she let her imagination run wild, she could easily believe that someone was following her, stalking her in the darkness.

What was that! Sally almost screamed as she heard a noise from the basement. Then she grinned self-consciously. It was only the boiler kicking in. The heating system at the Nisswa School was ancient. During the day no one noticed how noisy it was. But at night, when the building was silent, the clanking of the pipes was loud and frightening.

She was almost at the door now, and the light shining in from the parking lot was a welcome sight. Sally was fumbling with the security lock when she heard a sound behind her. She turned quickly, but no one was there. The building was old, she told herself sternly. Old buildings always creaked and groaned in the wind. The sound she heard was nothing at all.

There it was again! Sally stopped and listened. It sounded like someone crying.

Sally drew in her breath sharply. She remembered a story she'd heard when she was in college. A child was locked in the kindergarten room over the weekend. The little boy had been napping behind some play equipment, and the teacher had failed to check the roll when she dismissed her class. On Monday morning they had found the child, exhausted from crying and badly frightened by his ordeal.

Sally always checked her roll carefully at the end of each day. Perhaps one of the other teachers had been negligent. It was possible one of her children was locked in. She had to investigate. It was her duty as a teacher.

"Is someone there?" Sally tried to keep her voice steady. "This is Mrs. Powell. Where are you?"

Now she heard it plainly. The noise was coming from the bank of lockers at the dark end of the corridor. The lockers were big and roomy. A child could easily hide in one. And if the door slammed shut, it would be difficult to open from the inside. The lockers should have been taken out years ago. No one used them now. She'd certainly see that it was on the agenda for the next teachers' meeting.

Sally moved back into the dark corridor. She wished she knew where the light switch was. The child was crying now and scratching against the inside of the metal cabinet. It was coming from the locker on the end. She had to hurry.

The child was banging now, fists hammering against the metal prison. Sally started to run. The poor child was terrified.

"I'll help you, honey. I'm coming!" Sally hurried to the spot and dropped her purse and books on the floor. She tried to open the locker, but it was stuck fast. If some bully from the older grades had locked a young child in here, she'd see he was punished.

Sally put her shoulder to the locker and pulled

on the handle as hard as she could. The locker door flew open, and Sally held out her arms to the poor frightened child.

There was a moment when she froze, horror on her face. She screamed as she saw the fire ax gleam in the dim light from the street. The blade struck deeply, cutting into her neck. Another blow and her life spilled out over the polished wooden floor. Only a row of silent lockers witnessed the expression of shock in her unseeing eyes.

"Where's Sally?" Dan sat up and yawned. "I thought she was going to come home with you."

"She should be here soon." Marian checked the window to make sure it was closed tightly. It was going to get much colder tonight. "Have you been sleeping long, Dan?"

"I fell asleep right after you left, and I just woke up now. You shouldn't have left her alone, Marian. Harvey has a rule about that."

Marian laughed. "Harvey worries too much sometimes. Besides, she's locked in tight. No one can get in without a key. Do you want to play some cards later, dear? I stopped at the store on the way home and picked up some midnight snacks. You should have seen the lines! Betty says everyone's stocking up, just in case we get snowed in tonight. I thought we'd light a fire in the fireplace. Ronnie's coming over at eleven. The four of us could have an all-night card party."

Maybe a card party would be good for him.

Dan frowned. He was still upset from the dream. Another one! And his legs were trembling again.

"I ran into Jake when I was leaving the school." Marian shook her head. "I hope he gets home all right, Dan. The radio weatherman predicts a full-scale blizzard."

"Jake'll be fine. He's got enough antifreeze in him for forty below. Why don't you put on a fresh pot of coffee, Marian? Sally'll be cold when she comes in."

Marian hurried to put on the coffee. She wondered what was keeping Sally so long. Maybe she should take the van and check on her. The wind was blowing harder, and Sally might be having trouble with her car.

"I think I should check on Sally." Marian stuck her head in the den. "You know how temperamental her car is. If the wagon won't start, she'll try to walk over here. It's eighteen below!"

"Relax, Marian. Give her a couple more minutes. She's probably on her way over here right now."

As they waited, Dan saw Marian get more and more upset. She'd sit down, but she'd be up again immediately, running to peer out the window. Her hands began trembling, and her eyes looked wild. The suspicion struck him with the force of a physical blow. Marian had been alone in the school with Sally! He had to call Sheriff Bates right away!

Marian didn't object when he called the sheriff's office. Dan thought she seemed almost relieved when the patrol car drove up outside. Perhaps he was jumping to conclusions this time. Sally was Marian's best friend. Marian wouldn't hurt Sally.

* * *

"Now, Marian . . . there's no need to get upset." Sheriff Bates opened the door of his car for her. "I'm sure Sally's all right. She probably turned off the lights for a minute to rest her eyes, and she fell asleep at her desk."

"But she could be hurt!" Marian shivered. "Maybe she fell on the stairs or . . . or maybe something awful happened!"

"We'll check it out, Marian." Sheriff Bates gave her his best soothing smile as she got out of the car and they walked up the snow-covered sidewalk.

The door opened without a key. Sheriff Bates turned to look at Marian. "Are you sure you locked this door when you left?"

"I'm positive. I double-checked, Sheriff. Maybe Sally opened it."

At times like this, he wished he had a deputy. Sheriff Bates squared his shoulders. It was pitch-black inside.

"Where's the light?"

"I'll get it."

Marian switched on the light by the door. Now the hallway was partially illuminated.

"There's another switch, just beyond those lockers."

Sheriff Bates dropped his hand to his side. His gun was solid and heavy against his fingers. He really didn't expect to find anything wrong, but it was reassuring to know it was there.

"I'll get the other light." Marian stepped around the corner. There was a moment of silence, and then she gave a muffled scream.

He came around the corner at a run, gun drawn and ready. Marian was standing there swaying, one hand against the light switch. Her eyes were glazed and her expression was frozen as she stared down at the gruesome thing on the floor. They had found Sally.

For a moment neither one of them moved. It was as quiet as death in the empty school. And Sally, the hideous thing that had been Sally, was silent, too, lying in a seeping pool of dark red blood.

"Marian, come with me." Sheriff Bates moved to take her arm. "Don't look. . . . Just walk. That's it. Walk to the door now. Don't turn back, Marian. Just look straight ahead and walk."

Somehow he managed to lead her out, to push her into the car and drive to Dr. Hinkley's house. She sat so still in the seat that he thought she had fainted. He glanced at her as the streetlights flashed across her white face. Her eyes were wide open and staring.

CHAPTER 27

Who was talking? Marian heard voices. They seemed to be coming from her bedroom across the hall.

"She probably won't wake for hours yet. Let's go down and make breakfast for Dan."

"Have they told Ronnie? The poor man!"

"It's terrible, that's what it is."

For a moment Marian thought she was dreaming. Then she remembered, and she squeezed her eyes shut tightly. Edith and Midge were here, staying in her room. Dr. Hinkley had called them to take care of her. And she was in Laura's room, where she'd asked to sleep. And Sally, dear Sally, was dead!

She was slightly groggy. Dr. Hinkley must have given her another shot, but not as much as last time, because her head cleared rapidly. Marian waited until she heard them go downstairs, and then she sat up quietly. She wanted to cry, but she couldn't. Her best friend was dead!

Marian put her feet on the floor. Her slippers

and robe were folded neatly at the foot of Laura's bed. She put them on, each movement in slow motion. She had to wake up now. It was time to go down and see if Dan was all right. He would be terribly upset over Sally's death.

Was Laura's coloring book there last night? Marian tried to think. It was sitting in the very center of the table now, open to a page in the middle. It was a new coloring book, one Marian had bought only last week. She felt her knees shake as she moved closer to look.

There was a picture of a rainbow, done in lovely bright colors, though the lines were a little shaky. She'd never seen it before. On the bottom there was a note in red crayon.

To Mommy, from Laura.

Laura! A glad smile spread across Marian's face. Laura had been here just when she needed her most. And her baby had colored her a picture, a beautiful picture, just for her.

It took her a moment to pick it up. Every movement was a conscious effort. Then she held it in her hands and looked down, smiling. Laura had learned the colors of the rainbow. Red, orange, yellow, green, blue, indigo, and violet. And Connie had taught her. They had learned that lesson in art class only last week.

But where was Laura's diary? Marian turned around slowly. There it was, on the rocking chair.

For a moment, the words were a blur. Then Marian brushed away her glad tears and smiled.

> Oh, Mommy! Sally is here, and Jenny
> stopped crying. I love you so much.

The printing was not as regular as it usually was. Laura was getting out of practice. The important thing, though, was that Jenny had stopped crying. Marian was so relieved. Sally was there with her baby, and everyone was happy again. Things would be perfect very soon now.

Dan had been awake for hours. Edith and Midge were talking upstairs. They'd be down soon. He was grateful for their help, but he was glad they were going home today. It was a strain, acting normal, when he knew the truth. Marian had murdered Sally!

"How about some cereal, Dan?" Midge poked her head in the door. "Marian's got Wheat Chex and Cheerios in the kitchen."

"No, thanks. I'm not very hungry, Midge. I'd like a cup of coffee, though, as soon as it's ready."

At least she hadn't mentioned the murder. If he had to hear about it one more time, he'd scream. Why didn't Sheriff Bates arrest Marian last night? There wasn't time to wait for evidence.

He'd called the office first thing this morning. The sheriff had assured him something would be done soon. How long did it take to arrest a killer?

Dan took a deep breath and forced himself to be calm. Marian was coming down the stairs.

"Hi, honey." She stood in the doorway, looking radiant. There were no signs of grief on her face.

Her eyes were clear, with no traces of tears. And she was smiling!

"I thought you might be upset about Sally." Marian walked over and sat in the chair by his bed. "Don't be sad, Dan. Sally's not sad. Now she's happy. She's with Jenny again."

She reached out to take his hand, and Dan had all he could do not to pull away. He stared down at her strong, capable fingers. Marian's hands had held the murder weapon. Her arms had brought that wicked blade down on Sally's head.

"Here's your coffee, Dan." Edith breezed into the room. "Oh, Marian! I didn't expect you up so early. Would you like a cup of coffee?"

"I'll have it in the kitchen with you and Midge." Marian got up and walked to the door. "You two were just wonderful to come over here last night. I don't know how I can ever thank you."

Dan tried to get interested in a rerun of *The Six Million Dollar Man*. He had to do something to take his mind off Marian. Midge and Edith would be leaving soon. Then he'd be completely alone with her.

The phone rang as the segment was ending. Marian picked it up in the kitchen. A minute later, she came into his room.

"That was Jim Sorensen. They're holding a town meeting tonight at the Elks Lodge. Jim says they're organizing to protect the town."

"You'd better not go, Marian." Dan tried to hide his alarm. "Jim'll understand. He knows you're still upset."

"No, I promised him I'd be there." Marian's

voice was firm. "I'll go for both of us. Jim wants a big turnout tonight."

At least nothing could happen if she was in a crowd of people. Dan sighed, but he kept his thoughts to himself. Not one of the people at the meeting would suspect Marian. She was too good at hiding her madness.

Marian looked the same as always, sitting quietly in the chair by his bed. Dan was sure she didn't remember what she had done. She would deny everything if she were faced with the facts. She would be puzzled, then outraged, if someone accused her. She was innocent in her own mind. Her eyes were not haunted by the same hideous secret that plagued him.

Dan leaned back and closed his eyes. It was difficult to think when she was sitting across from him, reading the newspaper. He still loved her, even though he knew the horrible truth. When would Sheriff Bates come and release him from this constant torture?

"Look, Pete. We just want to help, that's all." Jim faltered a bit at the angry look in the sheriff's eyes. "The meeting starts at eight. You're going to be there, aren't you?"

"I've got some business to take care of tonight." Sheriff Bates frowned. "I can't get there until around nine. Just don't go stirring them up, Jim. We've got an explosive atmosphere here in Nisswa."

Gus spoke up. "That's why we called the town meeting. If the people think they're doing something to help, they'll feel better. We're going to calm them down, Pete. Jim and I have it all planned out."

"Well, you're the mayor, Jim." Sheriff Bates leaned back and nodded. "I guess you have a right to call a town meeting anytime you want. Just keep it orderly, and I'll get there as soon as I can."

Sheriff Bates motioned to Emma, and she brought the coffeepot. She gave him a smile, but it wasn't the big grin he usually got. Emma was upset over Sally's death. Everyone was upset. It was a bad time to hold a town meeting. Even nice people got hot heads when their community was threatened.

"Come on, Emma. Give us a smile." Sheriff Bates reached over to pinch her behind. "The day's never right unless I get a smile from my best girl."

"I don't feel much like smiling today, Sheriff." Emma's hand was shaking as she poured out the coffee. "Mrs. Powell's murder makes me scared. I told Joe I won't work the late shift anymore. I got a creepy feeling about being alone at night."

"A big girl like you?" Sheriff Bates laughed. "Come on, Emma. I know you. If that killer comes in here, you'll bash him over the head with Joe's frying pan."

"I guess I would, at that." Emma began to grin. "Maybe I'll bring it up at the meeting tonight. Joe could make a fortune selling those frying pans of his."

It was a pity, that was what it was. Joyce Meiers looked down at the papers on Dr. Hinkley's desk and sighed. Poor Mr. Larsen. She didn't believe for a minute that he was crazy, but there it was in the doctor's appointment book: *Sanity Hearing—Dan Larsen—8:00 p.m.* Of course, this was confidential and she wouldn't tell a soul, but Mr. Larsen was being steamrollered right into the state hospital.

Joyce picked up two half-filled coffee cups and emptied the overflowing wastebasket. Poor Mr. Larsen! He was the best teacher she had ever had, and it just wasn't fair. She remembered what he'd said in civics class. A person had rights. They were holding this hearing, and poor Mr. Larsen didn't even know about it. It seemed that the law ought to protect people from things like this.

There was nothing she could do about it. Joyce closed the appointment book and tidied up the doctor's desk. Maybe it would turn out all right. Judge Lawrence was coming in from Brainerd. Everyone said he was a fair-minded man. She sure hoped the judge would protect Mr. Larsen's rights.

Marian sat in the backseat of the Honda, wedged in between stacks of school papers and music books. The snowplows had done a good job clearing out the Elks Lodge parking lot. There were spaces for thirty cars, and Edith found one on the end. The lot was nearly full. The people in Nisswa had turned out en masse for this meeting.

At least it would be warm inside. They were due for another storm during the night. The radio said it would get down to twenty below. Marian turned up her collar and shivered. It seemed like miles to the door.

Folding chairs were set up in rows, and a podium was in place on the stage. Marian felt a stab of remorse as she entered the room. It was no longer cozy and intimate, the way it had been the night of the teachers' Christmas party. Fred Norby's band was gone, the mistletoe was gone, and Drew was gone, too. No one had heard a word from him since he left three weeks ago.

"It's a good thing we got here early." Edith waved at a group of people she knew, and found them a place near the back. Marian made a quick head count. There were close to forty people here already, and they were fifteen minutes early. There had never been a turnout like this for a town meeting before. There was a restless murmuring from the front rows, and the mood was tense and expectant.

"All right, folks, we're almost ready to start." Jim Sorensen took his place behind the podium. "Most of you have probably guessed why I called this meeting. With the recent trouble in Nisswa, I think it's time we did something to protect ourselves."

"Where's the sheriff?" someone called out loudly. "I want to hear what Sheriff Bates has to say!"

"Sheriff Bates is in a meeting, but he'll be here later." Jim held up his hand for silence. "In the meantime, Gus Olson has some ideas he'd like to pass on to you."

Gus took over the podium. He looked nervous and small up there on the stage all alone. Marian listened as he read off a list of suggestions.

No one was to go out alone at night. Parents were cautioned to keep a sharp eye on their children. Teenagers were encouraged to travel in groups, and smaller children should always be accompanied by a parent or adult.

If any strangers were seen in town, Sheriff Bates wanted immediate notification. Gus said parents should warn their children again about never talking to strangers.

Sheds and garages must be locked securely. Heino's Our Own Hardware had an ample stock of heavy padlocks. Frank Heino was selling them at cost as a community service.

There was a polite burst of applause, and Frank nodded to the crowd. This meeting was very well planned. Sheriff Bates should be proud of the way the community was responding. People in Nisswa stuck together in a crisis.

Some of the elderly widows in town had expressed concern. Jim was organizing a committee of men to install security locks for the elderly. All residents were urged to lock their doors, even in the daytime. Gus told them it couldn't hurt to be overly cautious.

Jim took over again. "I have a report from the sheriff to read to you. I know there're a lot of stories floating around about Sally Powell, and the sheriff feels you should know exactly what happened. I'll read it verbatim."

Marian watched Jim as he read the report. Several times he stopped to swallow hard.

"Death was caused by repeated blows to the head and neck with a sharp instrument." Jim winced as he read the words. Marian noticed that Edith looked very white. It seemed so cold and ghastly hearing it like this. It made her feel a little queasy, too.

"County coroner, Dr. Edwin Hinkley, establishes time of death at approximately eight thirty p.m. A fire ax covered with the victim's blood was found at the scene, along with a pair of blood-spattered coveralls. Janitor Chet Turner reports that the coveralls were taken from the janitor's closet on the first floor of the school. The closet was not locked.

"An investigation is also being conducted into the deaths of Clifford Heller, Constance Bergstrom, Jenny Powell, and Becky Fischer."

There was a stir in the front row as Donna Fischer got up and rushed toward the ladies' room. Her face was pale, and she held her hand to her mouth.

There was an excited buzz of voices. Jim banged his gavel for order, and finally the room quieted. Marian shivered and sat up straighter. Sally's death was hideous, but it was all over now. Sally was with Laura, and now Jenny was happy. She would think only of that.

Jim put down the sheriff's report and addressed the crowd again. "Are there any suggestions from the floor at this point? I know all of you want to help Sheriff Bates catch Sally's killer."

Ned Addams got up with a half-baked idea of blocking off the town and conducting a house-to-house search. Another man suggested turning the school upside down for clues. Now everyone was talking at once, and she was having trouble hearing. Marian shut her eyes and tried to think. There was something bothering her, something she had to remember about last night with Sally. She had the feeling that if she could only remember, it would help.

Judge Lawrence came in at 8:20 p.m. He was full of apologies for being late. Part of the highway was drifting shut again, and he had been forced to follow the snowplow in.

"It's customary to have the patient present at these hearings. I'm making an exception in this case, only because of the disability involved."

Judge Lawrence sat down and lit a cigar. "The law on involuntary committal is clear. Only a showing of pressing necessity can justify confinement. Now, let's hear your report, Doctor."

Sheriff Bates listened carefully as Dr. Hinkley read his notes. He'd never taken part in a sanity hearing before. It was sobering to think that a man's fate was being decided right here in his office. Judge Lawrence could send Dan to the hospital for only a thirty-day observation period, but the news would get out. Even if the doctors at the hospital decided he was sane, Dan Larsen would never work in Nisswa again.

It was eight thirty. Joyce tried to watch television, but she was too nervous to concentrate. Her parents had gone to the town meeting, and she was alone. She tried not to think of it, but she was still upset about the sanity hearing for Mr. Larsen. Dr. Hinkley seemed to think the judge would commit him. Poor Mr. Larsen. They were holding the sanity hearing in secret, and that made her doubly upset. Mr. Larsen should have a right to know what they were doing.

At the commercial break, Joyce reached for the phone. She'd call Mr. Larsen and warn him. He could get a good lawyer and fight this. At least he'd have a chance of saving himself.

* * *

Marian didn't remember until Jake Campbell stumbled in the door. He weaved from side to side and managed to knock over a chair as he sat down in the back. Jake had been there the night Sally was murdered. She had seen him leaning up against the doorway of the school building. What if Sally had felt sorry for him and let him in? And what if Jake had gone crazy and killed her!

Everyone in town had heard Jake's stories about the war. He bragged about killing the enemy. Jake had never done anything violent in Nisswa, but now his drinking was worse than it had ever been.

Should she say anything? Jake had been at the sledding party, too. He could be the insane killer.

"Edith?" Marian nudged her friend. "I just remembered something, but I'm not sure if it means anything. When I left Sally in the school last night, Jake Campbell was right outside. And he was there the night of the sledding party, too."

Edith's eyes widened. She turned to look at Jake. Then she grabbed Midge's arm and whispered to her.

Midge was sitting on the aisle. She got up quickly and hurried over to Gus Olson. The crowd was still discussing security, and no one seemed to notice their whispered conversation. Gus turned uneasily and glanced at Jake before he motioned for Jim Sorensen to join him.

What had she started? Marian's heart pounded fearfully as Jim hurried to the back of the room and took Jake by the arm. Several people turned to look, and there was an excited buzzing.

"Where were you last night, Jake?" Jim spoke softly, but the crowd was suddenly quiet. "You were seen outside the school."

Butch Johnson spoke up. "He was there at the sledding party, too. I saw him."

"And he was talking to Becky Fischer the day she died!" Mary Baltar stood up. "I was taking a Christmas basket to Mrs. Lupinski, and I saw them. It was about four o'clock, I think."

"You've got some explaining to do, Jake!" Jim grabbed for Jake's other arm. "Come on, now. We're going to find Sheriff Bates!"

"Lemme alone!" Jake swung around and wrestled free. "Lemme alone!"

He stumbled against the doorjamb, and then he was gone, moving faster than anyone expected. Suddenly the crowd was moving, too, running after Jake, shouting at him, pushing and shoving to get through the door.

Marian sat silently in her chair. A wave of fear swept over her as she realized what she had done. What if Jake wasn't the killer? Could she be wrong? She could hear the shouts of the men outside, and suddenly she was afraid. The ordinary people of Nisswa had turned into a mob. What would they do to Jake!

CHAPTER 28

Dan balled his hands into fists and hit the mattress hard. Sheriff Bates had betrayed him. Joyce's call proved it. All that talk about an investigation was a stall. The sheriff had been stringing him along, pretending to gather new evidence. This was treachery!

A sanity hearing! And they didn't even have the guts to tell him. He wondered if Marian knew. She might have gone to his sanity hearing tonight, instead of the town meeting. There was a wife for you. Good old loyal Marian.

At least his lecture on civic responsibility had made an impact on one student. Dan gave an ironic smile. Joyce hadn't done well on the exams, but she had learned. Now he wished he'd given her an A. She was the only one who cared enough to tell him.

What could he do? Dan felt like a sitting duck here in his bed. If he could walk, he might have a chance. At least then he could get out and convince people he wasn't insane. He concentrated until his face turned red with the effort, but his legs were still dead.

He was in big trouble now. Dan took a deep breath and tried to stay calm. He had to think of something to do, quickly. Judge Lawrence would send him to the state hospital. Dr. Hinkley and Sheriff Bates could be very convincing. And once people knew he'd been sent to the state hospital, they'd never believe him.

They locked up Dan Larsen. He's crazy, you know. The poor man was never right in the head after that accident. And Marian, she's such a saint. Imagine putting up with a husband who accused her of murder!

Joyce thought he should get a lawyer. Dan gave a bitter laugh. He wouldn't be able to find a lawyer to take his case. The minute he said that Marian was the killer, any lawyer would back off. Marian's reputation was impeccable. And when he claimed that Marian had fooled the sheriff and the eminent town doctor, his lawyer would be positive he was a basket case.

How soon would they act? Dan tried to remember his smattering of law. The papers had to be filed before they could take him away. That meant they'd come after him tomorrow. He had less than twelve hours to think of a plan.

Dan's hands shook as he turned off the television. It wasn't only the thought of going to the state hospital that terrified him. It was Marian. And what she would do when he was gone!

Marian would be free to kill again and again. The thought made Dan's stomach churn. She could go on making her ghastly sacrifices for Laura, and no one would suspect. Eventually, someone might catch her, but how many victims would she claim before then?

It was up to him to stop her. He was the only one who knew the truth, and his time was running out. Dan glanced at the clock. It was almost nine. They had been discussing his fate for nearly an hour. Soon they would make it official. Dan Larsen would be stamped as certifiably crazy. Tomorrow they would come to take him away, and then it would be too late. He had to stop Marian tonight!

"Are you sure the wife won't sign the necessary papers?" Judge Lawrence frowned. "I agree this man should be confined for observation. There's enough evidence to warrant a thirty-day committal, but in the absence of the patient, the case would be much stronger with the wife's cooperation."

"Marian Larsen is also my patient," Dr. Hinkley said. "She's had a series of shocks over the past six weeks that would have permanently incapacitated a lesser woman. I don't think it would be fair to ask her to make a decision of this magnitude at this time."

"Then we have no choice." The judge snapped his briefcase shut and glanced at his watch. He stood and gave them a brief nod. "I'll have committal papers drawn up and filed first thing in the morning. You can pick him up tomorrow. Tell the doctor on duty to give me a call if the papers haven't come in yet."

Sheriff Bates waited until the judge had left. "If it weren't for Marian, I'd never have done this."

"I know." Dr. Hinkley looked old and tired. "I

don't like it, either, Pete, but there's no other way. We had to do it for Marian's sake. Think of how we'd feel if he spread that crazy story around town. Marian's been hurt enough."

"I guess you're right, but that doesn't make me feel any better. Nine o'clock tomorrow?"

The doctor nodded. "We'll go together. It'll be easier that way."

"We'd better get over to that town meeting." Sheriff Bates checked his watch. "I hope Jim kept a tight rein on that crowd."

"We don't need any more trouble, that's for sure." Dr. Hinkley shook his head. "I think Nisswa's had its share for the next ten years."

"Come on, Marian!" Edith hesitated at the open doorway. "I can see the crowd from here. It looks like they've got him cornered over at the Conoco station."

"I'll be there in a minute." Marian watched the door close behind Edith. She didn't want to go, but she knew she should. She was the one who had started all this. It was her responsibility to see it through to the end.

She was the only one left in the building. Marian got stiffly to her feet. She didn't want to see Jake cornered and scared. She didn't want to hear the mob of people shouting. But her legs carried her to the door and out, across the cold street to the ring of people surrounding Jake Campbell.

"Come on, Jake. We just want to take you to the sheriff." Jim was still trying to reason with him. "You like Sheriff Bates, don't you, Jake?"

"Get away! I'll kill you!"

She could see Jake now, cowering against the cinder-block building. He thrashed out wildly with his arms, and Jim went down. He was like an animal in a trap, fighting for his life. For a moment Marian thought she was going to be sick.

The men in the front were moving now, circling around their wary prey. Jake's head was swiveling. He knew he was surrounded. Marian prayed that he'd give up quietly and let them take him to Sheriff Bates.

"You'll never get me alive!" His voice was crazed. Flecks of foam spattered from his mouth as he shouted, and his lips were drawn up in a frantic snarl. Jake was not going quietly. He was standing there, outnumbered fifty to one, but he wouldn't give in.

"We're going to have to rush him. Come on! On the count of three . . ."

As Marian watched, the men surged forward. Jake held them at bay, screaming threats. Another man went down as Jake swung desperately. He was holding his own, but it couldn't last long.

Where was Sheriff Bates? He must have heard this commotion. Marian stared up the dark street, hoping to see his squad car.

Jake was still defending himself, kicking out and swinging his powerful arms. No one wanted to get close enough to chance getting hit. Marian hoped the crowd would stay out of reach until Sheriff Bates got here.

Jake's movements were getting wilder. The huge man was getting tired, but he wasn't giving up. The expression on his face was one of pure terror.

Marian didn't blame him for being afraid. The people she lived and worked with were turning ugly out here in the dark.

"I'll take you bastards with me! Don't come any closer!" Jake brushed Tom Woolery out of the way.

One of the men brandished a plank. Gus Olson had a brick in his hand. Something glinted in the moonlight, and a tire iron waved above the heads of the crowd. Marian swayed slightly. She felt faint. The snowbanks were whirling around her, and it was all she could do to stay on her feet.

They were advancing now, tightening the circle, closing in for the kill. There was a rhythm about it: advance two steps, fall back one, advance two more, fall back to regroup. She could still see the tire iron slashing against the air. Suddenly it crashed down. There was a hollow, crunching sound and a hideous scream.

"Murderer!" It was Donna Fischer's voice above the shouts of the crowd. "He killed my baby!"

"Killer!"

"Get him! Don't let him get away!" Gus Olson was shouting now. Marian saw the brick being raised and lowered again and again.

"Hit him again! He's getting up!"

They were all screaming, high-pitched wails of terror from the women mingling with the shouts of the men. The sound built into something so loud and fearful that Marian reached up to cover her ears.

Then she was shouting, too, one thin voice raised in fearful protest. Stop! They had to stop! Dear God, they were killing him. They were bashing and battering and tearing him apart!

Now there was another sound, a sound that drowned out the screaming crowd. It was a siren. Sheriff Bates's car came around the corner, red lights flashing against the banks of snow.

Suddenly it was quiet. The crowd was frozen as the siren cut off and Sheriff Bates got out of the car.

"What the hell's happening here?" His voice was loud and demanding, but no one answered. The men who had been shouting moments before were silent and motionless now. It was as if time had stopped and everyone was caught in a freeze-frame forever.

The spell was broken. Dr. Hinkley came forward. There was a shuffling of feet as the crowd moved aside for the doctor. Through the break in the crowd Marian could see Jake on the snow. There were dark blotches of blood all around him. His body was crumpled and still.

Dr. Hinkley bent over him for a moment. The crowd waited. No one said a word.

"He's dead."

The doctor's words hung in the cold air. For a moment there was no sound at all, and then everyone started yelling at once.

"He was hanging around the school last night, right before Sally was killed. He murdered her!"

"He killed Jenny Powell, too! We all saw him at the sledding party."

"And he was talking to Becky Fischer the day she died. He must have waited for her in the icehouse."

"We were going to bring him to you, but he attacked us. He's guilty, Sheriff. He's the killer!"

Sheriff Bates did not raise his voice, but everyone heard him.

"Jake *was* at the school last night. That much is true. But I locked him up in jail to keep him from freezing. I waved at Sally when I took him away. She was in her classroom, just as alive as you or me."

There was nothing to say. The crowd shifted uneasily, and several women began to cry. Donna Fischer was sobbing openly now, and Earl put his arm around her shoulders. Marian could see Jim Sorensen's face. He was white and shaking.

"Go home now."

Sheriff Bates moved to stand in front of Jake's body.

"Go home and try to sleep."

One by one they moved, dark shadows with heads bowed. They were all looking down at the snow, afraid of meeting their neighbors' eyes. It took only a minute and the area was deserted except for three silent figures outlined against the stark building. Dr. Hinkley and Sheriff Bates. And the body of Jake Campbell.

CHAPTER 29

Dan tried to think of another way. In the agonizing hour that had elapsed since Joyce's call, he had gone through many possibilities. Only one remained. And that was so hideous, his mind balked. He loved her so much. Why did it have to happen this way?

Was his way kinder than theirs? Oh, he had no doubt that someday they would learn the truth. But by then it would be too late. There would be more suffering, more horror, and he could end all that now, if only he had the courage. Marian would be here soon, and then it would start. It was the only way to stop this horror.

There was paper and a pen in the drawer of the bedside table. Dan's hands were shaking so hard, he could barely form the letters. A note from Laura. It was the only way. Marian would believe a note from her baby.

Dan willed his hand to be steady. Images were flashing through his mind, wonderful memories of the joy they had shared.

Marian, radiant and smiling, dressed in bridal white, a look of expectant joy on her face, floating down the aisle of the flower-decked church to be his wife.

Marian, learning to drive the stick-shift van, the funny way she crinkled up her nose when she concentrated on finding second gear.

Marian, colored lights mirrored in her happy eyes, a strand of tinsel glittering in her hair, sitting cross-legged under their first huge Christmas tree.

Marian, pale and ethereal in a hospital bed, with baby Laura nestled in the crook of her arm.

Marian, serene, Madonna-like, baby at her breast, slowly rocking to lull Laura to sleep.

Marian in the fall, laughing and playing in a pile of colored leaves.

Marian in the winter, leaning against the snowman they'd built, reaching up to tip the hat at just the right angle.

Marian in the spring, planting their garden, marking the rows with the pictures of seed packages, a smudge of dirt on her cheek.

Marian in the summer, posing at the lake in cutoff jeans, a flopping sunfish held gingerly by the very end of the stringer.

Dan looked down at the note in his hand. It was finished at last.

Mommy, I need you. Please come here.
I'm sad without you.

He placed the note on the nightstand, where Marian would be sure to see it. What if he lost courage? What could he do? It would be so easy to relent.

The bottle of tranquilizers Dr. Hinkley had left was in the drawer of the nightstand. Dan shook out two and swallowed them. He would be sleeping when she came home. It was better that way.

His eyelids grew heavy as he waited. Merciful sleep was almost here. Just a few minutes more and it would be over.

She was here. Dan heard the front door open, heard the hangers rattle as she hung her coat in the closet. Now. It was time. Now.

She came in the door, brushing snow from her hair. Dan thought she had never looked more beautiful. Her back was to him, and her lovely dark hair curled in damp little ringlets on the nape of her neck. He remembered kissing her there, placing his lips against the warmth of her neck and breathing in the sweet scent of her.

I love you, Marian, he said in his mind.

She was so dear, so beautiful, he almost relented. His wife, his love, the only woman he'd ever really wanted. For a moment he almost convinced himself not to carry out his hideous plan. But there was no mercy.

She was turning toward the bed now, and Dan closed his eyes. He felt her lips brush his cheek. He had to stay quiet so she'd think he was asleep. It was the hardest thing he'd ever done.

There was a rustle of paper as she picked up the note. Dan could hear her sharp indrawn breath.

"She needs me!" Her voice was soft with joy. "My baby needs me!"

She was leaving now. Dan could hear her footsteps climbing the stairs. He had an almost palpable urge to call her back, to tell her that it had all been a lie. Then sleep came with a rush, and it was finished.

Marian flew down the hall to Laura's room. Her baby needed her. Laura needed her mommy!

"Are you here, baby?" Marian's voice was full of excitement. "I'm ready, Laura. Tell me what you want."

She listened carefully, nodding her head from time to time. Yes. It made perfect sense. She didn't know why she hadn't thought of it herself.

"Yes, darling." Marian began to smile. Then she laughed, a joyous sound of happiness. The sound of her laughter echoed and filled the room with gladness. It was a sound of celebration. Everything was very clear now.

She had to hurry. Marian didn't want to keep her baby waiting. Laura had waited much too long. Only a few more moments and she would be ready.

Laura's new blue coat was hanging in the front of the closet. Marian folded it carefully over her arm and carried it down the stairs. She was so happy. Laura wanted her!

It took only a moment in the kitchen. Marian looked at the thermometer hanging outside the window. It was twenty-four below. That was very cold. It was a good thing she had remembered Laura's coat.

The snow stung Marian's face as she stepped out of the house. The wind blew with blizzard force, and she had to fight her way through the drifts to the deserted cemetery. Laura was waiting for her there; she was certain. Laura was cold, and she had brought her new blue coat to keep her baby warm.

The sky was dark, and Marian heard the wind howl past the headstones as she knelt at Laura's grave. It was a lonely place for such a little girl. Marian was so glad to join her.

"Here, baby." The tears froze on her cheeks and stuck to her eyelashes. "I brought your coat, honey. Your new blue coat."

She was terribly tired. Marian sighed as she bent down and forced her numb fingers to spread out the coat. It covered the small grave like a blanket, warm and soft and comforting.

Now she was ready, at last. Marian dropped to her knees, listening for the sound of her baby's voice. She had to be very quiet and listen. Laura would come to her very soon now.

A smile spread over Marian's face. There was a cry in the wind, a high, hollow voice that she knew so well. Yes, Laura was calling for her, and she would come.

The wind blew so hard, she could not open her eyes. The bitter cold chilled her bones, and her fingers burned like fire. Marian was so sleepy that she barely felt the pain. She had to rest for a moment and then listen again. She had to sleep and wait for Laura's voice to free her.

There was a smile on her face as she fell forward. She was warm now, warm and at peace in her baby's love. It was so pleasant, cradled in the soft white snow. At the last moment, she saw Laura's dear face behind her frozen eyelids.

CHAPTER 30

There was no sound in the house when Dan awoke. It was nearly midnight by the clock next to the bed. He had been sleeping for over two hours.

He sat up in bed and winced. His mind felt sluggish and fuzzy. For a moment, he scarcely knew where he was.

The pills. He remembered now. He had taken two of Dr. Hinkley's pills. No wonder he was having trouble waking up.

"Marian?" he called out in sudden panic. *"Marian!"*

It was then he remembered. He had written the note. She had read it. Marian was gone!

Dan groaned once, a full-throated sound of agony. He had sent the woman he loved to her death. How could he live with that guilt?

No. He mustn't think that way. Marian was a killer. She was insane. He had done the right thing. But even though he knew he was right, it was no comfort. Marian was dead, and he had killed her.

Dan closed his eyes and prayed to his God to

forgive him. He had taken a life, the life of the woman he had sworn to cherish. Was she at peace now? Did she forgive him?

He tried to make himself believe Marian was happier now. She was with Laura. There had been no peace for her without her baby. But wasn't that the very kind of thinking that had pushed her into madness?

Dan coughed once, and tears ran down his face. Something was wrong with his eyes. They were so heavy, so terribly heavy, and his lungs felt as if they were bursting.

The gas! Dan's eyes flew open with shock. The gas was on. He could smell it now. It was coming from the kitchen stove.

The pitcher of water crashed to the floor as he pushed himself up and onto his side. Then he rolled, using his arms for leverage. There was a moment when he teetered on the side of the bed, and then he was falling out with a thump to the floor.

It was slow and painful pulling himself forward by his hands, his useless legs dragging out behind him. He had to get to the kitchen somehow and turn off the stove!

The heavy dresser helped. Dan grabbed the legs and pulled himself past it, sliding his body along the floor. He could smell the gas strongly now as he came to the doorway. There was still the length of the kitchen floor to crawl.

Dan pushed up with his arms and fell forward. The slippery linoleum was slowing him down. He wiggled and pushed with his hands, sweaty palms sliding against the smooth surface. Only a few more feet to go. He could make it. He had to shut off the gas!

The burners were up too high. He couldn't reach them. Dan pulled himself up on the oven door, but it was no use. There was no way he could shut off the gas.

Trapped! He was trapped! Dan's head hit the floor with a sudden jar. He was growing weaker now. His muscles weren't working. He was going to die!

Dan's eyes closed. A frightful weariness came over his senses. His hand brushed something. A piece of paper. He drew it nearer and opened his eyes for the last time.

Marian's handwriting. He knew it so well. A note from Marian. Dead Marian.

Darling, Laura needs her daddy, too.

Please turn the page for an exciting sneak peek of

Joanne Fluke's

DEAD GIVEAWAY

coming soon from Kensington Publishing!

PROLOGUE

The meeting took place in a high-rise office building, twenty stories above the Vegas Strip. The five men wore fashionably cut business suits. There wasn't a bodyguard in sight, the strains of an Italian aria did not fill the air, and no one's name was Guido.

The tanned, blond man looked uncomfortable as he addressed the senior member of the group. "I'm sorry it has to be this way, but our only option is to take a hard line."

Reluctantly, the older man nodded, perspiring heavily. "I know, I know. She thinks she's in love and she won't listen to reason. She doesn't realize he's playing her for a fool."

"She's already talked too much." The short, thin man frowned. "We managed to take care of it this time, but we can't take another chance."

The older man peered into their faces for some sign of compassion, but no one would meet his eyes. "But she's my daughter! There's got to be some other way!"

The fourth member of the group, a heavyset man with a ruddy complexion, sighed deeply. "You know we're reasonable men. If there's another solution, we're willing to consider it."

"What if I personally guarantee her silence? Put a guard on her day and night?"

There was silence for a long moment and then the heavyset man shook his head. "We know your intentions are good, but you can't control her forever. She'll manage to slip her guard sooner or later and then . . ."

The fifth member of the group, silent until this point, held up his hand. "I know that I speak for every man here when I say that we respect your feelings for your daughter." The heavyset man nodded along with the others. "And because of that respect which we all share, I have worked out a plan to keep her alive but eliminate the threat she poses."

They all leaned forward as he outlined the details. An expression of anguish came over the older man's face as he listened, but then he nodded reluctantly. It was better than nothing.

"It's settled then." The heavyset man sighed deeply. "So what about the boyfriend?"

The older man's expression hardened as he rose from the table. "Do what you think best. I have no interest in him."

* * *

Happy Smith wheeled another load of rubbish up to the industrial Dumpster. The wind whistled down the canyon and he shivered as he zipped up his Windbreaker. The foreman would be plenty surprised when he came up the mountain tomorrow and found all the construction trash and debris hauled away.

A strange set of circumstances had prompted Happy to start work one day early. It had to do with the mission and their Sunday schedule. First they fed you the food, a nice chicken dinner with soup and mashed potatoes and little green peas. But then, after the apple pie that Miss Alden made in a big pan for the men she called her lambs, she herded them all into the chapel to say prayers all afternoon.

Happy had already resigned himself when he'd heard Miss Alden tell another man that he'd better hurry or he'd be late to work. And that had given him the idea. The slip from the foreman was in his pocket and he'd folded it over so the date didn't show. Miss Alden had been so excited about his job that she'd given him a nice yellow Windbreaker and a pair of gloves from the charity box. And Sam, an old wino who'd been at the mission since they'd opened the doors, had loaned Happy his horseshoe ring for luck.

Happy turned around to stare at the building on Deer Creek Road. The foreman had told him it was almost finished, a high-rise with nine condos that took up a whole floor apiece. Even though he wasn't supposed to do any cleanup inside the building, Happy had been itching to see those million-dollar condos.

The parking garage was wide open, its iron security gates propped up by the entrance, waiting to be installed. Happy hurried in and climbed the stairs to the first floor. He knew he was snooping, but he wouldn't touch a thing. No one would ever know he'd been inside.

When Happy opened the door to the first-floor condo, he gasped out loud. It was carpeted with the thickest rug he'd ever seen, plenty soft enough to sleep on. And the rooms were so big they could hold every one of Miss Alden's lambs, without anyone ever bumping into anyone else.

There was a smile on Happy's face as he wandered through the rooms, trying to imagine being rich enough to live in such a place. The kitchen looked as if it belonged in a restaurant, with a walk-in freezer, a mammoth stove with four ovens, and enough shelves in the pantry to store food for a year.

After he had peeked into each of the rooms, Happy decided to head straight up to the penthouse. The foreman had told him they were putting a whole spa up there. Happy didn't see how they could build a pool without digging a hole in the ground, but the foreman had assured him that was exactly what they were doing.

It took time to climb up nine flights of stairs, and even though he stopped to rest at several landings, Happy was panting when he pushed open the door to the penthouse. The sight that awaited him made him gasp in awe. Metal girders curved around in a series of interlocking arches to make a domed ceiling. It wasn't finished yet, but several panes of glass were in place and Happy could see that there would be an unobstructed view in all directions. He stopped to look out at Mount Charleston and watched the pattern of the clouds just brushing its peak.

The view was so spectacular that, for a few moments, Happy lost himself in contemplation, forgetting the man-made marvels at his feet. Then he whistled in awe as he gazed down at the immense hole in the floor, lined with steel beams. He guessed they needed all that reinforcement because the pool was all the way up on top of the building. He'd watched some men put in a backyard pool once, but all they'd done was prepare the hole, install all the pipes, and drop in one of those premade shells.

There was the sound of a motor outside and Happy looked out to see a brown van pull into the driveway. When the doors opened and two men got out, Happy ducked behind one of the girders. His heart was beating fast and he rubbed Sam's horseshoe ring for luck. If the foreman was down there, he'd be in big trouble.

The men walked around to the back of the van and Happy sighed, relieved that he'd never seen those two men before. They opened the back door and helped another man out. He was staggering a little and Happy could see that he'd had too much to drink. They must have gone to a party and now they were taking their friend for a little walk to sober him up before taking him home.

The men looked startled as he leaned out and shouted, but they promised to give him a ride back to the mission. He should stay put and they'd come up to get him.

Happy was smiling as he walked back to explore the rest of the spa. If he'd watched just a moment longer, he would have seen that one of the men carried a gun. And that the third man was staggering because his hands were tied behind his back.

CHAPTER 1

The Castle Casino
Las Vegas, Nevada

Lyle Marshall was smiling as he threaded his way past a group of high rollers at the craps table. He'd signed the papers this morning and now he was officially retired. Since he'd made a hell of a profit by selling his share of Paradise Development to his partner, Marc Davies, he could afford to plunk down a sizable bet, but Charlotte was waiting in the banquet room and he didn't want to be late to his own twenty-fifth wedding anniversary bash.

A short, stocky man in his early fifties, Lyle was dressed in a custom-made gray linen suit. Charlotte always went to the tailor with him, choosing the material and cut that looked best. She also picked out his shirts and ties, even the smoking jacket she insisted on at home. Charlotte was a lady of impeccable taste.

A huge blond woman, slightly resembling Brün-
hilde in the one opera Charlotte had dragged him
to, hit a jackpot on the nickel slots. Bells rang, lights
flashed, and she let out a shriek that deafened
everyone within earshot. Lyle grinned; definitely a
soprano. Charlotte was the founder of the Friends
of the Las Vegas Civic Light Opera Company and
was always complaining about the lack of good
strong sopranos.

Lyle sidestepped the gawking tourists and entered the restaurant. An almost palpable sense of
relief came over him as the piped-in music muted
the clatter of the slot machines outside. Vegas was
hard on the ears. And on the savings account. If
Charlotte ever guessed how much of their money
had been converted into chips and scooped up by
the croupier, she'd kill him.

They'd come in the sixties as newlyweds. Charlotte had wanted to stay near her parents in Arling-
ton, Virginia, but he'd convinced her that a real
estate agent could make it big in a town like
Vegas. The casinos employed a lot of people and all
of them needed housing. There was a hell of a
turnover, too.

From day one Charlotte had complained about
the glitz, the heat, and what she called the gambler
mentality. It was true there wasn't much culture,
and the young city had little historical heritage. All
those things meant a lot to Charlotte, but she
missed the change of seasons most of all. Smack in
the middle of the desert, Vegas didn't really have
much weather to speak of. The wind blew a little
harder in the winter, and the nights got colder, but

that was about it. Shifting sand, bright lights, dry heat, and the feeling of being caught in the middle of a never-ending party—that described Vegas.

Marc and Lyle had formed Paradise Development fifteen years ago and it had been a going concern from the very first day. Marc was a wizard at finding prime building sites at ridiculously low prices, and Lyle pre-sold the houses he built. The only fly in the ointment had been Charlotte, but Marc had solved that one, too.

It had all started two years ago, when Marc picked up some great mountain property dirt cheap. One look at the land and Charlotte had fallen in love. There were trees that turned colors in the fall, snow in the winter, wildflowers in the spring, and real summer thunderstorms. They'd contracted with Paul Lindstrom, their architect of choice, to design the perfect apartment cluster, to feature an exclusive country club–type environment. Given the slope of their mountain site, Paul had designed a high-rise building, each unit consisting of an entire floor individually tailored to suit the occupant's needs. There were two common areas. The garage and the penthouse spa, complete with pool, Jacuzzi, sauna, tennis court, weight room, and jogging track. Totally enclosed by a climate-controlled glass dome, the spa afforded a spectacular view of the Mount Charleston area.

Charlotte and Lyle had moved in last year along with eight other couples who'd passed Charlotte's muster. Like one of those blue-blooded clubs back in Virginia, its members had to be perfect or they couldn't buy in. Charlotte loved the view from their eighth-floor condo, thirty-five minutes from Vegas on Deer Creek Road. "Mountain living at its finest" was the phrase she'd used two years in a row on their Christmas cards.

"Hi, Mr. Marshall." The hostess, a leggy blonde in a slit skirt that left very little to the imagination, greeted him with a perfect smile. "Everyone in your party is here except for Mr. Davies. He called and said he'll be delayed a few minutes."

Lyle grinned as he followed her to the plush private banquet room Johnny Day had reserved for the occasion. Lyle had always liked Johnny. He seemed like a regular guy, and Lyle had recommended him for membership in their Deer Creek Development, even though there were rumors about his womanizing. An Italian lounge singer who'd had a couple of hit records, Johnny's passion was mechanical musical instruments, and he had a whole warehouse full of antique music boxes of all sizes, along with player pianos and giant orchestrions. The orchestrions were fascinating—built in Europe before the turn of the century, the elaborately carved wooden cabinets contained string instruments, horns, woodwinds, and percussion. Johnny had explained that the orchestrions in his collection operated just like player pianos. The mechanical arms that drew the bows across the strings, the bellows that pumped air into the wind instruments, the levers that activated the drums, and the cymbals were all cued by a roll of pre-punched music. Charlotte, though a loyal supporter of classical symphony, admitted that the sound the orchestrions produced was nothing short of incredible for its day.

It had been touch and go overcoming Charlotte's aversion to anyone in show business, but now Johnny owned the fourth-floor unit. Johnny's collection had done the trick. When Lyle had first introduced them, Johnny had presented Charlotte with a heart-shaped music box he claimed had belonged to Queen Victoria. It might even have been true.

Charlotte was sitting at the head of a table decorated with white satin wedding bells and roses, an empty chair next to her. Lyle stopped in the doorway and gaped at his wife of twenty-five years. The long brown hair, always worn high on her head in a French twist, was gone. Through the wonders of modern cosmetology it had been lightened to a golden cap cut in a fluffy feathered style. Lyle blinked, then started to grin. It looked pretty damn good. She was wearing a bright pink jersey dress with a short skirt and it clung to her in all the right places. Charlotte's figure had always been good, but she'd been going to exercise classes for the past six months and there was definitely something to be said for all that toning and tightening. Lyle felt like he'd just been presented with a brand-new wife.

"Hello, darling! You're just in time." Charlotte had spotted him in the doorway and Lyle crossed the room to kiss her. Jayne Peters and Johnny Day were playing show tunes at the piano and Lyle noticed that Johnny was pale beneath his tan, a telltale sign to anyone who knew him well. Johnny had been gambling again and things hadn't gone well for him.

"Let's do our song, Jayne." Johnny switched on the microphone and they both started to croon.

> *Darling, when you're old and decrepit*
> *And liver spots make you look like a leopard,*
> *I'll stick with you through stormy or sunny*
> *'Cause you're the one with all the money.*

Charlotte giggled and pulled Lyle down into his chair. "That's awful! You must have written it, Jayne."

"Don't shoot. I confess." Jayne raised her hands in mock surrender. A petite woman in her late thirties with high cheekbones, her jet black hair was pulled back into two long braids. She was wearing a white satin cowboy shirt embroidered with red roses, white jeans studded with rhinestones, and red high-heeled cowboy boots. Since Jayne wrote strictly country-western songs, her agent had insisted on the cowgirl image. Public admission that her family name was Petronovitch and her parents had emigrated from Russia could be disastrous.

"Good afternoon, Lyle." Jayne's husband and Paradise Development's architect, Paul Lindstrom, stood up and extended his hand. A quiet man whom Jayne called her "textbook Norseman," Paul spoke slowly and precisely. As always, he was impeccably dressed in a snowy white shirt and dress slacks. At slightly over six feet tall and in his early forties, Paul was slim and fashionable, the only discordant note being his unruly halo of sandy hair. It reminded Lyle of pictures of Einstein and gave Paul the look of a sleepy lion.

"Hi, Paul." Lyle reached out automatically to complete the handshake. Paul had never dropped his Norwegian habit of rising to shake hands whenever anyone entered the room. When Paul and Jayne had first moved into the ninth-floor unit on Deer Creek Road, his firm handshake and polite bob of head had driven Lyle crazy. There were handshakes in the sauna, on the tennis court, and in the hallways. It had taken Lyle quite a while to get used to Paul's curious habit, but all the women in the building, including Charlotte, found the ritual utterly charming.

"Look at the lovely flowers Darby brought us." Charlotte gestured toward the centerpiece, a massive bouquet of roses.

Lyle turned to smile at Darby Roberts. Clayton and Darby lived on the fifth floor and Paul had designed a large, domed greenhouse garden. "Yours?"

Darby nodded. "The yellow ones in the middle are my own hybrid. I've been working on them for years, and Clayton registered them with the association last week. I named them Marshall Golds and that's my anniversary present. Smell 'em, Lyle."

Darby smiled as Lyle bent over to inhale the fragrance. She was a small, dark-haired woman, so thin her skin resembled white parchment stretched over a road map of blue veins. On the other hand her husband, their resident lawyer, wanted to look healthy, tan, and athletic and gave his workouts the same priority as his appointments with clients. At eight every evening, Clayton arrived at the rooftop spa, spending five minutes in the tanning booth, followed by twenty-five minutes on the exercise bike. Next came a fifteen-minute sauna and then thirty laps in the pool. Despite his efforts, Clayton still carried a roll of flab around his waist, and Lyle knew why. Clayton indulged himself with three-martini lunches at Alfredo's, where the entree was always pasta.

"Here's the paperwork." Clayton pulled a legal document from his pocket and presented it to Charlotte. "I personally checked the registration form. Since it didn't cover several salient points, I constructed an addendum which gives you clear title and protection against unauthorized use."

"Thank you, Clayton." Lyle tried to match Clayton's serious expression. He didn't give a damn if anyone wanted to grow Marshall roses, but it was obviously important to Darby and Clayton.

"I've got a present for you, too." Johnny Day stood up and motioned to a waiter who was hovering in the background. Almost immediately, twelve silver ice buckets were wheeled out, each containing a bottle of Dom Perignon.

"Oh, Johnny," Charlotte clapped her hands. "My absolute favorite champagne!"

"Your absolute favorite caviar, too." Johnny nodded and the waiter produced a crystal bowl filled with the finest Beluga caviar. "This is just the appetizer. I'll let Marc tell you about the rest of the meal when he gets here."

Moira Jonas got to her feet. A large woman with more muscle than fat, her red hair was twisted up into a knot on the top of her head, making her appear even taller. Moira's physical appearance matched her imposing presence as Vegas's leading interior decorator.

"That's simply a stunning outfit, Moira. You look wonderful."

Lyle noted genuine envy in Charlotte's voice and couldn't imagine why. Moira was wearing one of the caftans that had become her trademark. This one was a vivid blue embroidered in bright red thread, decorated with shiny gold beads interspersed with mirrored disks. Lyle thought she looked a little like the toy stuffed elephants found in a New Delhi bazaar.

"Aw, bullsh . . . I mean horsefeathers! I know I look as big as a house." Moira caught herself just in time and her roommate, Grace DuPaz, did her best to suppress a smile. As the only daughter of a career army sergeant, Moira's choice of expletives had been pretty colorful when Grace had met her ten years before. Since then, Moira had made a considerable effort to clean up her language.

"Thanks anyway, Charlotte." Moira tried to accept the compliment gracefully. "Can we bring out our present now? Grace has sixteen dancers on hold out there."

"Sixteen dancers?" Lyle was clearly puzzled as Grace jumped up to join Moira. Thin and graceful, she was the exact opposite of Moira, and wore her dark blond hair in a long ponytail. Grace had been the toast of Vegas, the featured dancer in all of the Castle's glitzy extravaganzas. She'd left the stage last year to become the head choreographer.

Charlotte had expressed her doubts when they'd wanted to buy into Deer Creek, as it was no secret that Moira and Grace were live-in lovers. Then, when Moira had offered to decorate all the units, Charlotte had quickly changed her mind. Since

Moira and Grace never discussed their intimate relationship and Charlotte refrained from personal questions, the three women were now good friends.

"I want to stage it perfectly, even though Moira said it really didn't matter, that you'd appreciate it anyway. And then, at rehearsal today, I noticed these perfectly lovely costumes from last year's show just hanging right there on the rack. Naturally, once I explained the situation, all sixteen girls wanted to help, so I asked for volunteers and . . ."

"Gracie dear, you're babbling," Moira interrupted gently. "What she really means is that our present's too dang big for one person to carry."

Charlotte winced. "This doesn't have anything to do with your inheritance, does it, Grace?"

"Yes and no." Grace laughed. "It's not the moose head, if that's what you're thinking."

"Thank God!" Charlotte gasped. Grace's father had been a taxidermist and Paul had designed a special climate-controlled storage room for their unit. When Lyle had seen Grace's collection and wanted to buy a moose head for their den, Charlotte had objected strenuously. Moose were ugly in the first place and she certainly didn't want some horrid dead creature on her wall, staring at her with its glassy eyes.

"Okay, guys . . . hit it!"

At Moira's cue, Jayne began an African melody on the piano. Grace crossed the room to open the door and a crowd of dancers dressed in Zulu costumes and carrying spears came in, holding a tiger skin rug, complete with head.

"Oh, Lord!" Charlotte began to laugh. "That animal has to be six feet long."

"It's actually a little over nine. I can take the head off if it really bothers you, but it adds such a nice touch of authenticity and it'll be on the floor, not the wall. Moira says it'll fit perfectly in front of your fireplace and I think it'll look very . . ." Grace stopped in midsentence as she felt Moira's hand on her arm. "Okay, Moira, I'll stop. But do you like it, Charlotte?"

Charlotte reached out to touch the fur. "It's beautiful and you can leave the head on. I can always put a sleep mask over its eyes."

"Since we're doing the presents . . ." Alan Lewis got to his feet. The owner of a chain of upscale building supply stores, Alan had provided Deer Creek materials at cost in return for his first-floor unit. An overweight man in his fifties with a cherubic face and a completely bald head, he placed his meerschaum pipe in an ashtray and cleared his throat. Alan's doctor had told him to quit smoking last year, and he'd tried everything: hypnosis, acupuncture, even aversion therapy in a famous clinic. Finally, the doctor had conceded that a pipe might be less harmful than chain-smoking unfiltered Camels, provided he didn't inhale, of course. Alan had left his doctor's office and ducked into the nearest pipe store. The salesman had been very helpful and Alan had emerged four thousand dollars poorer, with two hand-carved, antique meerschaums and a set of seven Dunhills, one for every day of the week, in a custom-fitted presentation case. His wife, Laureen, had picked out the tobacco, an aromatic blend that smelled a lot like cookies baking. Now Alan's doctor was happy and so was Laureen, and only Lyle knew that Alan still sneaked a Camel now and then.

"We wanted to give you something special." Alan beckoned at his wife. "Laureen? You do the honors, honey."

"I just want you all to know that this was Alan's idea." Laureen Lewis picked up a silver-wrapped box and carried it to Charlotte. An attractive blonde who was always watching her weight, she hosted a cooking show on the local Las Vegas television channel. Usually unflappable, Laureen's face was pink with embarrassment as Charlotte began to unwrap the package.

Charlotte lifted the lid and stared into the box with disbelief. "What is it?"

"It's a toilet seat." Alan grabbed it and lifted it out. "See? It's silver, that's in honor of your twenty-fifth anniversary, and it hooks on like this. The fixtures are genuine gold and that's mother-of-pearl inlay on the edges. I can install it in a jiffy if you tell me which bathroom you want it in."

Charlotte couldn't help it. She started to giggle. Leave it to Alan.

"I think it should go in the guest bathroom." Lyle took over when he saw that Charlotte was virtually speechless. "That way more people will get to admire it. Thanks, Alan. That was very . . . generous."

When Jack St. James stood up, Lyle gazed at him in shock. He was a short, muscular man in his early forties with light brown hair closely cropped in the military style. Today he was dressed for the occasion in a dark blue three-piece suit, quite a change from the chinos and NRA sweatshirt he usually wore. When Jack had applied for the job as live-in security officer, he'd told them that during his employment with a big security outfit, he'd designed the highly rated home security system that several of Charlotte's wealthy friends used. Jack was a lifelong member of the NRA, an organization that Charlotte abhorred, but his mention of a gold medal won in Olympic rifle competition had confirmed that Jack St. James was the man for the job. The tough little man inspired their confidence, important since their building was so isolated. In return for a small, one-bedroom apartment just off the garage and a reasonable salary, Jack had agreed to design a special security system for the entire building and to act as their in-house security chief.

"Twenty-five years and you're still together." Jack handed his gift to Charlotte. "I figure you and Lyle deserve medals for that."

Charlotte lifted the lid on the box and gasped, then held up Jack's gift for everyone to see. There were two silver medals inside, replicas of the ones from the Olympics. "Thank you, Jack. It says we won the silver in the marriage marathon. That's very clever! Wherever did you find them?"

"I didn't exactly find them. I just drew up the design and had a trophy place make them to order."

"It's your idea?" Alan Lewis put his pipe in the ashtray and got up for a closer look. "I bet you could market these. People are always looking for unusual gifts and these'd sell like hotcakes. It's a brilliant concept."

"And you could use silver for the twenty-fifth, gold for the fiftieth, and bronze for whatever the bronze anniversary is. What is it anyway? I've got a

Hallmark date book at home and I could look it up because they usually have a list of . . ." Grace realized that Moira was staring at her and she stopped. "All right, Moira. But I still think Jack is a genius."

As everyone began to tell him how clever he was, Jack sat there, obviously embarrassed, until Jayne took pity on him.

"Go fetch our gift, Paul. Jack's face is redder than a turkey waddle."

"A what?" Lyle turned to her in surprise. He hadn't been raised on a farm, but neither had Jayne. It must be a phrase from a song she'd written.

"A turkey waddle. You know those gross little things that hang down on the . . . oh, never mind. Just get it, Paul."

"If you will all pardon me, please?" Paul got up and bowed. "This will take only a moment."

Everyone watched as Paul returned almost immediately with a large box. "Jayne has told me this is appropriate for your happy occasion. It is only a small token of our friendship and affection, but we hope it will meet your favor."

"Lord!" Lyle's eyes widened as Charlotte lifted a miniature house out of the box. "That looks just like 247 South Haven Street."

"It is!" Charlotte bent closer to read the house number on the tiny door. "Look, Lyle, a replica of our very first house. Is that why you were asking me all those questions, Jayne?"

Jayne nodded. "Paul got hold of the original blueprints and his model man built it."

Charlotte lifted the roof and peered at the tiny furnishings inside. "I still don't know how you did it but it's simply perfect, all the way down to that awful living room rug."

"How'd you do it?" Moira leaned closer to look. "That pattern isn't even made anymore."

"Betty did the rug. That's her present."

"Our Betty?" Charlotte looked shocked by Jayne's emphatic nod.

"Dang-tootin'. I showed her what I needed and she hand-colored the pattern with felt tip pens."

"That was so sweet." Charlotte sighed deeply. "I'll go up to thank her when we get home. Do you think she's getting any better?"

Moira shook her head. "That's impossible, Charlotte. I read a book on it. It says that some days are better than others, but it's an inevitable decline. Of course Betty doesn't realize how confused she is and that helps, but Alzheimer's is a real b—"

"Bitch." Grace supplied the word before Moira had time to think of an acceptable substitute. With all these "shucks" and "dangs" and "horsefeathers" floating around, she sometimes felt like she was a character in a Jimmy Stewart movie. "Alzheimer's is a bitch of a disease."

Everyone was silent for a moment. Betty Matteo's lawyers had offered Marc the land on Deer Creek Road at a bargain price, provided it contain a unit for Betty and her full-time nurse.

Charlotte cleared her throat. "Well . . . Lyle and I thank you all for the wonderful presents. I think this is the nicest celebration we've ever had."

"It's not over yet." Hal Knight came as close as he ever had to smiling as he handed Charlotte a thin package. A handsome man whom Charlotte thought resembled the young Henry Fonda in *The Grapes of Wrath,* Hal was saved from a too-pretty face by a hairline scar, two inches in length, running across his left cheekbone. Most people imagined that it was a dueling scar, but Hal freely admitted that it came from a fall off his tricycle at age three.

Hal lived and worked in the third-floor unit. He was the cartoonist who drew Skampy Skunk, Benny Bunny, and Chiquita Chicken, whose antics made the whole country laugh. Few people acknowledged the subtle sarcasm that ran through every strip.

They'd all grown to know him very well, and one night at the penthouse spa, after one too many glasses of wine, Hal had revealed the source of his bitterness. Because he was handsome and successful, beautiful women continually made overtures toward him. Flattered, Hal enjoyed their company, but that was as far as it went. He'd tried all the remedies. Therapy. Sex clinics. Potency drugs. Even a desperate attempt at a homosexual liaison. Nothing had worked. Apparently, Hal had informed them wryly, he was lucky. One therapist claimed that he was sublimating his libidinal urges in his work, and that if that particular part of his anatomy was functional, he might not be nearly so successful.

"This is sweet, Hal. Thank you." Charlotte reached up to kiss him on the cheek. "Look at this, everyone. It's Skampy Skunk and Chiquita Chicken congratulating us on our anniversary."

Hal nodded. "Better hang on to that, Charlotte. It'll be worth big bucks someday."

"It's worth big bucks now." Lyle took the drawing from Charlotte and studied it. "A signed Hal Knight has to be worth at least a grand."

Hal almost smiled again. "More like five grand, Lyle, and just wait 'til I croak. Look what happened to the sketches Picasso drew on restaurant table-cloths. I'm probably a better investment than IBM."

"Sorry I'm late." Marc Davies burst into the room, shook hands with Paul who had automatically risen to his feet, and took his place at the table. "Some idiot backed into my car at the baseball game and dented my bumper."

"My goodness! I didn't know they played baseball in February!" Charlotte looked confused so Marc hurried to explain.

"It was college baseball. They start early so they can finish before the end of the school year, and I went out to watch the new pitcher at U.N.L.V. He's got one hell of a change-up and his slider's pretty decent, too. Those are pitches, Charlotte."

"Is he better than you were?" Lyle couldn't resist teasing his former partner.

"Of course not." Marc grinned. "I was the hottest thing the pros ever latched on to. Ask anyone who was around in seventy-two. This kid I saw today has got possibilities, though. All he needs is a little seasoning."

Charlotte frowned slightly. "I didn't know you played professional baseball, Marc. You never mentioned it."

"That's because I wasn't around long enough to

brag. One season and I was retired. It's a long story, Charlotte."

"It sounds fascinating." Charlotte reached over to fill his glass with champagne. "Tell us about it, Marc."

Marc raised an eyebrow. "You're really that interested?"

"Of course we are!" Charlotte smiled at him. She wasn't, but she knew that a good hostess always listened to her guests.

"All right. Just let me wet my whistle first. I've got some catching up to do."

Lyle studied his former partner as he drank. At first glance, he looked the part of a builder, sporting jeans and a blue work shirt open at the collar. But Lyle knew that Marc ordered his jeans from a tailor in London, and that the shirt was actually cut from the finest silk with an elaborate blue-on-blue pocket monogram. Marc's loafers were handmade in Italy, and his watch was a diamond-studded Rolex worth over ten thousand dollars.

Marc drained his champagne glass and set it down. His face was slightly flushed and Lyle was sure that he'd had a couple of beers at the game. He'd always been very close-mouthed about his aborted career before.

"On the night before the last game of the play-offs, I got a call from some guy who wouldn't identify himself. He said that if I came in to relieve, he'd give me fifty big ones to throw the game."

"Do you mean fifty thousand dollars?" Charlotte looked shocked as Marc nodded. "Whatever did you say?"

"I told him I wasn't interested, that there was no way I wanted to get involved in something like that."

"Well, I should hope not!" Charlotte pursed her lips together. "Did you report it to the authorities?"

Marc shook his head. "I figured it was a joke. We had some real bozos on the team and that was right up their alley. At the game the next day, I got called up to relieve in the sixth when the score was tied four-four. I got two strikes on my first man and then he caught a piece of my curve ball and lined one straight at me. I had to dive to make the catch and I racked up my elbow so bad they had to take me out of the game."

Grace was sitting on the edge of her chair. "That's exciting! I just love baseball except that I'm always working when the games are on television and every time I try to tape one to watch later, Moira ends up telling me how it came out before . . . Okay, Moira. I'll be quiet. But did your team win, Marc?"

"Nope, we lost. And the next day I got an envelope in the mail with fifty big ones inside."

"Good heavens!" Charlotte gasped. "They thought you got injured on purpose?"

"I guess so. I thought about turning it in, but the kind of guys who pay to fix a game don't like anyone to know about it, especially the police. And there was no way I could identify who'd sent it anyway. So I stuck it in a safe deposit box and went off to the hospital for elbow surgery."

"But the surgery didn't work," Lyle prompted. He'd heard this part of the story before.

Marc nodded. "That's right. After five different

doctors had worked on me, they told me to forget about pitching again. And since my career in baseball was finished, I used the money to start my construction business."

"No one ever asked you to return it?" Charlotte's hands were trembling slightly as she re-filled Marc's champagne glass.

"Of course not." Marc shrugged. "Everything turned out the way they wanted, even though my part in it was strictly unintentional. I've always regarded that cash as a kind of workman's compensation. And I've never told anybody about it before."

"Well, we certainly won't repeat it!" Alan nodded emphatically. "I don't blame you for keeping it, though. After all, how could you return it if you didn't know who'd sent it in the first place?"

"That's exactly the way I figured it. And that's enough about me. We've got just enough time for a few words from the happy couple before I present my gift." Marc drained his champagne glass again and motioned for the waiter to pour more. "You first, Lyle."

Lyle was solemn as he got to his feet. "Since Charlotte and I got married twenty-five years ago, I haven't regretted a single day."

"Isn't that sweet?" Grace started to applaud, but Charlotte reached out to grab her hands. She was well acquainted with her husband's sense of humor.

"And that single day was June fourth, nineteen fifty-seven."

"I knew it!" Charlotte was laughing as she got to her feet. "He doesn't mean it. At least, I don't think he does. And now, I have a surprise for all of you. My book is going to be published!"

"Your book?" Moira looked puzzled. "We didn't know you were writing a book, Charlotte."

Charlotte smiled modestly. "Well, some people might not call it a book, but I do. Remember the genealogy study I did last year?"

"Of course." Paul rose to his feet to shake Charlotte's hand. "I, for one, was very impressed. If I remember correctly, you traced your ancestors back to the fifteenth century."

Charlotte looked proud. "That's right, Paul. All the way back to Vicar William Henry Wingate's birth in fourteen thirty-one. But that's not the book they're going to publish."

"Tell us, Charlotte." Grace clapped her hands together, as excited as a child. "Who's your publisher? Is it a work of fiction, a murder mystery, or maybe a romance? You certainly could do one of those after being married for twenty-five years. No, I can't see you writing a romance. It's not cultivated enough. So I bet it's a family saga. I just love family sagas, I read one last week about some very valuable family jewels that were . . ."

Moira reached out to put her hand over Grace's mouth. "Never mind, Gracie. Be quiet and let Charlotte tell us."

"Thank you, Moira. My book is going to be published by the Clark County Historical Society. And I'm not sure what category it is. Let's just call it a genealogical study of our land on Deer Creek Road, since I'm tracing the lineage of ownership."

"That sounds fascinating." Moira tried to look interested even though the very idea bored her silly. "How long have you been working on it?"

"I just started the research a few months ago and

I've already discovered some things that are really quite shocking."

Laureen looked interested. "Like what? My mother traced the history of our family, but she quit when she came upon proof that my maternal great-uncle was a horse thief."

"Oh, it's much more shocking than that." Charlotte began to smile. "For example, I discovered that there was once a bordello right where our building stands."

Moira let out a whoop of laughter. "That's wonderful! Our own little red-light district. What else did you find?"

"I've barely scratched the surface, but I've been studying old assay records and I found several references to a silver mine that's reputed to be on our land. According to local legend, more than a dozen prospectors were murdered before they could stake a claim."

Alan began to grin. "Maybe Laureen and I should do a little exploring this summer. We'd own that mine if we found it, wouldn't we, Clayton?"

"Of course." Clayton nodded. "Our title includes all mineral rights."

Marc frowned. "Don't waste your time, Alan. The odds of finding anything worth excavating are even longer than the odds at roulette. Right, Johnny?"

"Oh, I don't know about that." Johnny flashed his famous grin, the one that made middle-aged ladies ask for his autograph after every show. "I think the odds at roulette are pretty good."

Marc snorted. "Only if you own the house. Roulette's a sucker's game and you know it. How about the double zero?"

Jayne put her hand on Marc's arm. "Hush up, you two. What else did you find, Charlotte?"

"Well, there is one other thing." Charlotte lowered her voice. "Now I'm not entirely sure about this, but one of my references alludes to some extremely unsavory individuals who may have held title previously."

Clayton, who was about to take a sip of champagne, set his glass down with a thump. "What on earth are you talking about, Charlotte? We went through a title search as part of our escrow and the title is clear."

"Oh, I'm sure it is, Clayton. What I'm interested in are the crimes that may have been committed while these individuals owned our land."

"What kind of crimes?" Hal leaned forward. "Come on, Charlotte. You can't leave us up in the air."

"I guess not." Charlotte's lips turned up in a mischievous smile. "All right, Hal. One more tidbit of information and that's it until I get the proper documentation. My reference alludes to several mysterious and unsolved murders."

"Holy . . . uh . . . cripes!"

Grace laughed out loud as Moira switched words in midsentence. "Go ahead and swear, Moira. What we just heard deserves more than a 'cripes.'"

"And I used to think genealogy was boring." Lyle put his arm around his wife's shoulders. "How about a toast to Charlotte, the genealogical sleuth?"

As soon as the waiter had refilled their glasses, Marc stood up. "To Charlotte's book. Come on, everyone. Drink up. And then it's time for my present. I'm treating Lyle and Charlotte to the best dinner money can buy."

"Thank you, Marc. We love to dine out." Charlotte took a sip of her champagne. Then she noticed that everyone was leaning forward in anticipation. Marc must be taking them to a very exclusive restaurant. "Where are we going?"

"I made reservations at the fanciest restaurant I could find. And I arranged a special dinner, just for you two. How does *langoustes à la parisienne* sound? Followed by *canard à l'orange* and maybe a little strawberries Romanoff with *crème Chantilly* and candied violets?"

Charlotte sighed. "That sounds heavenly. But where are we going?"

"Well, that presented a little problem, but I found the perfect place. Come on. Let's go."

Lyle looked around at the half-empty bottles of champagne. He knew how much this had set Johnny back and it was too good to waste. "You mean we're leaving right now?"

"Right now." Marc drained his glass and stood up. "Come on, everybody. You all know the plans."

Charlotte and Lyle exchanged puzzled glances as they got up and followed Marc out the door. Johnny whisked them into a private elevator and seconds later they stepped out on the sidewalk in front of the casino.

"This way." Marc led them to a silver limousine, idling at the curb. "Charlotte? Lyle? Climb in. I'm sending you to the Ritz for a romantic dinner."

"The Ritz?" Lyle frowned as the chauffeur held the door open for him. "Where's that, Marc?"

"In New Orleans."

"New Orleans? But . . . Marc!" Charlotte was so flabbergasted, she couldn't think of what to say.

Darby laughed. "Jayne and I packed your things, Charlotte. Your suitcases are in the trunk."

"That's right." Marc nodded. "You said you always wanted to go to the Mardi Gras and this year you're going."

Charlotte looked confused. "But where will we stay? Lyle tried to get hotel reservations over three months ago and everything was booked solid."

"I've got a little more juice than Lyle." Johnny grinned at her. "I called in a marker from a friend of mine and you're all set up in the bridal suite at the Orleans Hotel. What's the matter, Charlotte? Don't you want to go?"

Charlotte began to laugh. "Of course I want to go! But . . ."

"No more buts." Marc reached out to give her a hug. Then he shook Lyle's hand. "Now climb in. The chauffeur has your tickets and you'd better hurry. Your plane leaves in an hour."

Lyle opened the French doors and stepped out onto the private balcony. There was another parade passing in the street below, headed by a group of jazz musicians in white suits, and Lyle groaned as he heard the familiar strains of "When the Saints Go Marching In." He'd always liked that song, but he was sure he'd heard it a hundred times since arriving in New Orleans. The Mardi Gras was a perpetual party and Lyle was growing tired of celebrating. He felt like stretching out on the bed and going to sleep, but Charlotte was so eager to take part in the festivities that it wouldn't be fair to disappoint her on their last night.

He stepped back inside the suite, shutting the doors on the music, and glanced at his watch. Charlotte was still in the bathroom, putting the finishing touches on her makeup. If she didn't hurry, they'd be late for the costume party in the hotel banquet room. Lyle felt a little silly in black leotards, a black-and-white checkered tunic, and a hat with tassles and bells. But when he'd tried the harlequin outfit on this morning, Charlotte had convinced him that it was perfect for the occasion.

"Almost ready, honey?" Lyle sat down in the wing chair facing the fireplace and yawned. One more party and then he could go home and recover from this vacation.

The bathroom door opened and Charlotte stepped out. She was dressed in a powder blue velvet dress decorated with lace and pearls. Tonight she had long, plump curls piled up on the top of her head. Since Charlotte's hair had been short when she'd gone in to put on her costume, she had to be wearing a wig. "Well? What do you think?" Charlotte raised a blue velvet mask to her eyes and twirled around. "Do I look the part?"

"You look gorgeous, honey." Lyle evaded the question. He wasn't sure who she was supposed to be, but guessed it was someone like Marie Antoinette.

"Let's go then." Charlotte headed for the door and Lyle stifled another yawn as he followed. Ten more hours until he could catch some sleep on the plane. He'd never guessed that a vacation could be so exhausting.

There were several people on the elevator, and Lyle nodded to another harlequin, two devils, and a woman in a dark red velvet dress that looked a lot like Charlotte's.

Charlotte frowned as she checked the other woman in the mirrored walls of the elevator and when her lips finally turned up in a smile, Lyle breathed a sigh of relief. Charlotte had decided that she looked better than the other woman.

The elevator descended slowly, and at every floor more people in costume got on. Lyle found himself holding his breath. The scent of mingled perfumes and colognes made him feel slightly dizzy.

As the elevator started down again, Lyle felt a hand in his pocket. About to yell that someone was stealing his wallet, he felt a burning pain just below his shoulder blades. He tried to turn to see what was jabbing him, but the elevator was so crowded he couldn't move. Then, as his vision began to cloud, he heard Charlotte gasp in pain, and everything went pitch-black.